CUTIE
AND THE BEAST

FAE OUT OF WATER - BOOK ONE

E.J. RUSSELL

D1003252

RIPTIDE
PUBLISHING

Riptide Publishing
PO Box 1537
Burnsville, NC 28714
www.riptidepublishing.com

Cutie and the Beast
Copyright © 2017 by E.J. Russell

Cover art: Lou Harper, louharper.com/design.html
Editor: Rachel Haimowitz
Layout: L.C. Chase, lcchase.com/design.htm

ISBN: 978-1-62649-600-2

First edition
July, 2017

Also available in ebook:
ISBN: 978-1-62649-599-9

CUTIE
AND THE BEAST
THE

FAE OUT OF WATER - BOOK ONE

E.J. RUSSELL

RIPTIDE
PUBLISHING

TABLE OF
CONTENTS

CHAPTER ❦ 1

David Evans carried his aunt Cassie from her bedroom to the sun porch, laughing at her squeak of protest.

"Put me down, you dreadful boy. I'm capable of walking through the house on my own."

"I'm showing off for you. Stop fussing or you'll wound my masculine pride." He settled her on the chaise, angling it for a perfect view of her beloved garden. The morning sun was flooding the room with the crisp light of almost-summer. From a big cage in the corner, her zebra finches beeped in cheerful counterpoint to the lazy buzz of bees in the hollyhocks outside the window screens. "And you know how I love to pamper you."

She patted his arm, smiling up at him as he smoothed a coverlet over her knees. "You look very handsome this morning, Davey." A faint Welsh lilt still shaded her voice, even after six decades of living in Oregon. "I've not seen that tie before, have I?"

"What, this old thing?" David flicked the corner of the blue-on-blue polka-dot bow tie he'd saved for this exact occasion. "I start a new gig today, Auntie. Temporary office manager for a real live health care provider, so I dress to impress."

"Really?" Her fragile skin puckered between where her eyebrows used to be. "Ms. Fischer assigned you to a medical practice?"

David dodged her shrewd gaze by fiddling with the blinds, adjusting them so the sun didn't shine directly in her face. "Sandra's out with a nasty flu. Her assistant is the one who placed me."

When poor frazzled Tracy had called with the offer, he'd almost reminded her he'd been permanently exiled to telecommuting limbo. But then she'd told him the job was for Dr. Alun Kendrick.

Just once, a few months ago, he'd had a very small transcription assignment for the psychologist. He'd prayed for another, because, God, that *voice*. A British accent that put Colin Firth to shame. No doubt about it, the man was total ear candy.

So he'd neglected to mention that Sandra had banned him from office positions for life. On paper, he fit this position perfectly. In practice . . . well, there was always a first time. Besides, forgiveness? Way easier than permission.

"Are you sure this is wise?" Aunt Cassie's mouth quirked up in a ghost of her old sly grin. "The last time, you caused a riot. In a dentist's office."

"I did not *cause* the riot." He propped her cane within easy reach and dropped a kiss on her rainbow head scarf. "I was merely present when it occurred, and clearly those men were either unbalanced or laboring under the severe stress of looming root canals."

He nudged her hip gently with his knee and sat beside her, his arm around her thin shoulders. "It's the ideal job. Swing shift, two until ten, so I can still handle my billing and transcription assignments in the morning. Plus, it's indefinite, maybe permanent. Tracy hinted that the regular office manager might not return from maternity leave."

Aunt Cassie plucked at the blanket on her lap, pulling out tiny tufts of green and blue fluff. "Don't hope for someone else's misfortune, Davey. It's bad for your spirit."

"I'm not. Truly, I'm not. But if she chooses to spend longer at home with her baby, I'm more than happy to keep her chair warm and her desk competently staffed."

She sighed. "All right. You know best. Show me your lucky earring."

David turned his head to flash the onyx stud his aunt had given him on his thirteenth birthday. "Never without it."

"You have your worry stone?"

He pulled the purple quartz oval out of his blazer pocket, thumbing the shallow dip in its top face, the familiar shape smooth and cool in his hand. "Always. Now . . ." He stood up, brushing green fuzz off his gray trousers. "I won't be home until eleven, but I'll have my cell phone with me every minute. Lorraine should be here any second to sit with you until Peggy brings your dinner at six, but if you need me, you call. Understood?"

"Pooh." She scrunched her face in a near-pout. "I don't need a babysitter."

He picked up her pill bottle—just as full as it was yesterday. On days like today, when he'd sent off yet another partial payment to the clinic, begging for patience and an extension, he missed the time when the only things he had to worry about were studying for his next anatomy exam, or wondering why his latest sort-of-boyfriend had suddenly turned into a jealous douche bag.

And when Aunt Cassie wouldn't even comply with the doctor's orders for the treatment that kept David working as many hours as he could swing—and still barely earning enough to keep them from losing their home? *Argh*.

"Auntie, how many times do I have to—" He took a deep breath. *Don't be a jerk. You can't browbeat someone into getting better.* He rattled the pill bottle, waggling his eyebrows. "Could you at least *try* to do what the doctor says?"

Pink tinged her pale cheeks, but she met his gaze calmly. "I've been an adult for several times your lifetime. I've earned the right to control the end of my own."

David's heart tried to scrunch itself into a fetal position. No. No. No and no and no. Life without his aunt? The thought made him want to lie down on the floor and drum his heels against the hardwood like he'd done as a temper-prone toddler, or hide in the closet and rock in denial like he'd done during his years in foster care.

Instead, he dropped to his knees and took her hands. "Auntie, you're the only family I've got. I want to keep you around as long as possible. Please?"

"Ach, Davey. How can I say no to that?" She sighed and took the pills from him. "Revolting little objects."

"I know, so thank you." He kissed her forehead. "Love you. I'll see you tonight."

"Be careful, *cariad*." She rested one palm against his cheek. "You leap into things, heart first. Don't be too quick to believe this your belonging place. Wait a bit. Learn how the days play out."

David dropped his gaze from her bird-bright eyes. She had a point, but he couldn't help it. Something about this job felt so right, as if the ultimate assignment had come along exactly when he was able to snag it.

His cheerful honorary aunt Peggy, one of his aunt's six closest friends, would say his stars were in alignment. Aunt Regan, the more mordant one, would call it fate. But he didn't care what any of them called it; he called it perfect.

He'd *make* it perfect, damn it. This time for sure.

A beast loomed in the stairwell, hulking and monstrous and far too savage to be contained by the glass door panel with its flimsy safety mesh.

Alun Kendrick's pulse bucked like a frightened mare. He grabbed the door handle, teeth bared in the battle rictus of a Sidhe warrior.

Undeterred, the beast mirrored him, grimace for grimace, scowl for scowl, glare for glare.

Oak and thorn, not again. He released the doorknob with a groan. *It's been two hundred years, Kendrick. You ought to be accustomed to your own reflection by now.* But intellectual acceptance didn't trump his instinctive revulsion at the sight of his grotesque features.

Beauty was a prerequisite for admittance to the Seelie Court, a tenet so basic he'd never thought to question its fairness. There'd been no need—he'd met that restriction for millennia—but he bloody well violated it now.

As long as he wore this face, the gates of Faerie were barred to him. He'd have preferred a death curse to this exile and all-consuming guilt, but he'd not been given that choice.

He shoved the stairwell door open and took the stairs two at a time, down the six flights from his top-floor flat to his clinic offices. With the curse robbing him of nearly all his former abilities, he knew better than to take the elevator. He could pass unnoticed as long as he was moving, but his paltry *glamourie* of *not-here* couldn't stand up to the scrutiny of a bored human in an enclosed space.

Stairs were by far the safer choice.

When he emerged from the stairwell into the corridor that led to his clinic, his nerves flared again.

Intruder.

Stomach jolting toward his spine, he rushed halfway down the hall, reaching reflexively for his sword. *Fool. You haven't worn a scabbard in two centuries.* He stopped and rested his hand against the wall, willing his battle reflexes to stand down. *You carry a briefcase now, not a broadsword.*

Besides, this intrusion, while not welcome, was anticipated. His office manager, a werewolf expecting her first child, had taken early maternity leave, collateral damage in the F1W2 flu that had approached epidemic proportions in the shifter community. Although it only affected the big cats, her father-in-law had demanded she retire to their compound to await the birth. Something about impending grandfatherhood had turned the normally tough and pragmatic alpha of the Multnomah wolf pack into a skittish old hen.

Alun opened his clinic door and slipped into the reception lobby. While the need for a temp irritated him, he had no intention of frightening her senseless before she brewed the coffee. He might be a monster, but he wasn't an idiot.

"Hello? It's Dr. Kendrick."

A narrow band of sunlight spilled through open blinds, gilding the carpet with a stripe of gold, and Alun rethought his don't-frighten-the-temp-senseless policy. Damn it to all the hells, hadn't she bothered to read the office procedures manual?

Blinds must remain closed during daylight hours.

Throughout most of the year, the north-facing windows wouldn't admit enough sunlight to injure any but the most helio-sensitive of his clients, and his clinic hours—midafternoon through evening—were arranged to further minimize exposure. This close to the solstice, however, the sun's angle was acute enough to bleed into the room. She should know that. Every supe in the Pacific Northwest knew that.

A growl rumbling in his throat, he yanked the cords, plunging the room into soothing shadow. He stalked down the hallway, searching for the temp. No one was cowering in the break room, nor the restroom, nor the supply closet that housed the copier and printer.

Where the bloody hells was she? As a rule, people didn't run until *after* they'd gotten a look at him, although few supes had cause to balk. Many of them looked nearly as bad at certain phases of the moon or after an ill-considered blood bender.

Cursing under his breath, he threw open the door to his inner office and came face to posterior with the most perfect arse he'd seen since the day he left Faerie.

A *human* arse.

Flaming abyss, had everyone at Fischer Temps run mad, or only Sandra Fischer herself?

The slender man in indecently well-cut trousers and a fitted dress shirt was standing on Alun's desk atop the latest *Physician's Desk Reference* and two of Alun's heftiest old text books, arms stretched overhead as he fiddled with the light bulbs in the track lighting. His shirttails, partly untucked, displayed a tantalizing arc of skin over one hip.

Alun's mouth went dry, an unexpected surge of want sizzling from the base of his outsized skull to his bollocks.

No, damn it. *He's human.* Humans were off-limits for so many reasons, not least of which was that heavy sedation and years of therapy lay in store for any unlucky enough to see his face. No non-supe was allowed knowledge of the supernatural world without the express permission of the all ruling councils, under pain of . . . well . . . pain.

Excruciating, never-ending pain.

He thrust his unwelcome desire away, which his strict century-old vow of abstinence made more difficult than he wanted to admit. He tossed his briefcase on the love seat next to the door and stalked across the office to stand behind the human.

"What in all the bloody hells do you think you're about?"

"Dr. Kendrick." Despite Alun's less than hospitable words, the man's mellow tenor held welcome, not alarm.

He turned. Eyes widening under a slash of dark brows, he inhaled sharply and his smile faltered. Alun caught a brief impression of an upper lip shaped like the longbow he had last held the day he left Faerie. *Enchanting.*

Then the man lost his footing on the teetering pile of books, and stumbled backward, slipping on a stack of *Psychology Today*. His feet flew out from under him, along with a spray of magazines, and he toppled right into Alun's arms.

Merciful Goddess. Alun hadn't been within intimate-touching distance of a man since 1898. No wonder then that his breath sped up, his blood burning like molten silver in his veins. His cock suddenly hard behind his fly.

He inhaled, slow and deep. *This* was what a man's skin smelled like when he was fresh from the bath and not the battlefield. Vivid and forest wild, with a faint undertone of salt and a hint of musk. *This* was what a man's hair looked like, shiny and flyaway, gold threads glinting among the peat brown, finer than any pelt yet coarser than a woman's or child's. *This* was what a man felt like in his arms, alive and warm and—

Shite. Human.

To the human's credit, he didn't shriek or faint, nor did he struggle or try to escape. Instead, he remained cradled in Alun's arms, tilted his chin, and blinked eyes the color of a storm-clouded lake. An erratic pulse beat in the angle of his jaw, betraying that he wasn't as calm as he pretended, a bright—and undoubtedly false—smile curving that tempting mouth.

"How do you do? I'm David Evans, your new temp office manager."

"I don't think so."

Alun set the man on his feet and escaped behind his desk before the state of his trousers could reveal his inconvenient reaction. Thank the Goddess he no longer wore doublet and hose.

The human, David—although despite endless years in exile, Alun mentally translated the name to its Welsh form, *Dafydd*—sidled away under the guise of picking up the scattered magazines and reshelving the books he'd used as an impromptu stepping stool.

"Yes, indeed I am." He didn't lift his gaze to Alun's face, and who could blame him? "Don't worry. Tracy filled me in—"

"Not Sandra?"

David shook his hair out of his eyes. "Sandra's out with that bug that's going around, I'm afraid, but you know she trusts Tracy to fill in for her or she wouldn't employ her. Sandra insists on the best."

She did, and she'd hear about this outrageous infraction, flu or no flu. Supe business, supe temps. That was the foundation—the absolute guarantee—of her company. She was a panther shifter, damn it, with the responsibility to adequately brief her staff.

"You've no business in here. My office is off-limits." Especially to humans, however beautiful they might be.

"The lights above your desk. They . . ." David cast a brief glance at him from under unfairly long eyelashes and swallowed, his Adam's apple sliding beneath the honey-smooth skin above his collar. "They were failing. I wanted to change them before they burned out so—"

"Did you not consider that I keep them dim on purpose?" Alun thrust his head forward into the merciless light. Flinching, David stumbled back, the unmistakable tang of fear tainting his seductive clean-man scent. Good. He should be afraid. He should be afraid, and he should be gone. "You think anyone wants to look at this face too closely while they're spilling the secrets of their soul?"

David pressed his lips together, no doubt to hide their trembling. Alun should have felt gratified that he'd succeeded in intimidating the man. A necessary evil, for his own sake as well as for the safety of the supe communities. But a whisper of regret, the shadow of sorrow for something he could never have again, raised a lump in his throat and tightened his chest.

Yes, the human must leave, no matter how much Alun's awakening libido regretted the necessity.

Instead of bolting out the door, however, David took a deep breath, a mulish cast to his pointed chin, and stared Alun straight in the eye. "If you prefer to remain in the dark, that's your choice and privilege. After all, you're the doctor."

CHAPTER 🔗 2

With his pulse thumping like a techno dance beat, David clamped his teeth together to keep his chin from wobbling. This was so not the way he'd envisioned meeting the owner of The Voice.

Dr. Kendrick picked up the handset of the desk phone and punched a button so hard it was a miracle the unit didn't shatter. "Don't get comfortable. I'm getting a replacement."

While the doctor growled into his phone, David reached instinctively for his worry stone. Damn it. He'd left it in the pocket of the blazer currently draped over the back of his chair in the lobby. Out of reach, it did him precisely zero good in his face-off with his new boss.

And, judging by David's slam-dancing nerves, Dr. Kendrick was winning that particular contest on points alone.

That face. What kind of birth defect or unfortunate medical syndrome caused skull disfigurement that severe? He looked like the victim of a failed experiment on the island of Dr. Moreau who'd tried to get the results fixed at a cut-rate back-alley plastic surgeon.

David's compassion circuits would have been firing on all channels if it weren't for the attitude.

Dr. Kendrick slammed his phone into its cradle. "Voice mail. Bloody hells." He glared at David from under a brow ridge as craggy as the Nehalem jetty. "This situation is completely unacceptable."

Maintain, Evans. You can do it—just imagine you're Luke Skywalker, and he's . . . he's . . . David's gaze drifted up and up and up. *He's Darth Really Freaking Huge.* But if David bombed at this assignment before he'd been on the job for half an hour, Sandra would never let him near a medical office again.

Not that she'd let him near this one, but David never sweated the details.

"With all due respect, Doctor, you've known me for two minutes. How do you know it's unacceptable?"

"In that time, you've violated at least three office policies. You." He drew his shoulders back, making him even more ginormous than before. "Opened. The. Blinds."

Seriously? The blinds? This was the unforgivable sin? "I could barely see to cross the room. Safety first, you know. I would have closed them before—"

Dr. Kendrick marched around the desk and invaded David's personal comfort bubble. "You entered my office without permission."

David loved big men, but he didn't like bullies, and the good doctor's body language was all *me-Tarzan-you-twink*. He took a baby step forward, tipping his head back so he could focus on Dr. Kendrick's face and not his necktie. "You weren't here. I knocked. According to the procedures manual, it's the office manager's job to make sure your office is ready for the day."

"You changed my light bulbs. *Without asking.*" Dr. Kendrick took the last step, so they were practically toe-to-toe. As his nostrils flared, chest rising on a long inhale, something flickered across his misshapen features and in the depths of his shadowed hazel eyes.

With the nursing training David had already completed, and with his experience caring for his aunt, he had no trouble recognizing that something.

Pain.

Whether Dr. Kendrick wanted to admit it or not, and no matter how he camouflaged it with anger, he was in pain.

Maybe not physical pain, but if emotional pain was great enough, the brain processed it exactly the same. If David knew anything, he knew how to deal with pain, and it didn't start with giving up or— unfortunately, drat it—getting confrontational. But that didn't mean the man could get away with being a jackass, no matter how good it had felt cuddled up against his acres of chest.

David dialed his inner Jedi down a few notches.

"I'm sorry about that." He backed up and reshelved the last of the scattered books. "I didn't realize the lower light was intentional. Shall I put the original bulbs back?"

"No," Dr. Kendrick barked. "Just go."

"Very well. I'll be at my desk. Buzz if you need anything."

He closed the door of Dr. Kendrick's office and was immediately plunged into gloom, the lobby blinds once again shut tight against the glorious afternoon sun. This was Oregon, for goodness sake. Wasn't it gloomy enough most of the year to suit the man?

David flicked on the track lighting in the patient seating area. Ooorg. Whoever had decorated this office must have fond memories of fog banks and rainstorms because gray was a definite theme.

The L-shaped speckled gray Formica reception desk—*his* desk, damn it—and matching credenza guarded the doctor's inner office door. Gray carpet extended down the hallway. Gray faux-suede chairs lined the gray walls. Gray granite end tables sat in each corner with accompanying gray ginger jar lamps.

Good grief. Whatever the patients' diagnoses were when they arrived, they'd add clinical depression by the time they left. Luckily, David had come prepared with anti-gray accoutrements of all sorts. Since the procedures manual, holy of holies, said nothing whatsoever about the display of personal items, he intended to spread the love— and the color.

His practical pagan aunts—the real one and the six honorary ones—had gifted him with enough gorgeous handcrafted cheer on each solstice and equinox to transform a dozen dreary offices. He hummed the theme from *Raiders of the Lost Ark* as he unpacked his treasures. Blown-glass candy dish in flaming orange-red? *Check.* He filled it with Aunt Peggy's pastilles and stationed it on the corner of the desk.

Hand-woven coasters in all the colors of the rainbow? *Check.* After stacking them on the coffee service table, he snagged his favorite green one for himself, and crowned it with his cobalt-blue ceramic mug.

Inspirational action figures? *Check, check, check,* and *check.* Arranged in heroic lockstep under the flat-screen computer monitor—Dr. Who (the eleventh incarnation, because bow ties truly were cool), Chewbacca, Legolas, and Lt. Commander Data—they'd have his back every time, no matter what poo Dr. Curmudgeon decided to fling at him.

Although he hunted for ten minutes, he couldn't locate a sound system, but no worries. Once he got the word on acceptable lobby music, he could cue up mental-health-appropriate tunes on his phone so the place didn't feel quite so much like the inside of a sensory-deprivation chamber.

He crawled under his desk, iPhone dock cord in hand, but while he was wrestling the cover off the outlet, the clinic door whooshed open.

Shoot, he hadn't made the coffee yet, and his blazer was still hanging over the back of his chair. He'd planned to be sitting behind the desk when patients arrived, welcoming and professional and perfectly turned out. He scooted out, misjudged his position, and whacked his head on the edge of the desk.

"Ow. Son of a—" Oops. No swearing in front of patients. He peeked over the desktop and met the amused gaze of a guy who had obviously mistaken the clinic for the location of a photo shoot for Hot Men and Their Harleys. Leather bomber jacket (in June?), blinding white T-shirt (tight!), black leather pants (tighter!), windblown dark hair, and blue eyes that put David's coffee mug to shame.

"All right there?" His voice had the same swoon-worthy British flavor as Dr. Kendrick's.

"Absolutely. Nothing dented but my pride." David stood up without any further close encounters with the furniture, and shrugged into his jacket, tugging the sleeves straight and smoothing his lapels. "How can I help you?"

"Depends on what you're offering." Dimples quivered in the man's stubbled cheeks, a matched set to go with the chin cleft on his square jaw and his bad-boy attitude.

David didn't roll his eyes, but it was a close call. He sooo knew this type. The Handsomeness God's gift to horny club boys everywhere. No, thanks. That kind of arrogance didn't get invited to play in David's sandbox. "Depends on whether you have an appointment."

"I don't, but I rate special treatment. Mal Kendrick." He jerked a thumb at the closed office door. "Brother."

Holy cats. If poor Dr. Kendrick had had to grow up comparing himself with this pinnacle of male hotitude, no wonder he was Dr. Grumpypants. "In that case, I can offer a cup of coffee and the announcement of your arrival."

Mal chuckled and raised one shoulder in a negligent shrug, conceding with more graciousness than David expected. "Half-and-half would be grand. No sugar."

David delivered his best customer-service smile. "Coming up." He lifted the phone handset and buzzed Dr. Kendrick.

"Aren't you gone yet?"

"Your brother is here, Doctor."

"Wonderful." His growl implied the exact opposite.

"Shall I send him in?"

"I doubt you could stop him."

The doctor hung up with a bang. David smiled with only a hint of teeth-gritting and settled the handset into its cradle.

"Please go right in. He's thrilled."

"I'll just wager he is." Mal grinned, and David was surprised sparkles didn't glint off his teeth. "Thanks, love."

As soon as the door closed behind Mr. Hot-and-knows-it, David leaped up from his chair. God, if he expected to keep this job, he had to pull a rabbit out of his ass *tout de suite.*

Luckily, he had the perfect secret weapon. He dug the precious package out of his messenger bag.

Coffee. Aunt Cassie's special blend.

David chuckled to himself in his best evil minion impression. Oh yeah. The brothers Kendrick were freaking toast.

CHAPTER ✤ 3

Two years. Two bloody years since Mal had last crossed this threshold, yet now he was lounging in the doorway, as if he dropped by for a visit every day. Maybe in Mal's eyes, his last visit *was* only yesterday, since he was still living under the stars of Faerie, where time passed at a different rate. But Alun had felt Mal's absence—indeed, the absence of both his brothers—every minute of every Outer World day, making his exile all the harder to bear.

Alun glared, derailing the prickle in his eyes. He gathered up half a dozen issues of *Psychology Today* to hide the trembling in his traitorous hands, and whacked their edges on his desk until they lined up. "What do you want?"

Chuckling, Mal kicked the door closed with one booted foot. He placed a hand on his chest and bowed. "A gracious good afternoon to you too, brother." He sauntered forward at perfect ease, his thumbs hooked in the pockets of his leather pants, as if Alun's office were his own personal domain. "You're looking slightly better these days. Brow ridges less pronounced. Jaw not as Neanderthal. Cheekbones still capable of slicing a tough steak, but promising, brother, promising."

"I can't say the same for you. What in the hells is that on your face?" No high fae sported facial hair, yet stubble shadowed Mal's jaw and chin.

Mal snagged Alun's framed diploma off the wall and angled it to preen at his reflection in the glass. "Like it? They call it scruff."

"You're using *glamourie* to emulate poor grooming?"

"Men find it sexy, and it's such a small illusion. Simple to maintain, expends no power to speak of. I recommend it." He replaced the diploma, then flicked the corner so it hung a fraction off true, laughing at Alun's resultant growl. "You're so easy to wind up, Alun. Especially when you're horny."

The back of his neck heated with the memory of his reaction to David. "I'm not horny."

"Don't try that on with me, brother. The lad at the front desk? Exactly the type to make you play the fool."

"You're just as likely as I am."

"Nah. The soft, pretty ones were never my taste. I like mine with a bit of steel. An edge."

"Well he's not my type either. He's human."

"So?"

"He doesn't belong here. Humans aren't equipped to face our world. They have enough trouble interacting with normal supes—"

Mal snorted and picked up the geode paperweight from the corner of Alun's desk, tossing it from hand to hand. "Assuming any supe is ever normal."

"Precisely my point. All my clients, with the exception of the PTSD group, are disturbed supes. Even if the councils tolerated the threat of human exposure, the danger to his psyche is too great." Alun stood up and snatched the geode out of the air mid-toss. "To what do I owe the honor of this visit?"

"I'd stop by more often if you acted happier to see me."

And I'd act happier if you could bear to look *at me.* "That doesn't answer my question."

"Maybe I just want to catch up." Running a negligent finger down the stack of magazines, Mal shoved them into a sloppy fan over the polished oak desk. "Seen any good movies?"

"No."

"Any new restaurants?"

"No."

Abandoning any pretense of nonchalance, Mal actually met Alun's gaze. "Goddess save us all, what do you do with your time?"

"I read. I listen to music."

"What do you read?"

"Psychology texts. Magazines. I write self-help articles for the supe community."

"There's a bloody irony for you," Mal muttered. "Who do you kick back with? Friends? Acquaintances?"

Alun raised a heavy eyebrow. "Brothers?"

Mal had the grace to flush. "A point. Sorry. I plan to do better. But what about supes? Do you socialize with any of the families you treat?"

"That would be unprofessional."

"But it might be fun."

Could his brother truly be that oblivious? He was the Queen's Enforcer—did he restrict his knowledge of the supe races to what he required to track and kill them?

"I dare you to play poker with a clutch of dragon shifters. None will ever place a bet. They're too busy hoarding their chips." Still holding the geode, Alun ignored Mal's wicked chuckle and walked to the wall to straighten the off-kilter diploma. "The top flight of the vampire council invited me out once. For drinks. It struck me as ill-advised."

"All right. I can see how that might turn . . . unfortunate. What about sex? When was the last time you had a date?"

Alun snorted. "The last man who agreed to sleep with me— whom I *paid* to agree—couldn't bear to look me in the face."

"He doesn't have to look at you for you to shag him."

Goddess preserve me. "Mal. I don't have time for guessing games. Why are you really here?"

"Have you seen Gareth?"

Alun flinched, his fist clenching around the geode, and its rough surface bit into his palm. He hadn't seen Mal for two years, but his youngest brother hadn't spoken to him since the day of his exile. The day of Owain's death. He forced his hand to relax and set the stone in its rightful spot on the desk. "Of course not. He's still in LA, partying like a rock star." He restacked the magazines and moved them out of Mal's reach.

"He *is* a rock star. But I expected him to . . ." Mal took a deep breath, his shoulders rising under his leather jacket. "He's in Portland. His band has a gig at the Moda Center."

So close. Anger warred with hurt in Alun's chest. He sat down heavily. "I didn't know."

"Here." Mal removed a CD case from the pocket of his jacket and tossed it on Alun's desk.

"What is it?"

"Gareth's latest solo work."

Anger won, burning like basilisk venom in his belly. Alun shoved the CD away with extra force. "Keep it."

"Gwydion's bollocks, man." Mal flicked the case with his finger, sending it skating across the desk's slick surface. Alun slapped his hand on it before it could fall into his lap. "You're both over twenty-five hundred years old. When will you grow up?"

"He's the one who turned away."

"But you're the one who let him." Mal planted his fists on the desk. "Aren't you over this shite by now? Stop wallowing and break the damn curse."

"I can't."

"Have you ever tried? There must be a way. The end is always contained in the beginning."

Alun stared his brother down until Mal's gaze shifted to the corner, away from his unlovely features, as it always did. "I walked into the Stone Circle as a lord of the Sidhe. I walked out as something from a demon's nightmares. Draw your own conclusions."

Mal's dark brows snapped together over the Roman nose so like what Alun's once had been. "The *achubyddion* cursed you? Not bloody likely. They were healers. Pacifists."

"Even the most peaceable will call down vengeance when pressed."

"That wasn't your fault. The Unseelie hordes had been tracking them for months."

"They'd never have found the camp if I'd been more careful. If I'd—"

If he hadn't been so thrice-damned arrogant to believe Owain willing to forsake his home and family for an oh-so-exalted position as Alun's consort.

His jaw tightened and he shut his eyes, the memory of that night crashing through him as it did every single day, every single night. The fire in his chest and belly, as if he were being gutted by his own sword. The blinding, knee-buckling pain as the bones in his face contorted and reformed. And Owain—his poor broken body abandoned on the altar stone under the lowering clouds while the carrion birds circled overhead.

How could he ever atone for that? He deserved every moment of his curse, and more.

"Alun." Mal's voice was uncharacteristically gentle. "Don't. I know you loved him. You wouldn't have done anything to hurt him. His death was not your fault."

Alun's throat constricted, throttling his voice. He swallowed once, twice, and spun his chair toward the window, the reflection of his harsh, misshapen features an easier penance than any potential pity on Mal's face. "This is what I am now. What I will likely be until the End of Days. It's time to accept that the curse is permanent."

"Have you accepted it? Truly? Because—"

"Yes. I have." He swiveled back to face Mal, and his brother's gaze shifted once again to the bookshelves. Despite his swagger, his words of support, his brother was still Seelie fae, the tenets of the Seelie Court branded on his soul. Alun's curse—its cause and its result—violated nearly all of those. No wonder his brothers avoided him. "It's only right. I was responsible for the slaughter of the last enclave of an entire race."

With a muttered oath, Mal sat on the love seat. "About that. We found another enclave."

Alun's breath stilled in his chest. "Of *achubyddion*? You mean they're not extinct? Did you— Were they—"

"I'm sorry. We were too late. Someone got there first."

Eyes burning, Alun let his head fall against the high back of his chair. "How many?" he rasped.

"Two bodies. Completely drained. No soul, not a spark of life force left to regenerate."

"An Unseelie attack?"

"Maybe not."

"Oak and bloody thorn, you really think someone from the Seelie Court would do this?"

Mal shrugged. "No hard evidence one way or the other. However, there were signs that the colony may have had more members."

"Some escaped?"

"Or were captured. For—" Mal swallowed hard, his expression darkening. "For later use."

Alun squeezed the back of his neck. "Shite."

"They had records. Computers. Those were gone, but we don't know whether they were taken by the survivors or the attackers."

"So the hunt may still be on?"

"If word of an enclave of *achubyddion* gets out? It'll be worse than the last battle of the Oak Wars."

"The Queen—"

"You know what she's like. If it doesn't happen in Faerie, then it doesn't exist as far as she's concerned, and this attack happened in Vermont."

"Shite." Alun moved from his desk to the wingback chair across the coffee table from Mal. "I— Thank you. For telling me."

"I didn't want you to hear it from anyone else."

"I appreciate it."

"There's more. There's rumor of a power play by the Daoine Sidhe."

"Again?"

"Fair warning—it might amount to something this time, since you're not around to counter them."

"I haven't been around for two centuries."

"Two centuries in the Outer World. Less than a year in Faerie, depending on who's counting. At first I thought it wasn't anything, but I've heard talk from more than one source, and both of them mentioned the Midsummer Revels. Something's going down then, but I don't know—"

A knock sounded at the door, and David entered without invitation, carrying a tray with two steaming cups.

Alun scowled, fisting his hands on his thighs. "I didn't ask for refreshments." Although he counted it a blessing that the dark aroma of coffee was masking the maddening scent of David's skin.

David grinned, bright as a sunny meadow. "No, but your brother did, and he doesn't look the sort to be rude enough to indulge when you don't."

Mal rose and took the cup David offered him, standing a little too close, damn him. "Don't know me very well, do you, boyo? Want to change that?"

"Mal." Alun let his voice dip in warning. His brother grinned wryly, but he retreated to the love seat, cradling the mug in his hands.

David flipped a woven coaster in eye-watering yellow onto the low table and set an oversized orange cup on it. Alun's mouth watered at the smell of the coffee. Or maybe it was the proximity of David's arse.

Oak and bloody thorn, he needed this human out of his sight, out of his office, out of his life. The fae were notoriously susceptible to human charm, and it never ended well—not for the fae, but especially not for the human.

"I didn't tell you how I like my coffee."

David cast him a sidelong glance from under his lashes. "Black. No sugar."

Mal laughed and raised his cup in a toast. "You are so very right, boy *bach*. Gods forbid he should indulge himself, even in something as trivial as sugar and cream."

Alun's gut tightened, and he clenched his teeth, waiting for the inevitable smile and melting body language that his brother never failed to invoke in fae, supe, or human, but it didn't come. Instead, David turned his back on Mal and faced Alun, swinging the tray at his side.

"Your first appointment should be here in twenty, Doctor. I'll buzz you when he arrives."

"I told you—"

David exhaled on a barely perceptible sigh. "Yes, you told me to go. But I doubt you could run the office by yourself, so why not let me do my job? I'll be at my desk."

He left, Mal ogling his backside until the door *snick*ed closed.

When Mal turned around, he burst out laughing. "Goddess bless, Alun. Upgrade your bleeding wardrobe. Hair shirts went out of fashion in the Middle Ages."

"What are you talking about?"

"You and your self-immolation fetish. Why are you trying to get rid of this man? He's cute, past the age of consent, and seems competent."

Alun's scowl would have sent anyone but his brother scurrying for the nearest exit. "He's human."

"So you said. Get that stick out of your arse about consorting with humans or you'll never get laid."

"Setting aside the ethics of fae/human pairings—"

"Nobody cares about the ethics except you, brother."

Alun lowered his heavy eyebrows and glared at Mal. "Ask the families of the humans whom randy Sidhe lords co-opted for their pleasure. Ask those humans, after they were expelled from Faerie when those same lords grew bored, only to find a year had passed for every day, the world changed, and them with no place in it. Ask Gareth."

Mal fidgeted with his cup, pivoting it in precise quarter-circles on a lopsided knot in the burled oak coffee table. "I'm not advocating that whole changeling shite, or old-school flitting, or spiriting unwilling humans from their beds and into Faerie. I'm talking a couple of drinks at a bar and some consensual Outer World good times. Nothing wrong with that."

"What of the unfair advantage? No human can resist fae *glamourie*. None could ever say no."

Mal grinned. "Why would they want to?"

"Are you saying you'd be happy with love based on compulsion?"

"Who's talking about love?" He leaned back, cradling his cup in his hands. "Attraction of any sort is its own compulsion anyway. I don't see the problem."

"The *problem* is that they deserve a choice. A true choice. If you're using *glamourie* to pull men in your infernal clubs—"

"Don't get your knickers in a twist. Of course I don't."

"Other than your ridiculous facial hair."

"That's nothing but a minor decoration. For fun. I don't *need* it. You, now—"

"Out of the question. Even if I could reconcile it with my conscience, high-level *glamourie* is lost to me under the curse." *And without it, no one could want me anyway.*

Mal shrugged and sipped his coffee. His eyes widened, and he took another sip, then a gulp. "Gwydion's bollocks. If nothing else, keep the lad for his brew skills. Have you tasted this?" He pointed to Alun's untouched cup. "Better than anything on the Queen's table."

Alun crossed his arms and grunted. Like all the Sidhe of the Seelie Court, Mal was a hedonist. Alun preferred Unseelie fae psychopaths. Those, he could treat.

Mal took another sip, and the look of bliss on his face robbed it of its usual cynical smirk. Alun glanced at the steam rising from the cup, beckoning him to taste, to yield.

"Drink the damn coffee, Alun." Mal took another gulp of his own and chased it with a contented sigh. "You know you want to."

Tempted as he was to dump the whole thing in the ficus pot in the corner for spite, he rose to the challenge of Mal's lifted eyebrow. He took a sip, and his eyes nearly rolled back in his head. Smooth. Dark. Secret. The coffee wasn't just a flavor—it was a seductive whisper, a stroke of sin down his throat to his belly.

"Goddess strike me—" He took another gulp. "Gaaah."

"I'm saying. You've got to keep this lad. If you don't make a grab for his balls, at least find out where he buys his beans."

CHAPTER ❀ 4

David hummed as he settled back in his chair with his own cup of coffee and punched up the schedule on the computer. He still couldn't access the patient records, dang it. Their names, period. Nothing else, not even their age or gender. If he had a clue about the patients, he could do a much better job anticipating their needs.

In his sparse transcription work for the doctor, the patients had been adults, victims of some form of relationship trauma. Standard beverage choices and waiting room reading material would do for them—not that Dr. Kendrick had so much as an outdated *People* magazine in sight. But what if he treated children? There were no toys, no children's publications, no amusements of any kind to keep kids entertained while they waited to have the doctor poke around in their little psyches.

He'd have to discuss that with Dr. Kendrick when he was in a better mood. Assuming the man was ever in a better mood.

But to be here for that discussion, he needed to solidify his position. Time to make double damn sure he couldn't be replaced.

He grabbed his iPhone and keyed the speed dial for Fischer Temps.

"Hello?" Multiple phone lines jangled in the background. "I mean, thank you for calling Fischer Temps, Portland's best choice for all your staffing needs. This is Tracy. How may I help you?"

"Tracy, it's David Evans."

"God, David. Please tell me you're still on the Kendrick assignment."

"No worries, sweetie. I've got it covered. More important, how are *you* doing?" She sounded twice as frazzled as yesterday, poor boo-boo. "Tough morning?"

"It's awful." Tracy lowered her voice to a rough whisper. "It's like half of Portland is down with the same flu Sandra's got, including two of our other employment specialists and three-quarters of our associates."

"That's why I'm calling." David doodled a spiderweb on the pad of Post-it notes next to his keyboard. "I suspect Dr. Kendrick may have a tendency to be . . . shall we say . . . difficult?" He added a spider in the center of the web. "He seemed to take issue with me at first meeting."

"Don't tell me he's one of those assholes who objects to men in support positions. Or, God, is he a homophobe? Because if he is, we'll terminate our agreement with him, David, I swear."

"Nothing so dire." He gave the spider a fetching polka-dot bow tie. "But if he should call, I hope you'll encourage him to stick it out with me?"

"All our other qualified health care support associates are out sick. He doesn't have a choice."

Dr. Pissy might not have a choice, but he'd have no cause for complaint either, dang it. "Then have no fear, my dearie-dear." He drew a giant grin on the spider. With fangs. "I won't let the team down." An irritated voice demanding attention joined the phone racket. "Sounds like you have your hands full. I won't keep you. Thanks, sweetie."

"You can count on me, David. I'm behind you, one hundred percent. That is, if I'm still alive by the end of the day."

David disconnected the call. He sat back in the (gray) Aeron chair, tapping his lower lip with his steepled fingers. Hmmm. Good news and bad news. At least Dr. Kendrick didn't have a Fischer Temps option, but there were dozens of other agencies in town.

Don't screw this one up, Davey. Technically, he hadn't screwed the others up. Exactly. But for some reason, no matter how soothing and helpful he tried to be, he ended up in the middle of a standoff. Literally. In the middle, with a pissed-off guy on one side and a second—sometimes third and fourth—guy on the other.

When items started flying—magazines, coffee mugs, the odd piece of furniture—the collateral damage to expensive office equipment was inevitable, as was the pink slip that followed. David mentally hefted the extra-wide (gray) waiting room chairs. He darted over to the nearest one and gave it an experimental nudge. Ooof. The brushed-metal frames were solid, not hollow tubing.

Another good news/bad news thing. The good—harder for agitated not-so-gentlemen to pick up. The bad? "They'll pack one hell of a wallop when they land."

"Talking to furniture?"

David spun around, his heart tripping over itself. Mal was standing in the office doorway, empty coffee cup in his hand, with Dr. Kendrick glaring over his shoulder as if he wished he could incinerate David with his gaze.

"A little desperate, don't you think, love? I'm much more entertaining."

David squared his shoulders and fought the urge to back up a step. Five ten was a perfectly respectable height, but given the size of the Kendrick brothers, he felt like a hobbit on the set of *LOTR*. Mal would be one of the battle elves, or maybe one of the buff human warriors, a little disheveled by living rough, but *tres* hot nonetheless. Dr. Kendrick? A ringer for Aragorn, transmogrified into an Uruk-hai who'd had the advantage of a Gandalf nose job and the finest orthodontist Middle Earth had to offer.

He ignored Mal's come-on, which seemed a reflex, a goad to his brother more than real interest in David, and retreated behind his desk. "If you're looking for company, Mr. Kendrick, I can provide you with the names of several bars and clubs in the area. I, however," he smiled and settled into his chair, fingers poised over his keyboard, "am working."

Mal laughed and ambled over to David's desk, nothing but ease and confidence in the way he held his shoulders and the angle of his perfect jaw. Dr. Kendrick hovered in the doorway at the precise spot where the doorjamb cut a shadow across his face, his body so rigid he could be mistaken for a gargoyle escaped from the nearest Gothic cathedral.

Jeez. Brotherhood must be a real bitch. David was suddenly grateful that he was an only child.

"Any chance for more of your extraordinary coffee?" Mal extended his empty cup.

"Will you be staying, then? Dr. Kendrick's first appointment should arrive momentarily."

"No." Mal shook his head, his dark hair flopping over his forehead, just exactly shy of his eyes. *You practice that in the mirror, Mister Sir?* "On my way out."

"No worries." He took the ceramic mug and pointed to the side table where he'd set up coffee and tea service for the patients. "To-go cups are over there. You'll excuse me if I don't get it for you? Dr. Kendrick and I need to review his schedule for the day."

"If you're trying to keep me from ogling your backside, it's too late." His smile glinted behind perfect lips. David glanced between the two brothers and noticed that despite the obvious other differences in facial structure, their mouths were identical. "Thanks for the coffee." He shot David one last grin set on kill. "Later, Alun."

Dr. Kendrick grunted, his fulminating glare following his brother out of the room.

"So." As soon as the door closed behind Mal's world-class butt, David folded his hands on his desktop and met Dr. Grim's evil-eye glower with one of his own. "We have a few things to discuss."

Alun retreated farther into the shadows of his office in the face of David's unrelenting stare. Oak and thorn, the man had just been exposed to a Sidhe lord who was in full possession of his abilities and not shy about using them. Mal, damn him, was the acknowledged epitome of Seelie Court male beauty, even without the coercive spell of *glamourie*.

How could David bear to look at Alun now? Yet his spine was as straight as a birch sapling, and he never glanced away.

Shite. The tenacity of the human will. How could he have forgotten? Dragon shifters in the throes of gold lust had nothing on the single-mindedness of a human with an agenda.

"I'd like to clarify a few things about the job so I can best serve you and your patients."

"Clients."

David lifted his gull-wing brows. "Beg pardon?"

"The people I treat. I call them clients, not patients."

"Duly noted." He gestured to the computer screen on the short arm of the L-shaped desk. "I think I'd be more effective if I had broader access to the client charts. Since I can only see their names and—"

"No."

David's mouth dropped open, then snapped shut with an audible click of his teeth, his eyes narrowing.

Before Alun could weaken, he retreated into his office and slammed the door. It would be so easy to give in to the unwelcome desire; linger by the reception desk, inhaling lungfuls of air laced with that seductive scent; allow his soul to feast on that face, a beauty as far from Alun's grotesque features as it was possible to be. David's slightly tilted eyes, finely modeled cheekbones, pointed chin, and artfully tousled hair made him resemble an Arthur Rackham wood sprite. The artist had gotten those details right too—half the page boys and attendants at the Seelie Court had a similar look, although none were as enticing as David.

Alun stalked to his desk, spun his chair with a vicious jerk, and sat. Ironically, his own appearance was an advantage in his practice among the supe communities, his monstrous visage perversely comforting to them. No matter how extreme their problems, they sussed that he had it worse.

Likewise with the double handful of humans he treated, all of them in council-ordered treatment for PTSD following unfortunate close encounters with supes. His appearance validated their experience—yes, monsters existed in the world—while offering assurance that not all monsters were threats.

While ugliness didn't guarantee evil any more than beauty guaranteed goodness, in Alun's case, his appearance precisely reflected the blackness of his soul.

In the days before his curse, he'd been arrogant and entitled. As Court Champion and a favorite of the Queen, he'd been granted more privileges than he'd deserved, including that of leading the hunt. That night, the one that had forever changed his life, he'd ridden out with a score of other courtiers who'd sought either the thrill of the chase or the reflected glory of being part of his entourage.

Before, his longbow had always struck true, but that night, it had not. The buck had spooked at the last second. He'd caught it in the flank instead of the breast, and it had bounded into the brush.

"Shite." Alun had slung his bow over his back. "You lot stay here. I'll take care of this."

He urged Cadfael forward, trusting the stallion to pick a path through the dense foliage. Leaves crackled under the horse's hooves, but the night was silent otherwise—eerily so.

When Cadfael broke into a moonlit glade, Alun discovered why. The buck lay on its side, flanks heaving, eyes showing white in terror and pain. A man was kneeling beside it, drawing Alun's arrow from its flesh.

A man? No. For one thing, he was too beautiful to be real. His white-blond hair shone silver in the moonlight, his eyes were as dark as a secret forest pool. His full mouth would make the gods weep, were it not drawn down in fierce concentration.

But he was more than his beauty. Awareness skittered along Alun's skin, drawing him forward with a wanting that would be pain if it weren't so sweet.

Achubydd.

He'd never thought to see one. They kept themselves apart, nomadic, their clans ghosting through the lands of both Faerie and the Outer World. At one time, they'd lived only in Annwn, the Welsh Otherworld, but with Arawn's disappearance, its gates had closed forever, putting the *achubyddion* at the mercy of fae who lusted after their abilities.

"If you must hunt the night," the man said, his voice low and musical, "you should be sure of your aim."

"Usually I am."

He tossed the arrow aside. "Do not try unless you know you will succeed. Otherwise you do naught but scatter pain in your wake."

Alun shifted uncomfortably in the saddle under the accusing glare. "I intended to put an end to him swiftly." He swung to the ground and unsheathed his hunting knife from his belt. "Stand aside and I will do so."

"No." The man placed one hand over the buck's wound. "You forfeited your claim when you failed in your covenant for a clean kill."

"I can't in conscience leave him like this—suffering, unable to flee from predators."

He lifted one slanted eyebrow, nearly white against his brown skin. "Such as yourself?"

Heat stole up Alun's throat, and he thanked the Goddess for the dappled moonlight that hid his telltale blush. How long had it been since anyone had shamed him? They had tried, with insinuations and petty Court politics, but nothing had ever touched him until this accusation of clumsy brutality.

He strode forward, ready to end the unpleasant feeling. "Let me—" Before he got halfway across the clearing, the buck heaved to its feet and bounded off, its gait unmarred. Alun's mouth fell open. "He's . . . he's—"

"He is well." The man rose slowly. "And no longer susceptible to a hunter's ill-aimed arrows."

"Forever?" At the man's nod, Alun fumbled to stow his knife. "I never knew— That is, I'm aware that your kind can work near miracles on people—at a cost. But to make an animal invulnerable?"

"There are many things you do not know—that you'll never know—about . . . about . . ." The man's eyes rolled back in his head, his eyelids fluttering, and he began to topple forward. Alun caught him, and let the momentum carry them both to the ground.

His legs were twisted uncomfortably beneath him, but he was loath to risk disturbing the man draped over his lap. He stroked the man's silky hair back from his high forehead. Traced the arc of a cheekbone to the ever so slightly pointed ear. Breathed in the scent of his skin, like rain on heather.

And there, curled awkwardly on the ground with Cadfael cropping grass at his elbow and a full party of hunters waiting for him on the other side of the grove, he had fallen in love with Owain Glenross, and sealed both their fates.

He could never be forgiven for what had followed, but at least he could atone somewhat by helping others—and prevent another stubborn man from destruction at his own hands.

David Evans had to go, for his own good as well as the safety of the supe communities and Alun's own fragile peace of mind.

Alun punched up Sandra Fischer's number and got her voice mail again, damn it.

"Sandra. Alun Kendrick. I'll grant you some slack since you're an F1W2 victim, but are you insane? You sent a human to staff my office. Are you trying to call down the wrath of every supernatural council in the Pacific Northwest? Because you've definitely called down mine. Fix this. Immediately." He lowered the handset, ready to slam it, but raised it to his ear again instead. "Get well soon."

CHAPTER ✿ 5

David remained rooted in his chair for two minutes while he waited for the virtual steam to stop shooting out his ears. Of all the arrogant, self-righteous, pigheaded . . . Gah!

This was a psychology practice, right? Well, time to stage a little intervention of his own.

He marched into the inner sanctum (without knocking—ha!) and planted himself in front of Dr. Kendrick's desk, hands clenched at his sides so he wouldn't pick up the nearest ten-pound textbook and wing it at the doctor's plus-sized skull.

"You make it sound as if you don't think I can handle the job."

Dr. Kendrick opened a copy of the *Portland Business Journal*, holding it up so it blocked David's view of his face. "You can't."

"I'll have you know I've taken many"—*one*—"classes on clinic office management. I've completed most"—*about a third*—"of the coursework for my RN degree, and I have extensive experience in"—*getting fired from*—"medical and dental practices of all types and sizes."

Dr. Kendrick lowered the journal, and David flinched. He couldn't help it. When he'd only heard The Voice, he'd fit his vision of a matching fantasy man to it. The sight of that tortured face—overlaid by the odious attitude—was a shock. Unfortunately, the doctor caught his reaction, and the perpetual frown deepened.

"Yet despite your impressive credentials, you've chosen to temp for a one-man psychology practice. On sabbatical from your stellar career?"

David sniffed and tried his best to look confident. "I'm considering my options. Of which there are many, before you ask."

"Doing me a favor, are you?"

"Yes. I mean no. I'm here to do the best job possible. It's to both our benefits if we can put together a workable professional relationship."

Dr. Kendrick grunted and raised the journal again. "No point. I've already logged the request for your replacement."

Was that so? In that case, Dr. Smug was in for a surprise. In the meantime, David would simply pretend that the doctor was a reasonable human being. At least one of them could be professional.

"Here's your schedule. The charts are cued up on your laptop." He slapped the agenda printout and a handful of take-out menus on the desk. "IM me with your food choice by four and I'll have your meal here in time for your dinner break at six." He bared his teeth in a dare-me smile. "Have a nice day."

He pivoted smartly on the toe of his perfectly polished loafers, lifted his chin, and put an extra slug of confidence into his walk out of the room. With each step, he repeated *pretend, pretend, pretend* in his head, waiting until he'd closed the door before the breath whooshed out of his lungs and his chest deflated.

Sheesh, usually altercations occurred *around* David. This was the first time that he might not only have been part of the melee, but the direct instigator. If anything was likely to put an end to his hope of landing a permanent gig, this was it. Attacking your boss with a blunt instrument? A sure way to get fired.

He plopped into his chair and poked at his keyboard until his abbreviated menu appeared, glancing at the time in the corner of the screen. The first patient—oops, *client*—was ten minutes late. Since one of the many things David didn't have access to was the client contact information, he couldn't call and confirm the appointment. It would serve Dr. Douche right if he was reduced to playing solitaire beer pong in his office for the next hour, perfecting his snarl.

The outer door opened, and a man in a muted brown plaid Hugo Boss suit sauntered in, his gait as smooth as his medium-brown hair. If this was the missing client, David would bet his entire collection of Star Wars memorabilia that the lateness was deliberate. *Passive-aggressive macho posturing much?*

From the corner of his eye, David studied the client, who took a detour to the coffee service without bothering to acknowledge that there was anyone else in the room. David never trusted guys who were that . . . smooth. He liked his men—when he could get one—a little rougher around the edges. Perfection was a skosh too intimidating for someone so . . . well . . . he refused to cop to awkward. Alternative. Idiosyncratic. Somewhere on the sliding scale between *GQ* and nerd-tastic. But with great hair.

Unlike Mr.—he checked the schedule on his monitor—Hoffenberg, whose slicked-back do sported a tad too much product. David found it difficult to trust a man who couldn't conquer his own personal grooming supplies.

Still, he shouldn't make any judgments. If the man was here, he had already admitted that he needed help with some knotty life issue, and David had only the highest respect for that kind of self-awareness.

He donned his best smile. "Mr. Hoffenberg? Shall I tell Dr. Kendrick you're here?"

Hoffenberg eyed him, swirling his coffee with a slow figure eight of the red plastic stir stick. "Where's Vanessa?"

"The regular office manager? She's on maternity leave."

Something flared in the back of Hoffenberg's frost-gray eyes, a glint of red. David's smile slipped and throat constricted, his hand creeping to his pocket to rub his thumb across the smooth surface of his worry stone. *Did I really see that? Sure, his tie has red flecks, but his eyes?* Maybe it was a freak reflection off David's flame-colored candy dish, but whatever it was, it was damned eerie. And he *must* be imagining the shock wave of fury that rolled over him from that red-speckled glare.

Surely Dr. Kendrick didn't treat any violent clients. Maybe he needed to rethink this assignment after all. Getting murdered in the workplace? Not part of his master plan.

He clenched his fist around his worry stone once and released it. *Man up, Evans.* He'd nail this job, damn it, despite the dreary decor and curmudgeonly boss and possibly homicidal clients. For Aunt Cassie's sake as well as his own.

He cleared his throat before lifting the phone, his finger shaking as he pressed the intercom button. "Dr. Kendrick, Mr. Hoffenberg is here."

"Shite." The doctor's response was a barely audible growl.

Hmmm. Good to know David wasn't the only one with that reaction to Hoffenberg.

He placed the handset back in the cradle and smiled. "Dr. Kendrick will be—" The door to the office flew open, and the doctor loomed just inside the threshold, his face in shadow again. "Why, here he is now."

"Good afternoon, Jackson."

"Alun." Hoffenberg pivoted toward the door, thrusting his nearly full cup at David, who fumbled the unexpected handoff. The still-hot coffee soaked the sleeve of his jacket and spattered into a steaming puddle on the desktop.

Hissing through gritted teeth, he shook coffee off his hand as Dr. Kendrick surged out of his office and crowded behind the desk.

"Take off your jacket. Hurry. The fabric will hold the heat in."

"I'm all right. Really. I can take care of it myself."

"Like bloody hells you can. Jacket off. Run your hand under cold water. Now." He grasped the lapels of David's blazer as if he were about to forcibly assist in its removal, like some kind of goblin valet.

"Can we start my session?" Hoffenberg straddled the office threshold. "I have an appointment downtown at three thirty."

Dr. Kendrick shot him a lethal glare. Lord. The client must be made of stern stuff if he could withstand *that* with nothing more than a lift of one eyebrow. "This doesn't speak well for your progress, Jackson."

Hoffenberg scarcely glanced at David. "I'll wait for you inside."

David closed his hands over Dr. Kendrick's and removed them from his jacket, swallowing against the pain. The doctor's eyes widened at the contact, and David noticed they were a beautiful gold-flecked hazel, as incongruous in the disfigured face as the sensitive lips.

"I'll be fine. The client should be your first priority." He shooed the doctor toward the open door and forced a smile. "The sooner you go, the sooner I'll be able to treat my poor wounded paw."

Dr. Kendrick went, but his over-the-shoulder glance at the office threshold made David's breath hitch in his chest. God. Who'd have thought that Dr. Dementor could ever look that *caring*?

Alun closed the door, flattening one palm against it, his vision tinged with red, the muscles in his neck tight from fighting the urge to slam his client against the wall—not accepted clinical practice, even among supes. But Goddess, David's pinched lips, his uneven breath, made Alun want to roar. He inhaled, chest expanding, eyes closed. Exhaling slowly, his fury once more in check, he turned to his client.

Jackson Hoffenberg, eldest son of the alpha of the Clackamas wolf pack—handsome, rich, educated, and angry as all the hells because despite his pedigree, his shifter gene was dormant. Effectively human, he was ineligible to assume pack leadership when his father stepped down.

"I believe you owe David an apology."

Jackson sat in the precise center of the love seat and rested his arms along its back, a pretense of openness that Alun saw through as easily as if the man's skull were made of glass.

"Why? He's just a human. Surely it's beneath you to employ one." Jackson crossed his legs and smoothed the line of his trousers over his knee. "It's certainly beneath me to apologize to one."

Alun settled himself in the wingback chair, his elbows on the padded arms, his fingers laced loosely in front of him. He didn't need to take notes because his recall was perfect—unfortunate when it came to eluding his past, highly advantageous in his current occupation.

"You could have seriously injured him."

"He's fine. He said so himself. Now. I'd like to discuss terminating this farce."

Alun leaned back, perversely glad of his curse because he knew that despite Jackson's attempts at indifference, he was one of the few clients who found Alun's appearance unsettling. "Your alpha reported the incident at the last council meeting."

Nostrils flaring at the mention of his father, Jackson shrugged without lifting his arms from the back of the love seat. "Trivial."

"He felt it significant enough to inform me of it. And what about your behavior to David just now? A week ago you wouldn't have been so cavalier about injuring my office manager."

Jackson's eyes turned flinty, pinpricks of red flashing in the pale gray of his irises. "A week ago your office manager was Vanessa."

Ah. As he'd suspected, Jackson still harbored resentment because Vanessa had mated a were from the Multnomah pack. Setting aside that Vanessa was ears over tail in love with her husband, Jackson's inactive status barred him from mating anyone. Chalk up another grievance in the tale of Jackson Hoffenberg versus the Unfair World.

"Despite your claims to have overcome your anger-management issues, I don't believe you've progressed enough to justify an end to our sessions. In fact, we may need to increase the frequency of your visits."

Jackson's brows lowered, and his lip lifted in a sneer. "I don't have to listen to you."

"Perhaps not. However, as long as you're in pack-mandated treatment, *I* must listen to *you*. Let's begin with the incident at the council meeting."

"I have important pack business at the courthouse this afternoon." He crossed his arms and lost his last shred of affability. "I don't have time to waste with this nonsense."

"Then I suggest you start talking."

CHAPTER ✥ 6

D avid waited until the door closed behind doctor and client, then
stripped off his jacket.

"Ow ow ow, damn it, ow." Now that Dr. Stoic wasn't watching
him, he could be a big baby and give in to the pain. The left sleeve of
his blazer was completely soaked. It might never recover unless Aunt
Cassie had a special stain remover in her bag of herbal tricks.

One thing she did have was the world's best burn ointment,
and after an accident-prone childhood that included far too many
excursions outside without sunscreen, David never left home
without it.

He pulled the little pot out of his messenger bag and unscrewed
the lid, unleashing the scent of mint and rosemary and something she
would never divulge and he could never identify. All he knew was that
it smelled like comfort. He smeared some on the back of his reddened
hand and breathed a sigh when the pain dulled.

He rolled up his sleeve and checked his forearm. Once exposed to
the cooler air, it felt tingly, but mostly unharmed. His shirt, however,
was worse off than his blazer because it was white, not charcoal. He
rolled up the other sleeve to more or less match. Not the perfect
professional image he wanted to convey, but there wasn't a lot he
could do about it in the absence of a boatload of laundry supplies or a
dry cleaner who made house calls.

The outside door opened, and he braced himself for another
onslaught of not-so-veiled aggression, but this time the arrivals were
much less alarming. A zaftig woman in a black dress so flattering
it had to have cost a fortune, accessorized with a triple strand of
freshwater pearls that hung halfway to her waist, was leading a little

dark-haired boy, no more than five or six, who stared at David with wide brown eyes.

"Good afternoon. You must be Mrs. Tomlinson, and this is Benjamin."

The kid ducked his head, pressing against his mother's side, and peeked at David from the folds of her skirt. In his gray flannel shorts, white shirt, and red tie, he looked like a refugee from a high-end prep school, complete with a stylized red-and-gold crest on the breast pocket of his navy blazer.

Mrs. Tomlinson glanced around, a slight frown marring her patrician face. "Where is Vanessa? I hope nothing's wrong with the baby."

"Not a thing. She just opted for early maternity leave."

Her face relaxed into a smile that would have charmed anybody within a two-mile radius. Why did she make him think of royalty? He couldn't tell, other than that she held herself with the regal bearing of a Princess Diana who wasn't as obsessed with her diet.

"Please have a seat. Dr. Kendrick will be with you shortly."

She nodded and led her son to a chair next to the bare end table. Benjamin settled in docilely enough, poor kid. His little legs were too short for the seat depth and his feet stuck out in the air. He folded his hands in his lap, and his thin chest rose in an unmistakable sigh.

See? Exactly as David had suspected, the poor little guy was bored, bored, bored. This office totally needed a play niche, or at least a shelf of Dr. Seuss classics, to occupy kids who didn't come equipped with their own amusements.

"Wait here, Benjamin," his mother said, and glided to the door in her sensible heels. When she opened it, David spied two men outside, holding up the wall on the opposite side of the corridor with their massive shoulders. They were bigger than Dr. Kendrick and his brother, and that was saying a lot. Bodyguards? The royalty notion might not be so far-fetched, even if royalty these days was more likely related to money or corporate power.

He glanced at the boy and caught him staring. His big eyes got even wider, as if he thought he'd done something wrong. David grinned and displayed his one undeniable talent.

He wiggled his ears.

Benjamin giggled, then clapped his hands over his mouth with a scared glance at his mother. She was still conversing in a low tone with the bruisers in the hallway, though, and didn't catch it, so David laid a finger across his lips.

And did it again.

This time Benjamin muffled his laughter behind his hands, but he looked way happier than he had when he'd walked in. *My job here is done.*

But when Dr. Kendrick opened his office door, default glower back in place, and strode into the lobby with Mr. Hoffenberg, the boy cowered in his chair again. *Never mind. My job here is just beginning.*

He frowned at his monitor, then cut a glance at Mrs. Tomlinson, who'd taken a seat next to her son but seemed oblivious to his distress. David, as an adult with an interest in health care, could make allowances for conditions that would distort Dr. Kendrick's features so far off the norm. But to a little kid without that understanding? He'd look like the monster in the closet come out to munch on a random leg or two.

When he tore his attention away from the couple in the corner, he realized Mr. Hoffenberg was standing in front of his desk, staring at him with that same matching-tie-and-eye-fleck intensity.

"How's your hand?" Hoffenberg's voice matched his suit—a brown plaid voice if ever David had heard one. "You sustained no lasting injury, I trust."

"No worries." He held up his hand, where Aunt Cassie's ointment had already worked most of its magic. "See? All better."

"But your shirt. Your jacket." Jeez, the guy could drill holes with that stare. "To make amends, allow me to take you for lunch."

Seriously? Between Hoffenberg and Mal Kendrick, he'd gotten more action in a half day on the job than he'd gotten in a month of club nights. Yeah, most of those club hookups had started with a similar come-on, and every single one of them had imploded—sometimes before the end of the first drink.

"Jackson." Dr. Kendrick's voice was as hard-edged as a knife. "The gesture is appreciated, but David has a job to do. I'll see you next time."

Hoffenberg pointed a last creepy-ass stare at David and nodded once before he allowed Dr. Kendrick to walk him to the door.

He did a visible double take at the sight of the two guys in the hallway, although the doctor didn't seem surprised to see them.

Dr. Kendrick waited until the *ding* of the elevator marked Hoffenberg's exit before he nodded at the bodyguards or bouncers or whatever the heck they were, and closed the door. He stalked across the lobby, circling behind the desk to loom over David's chair.

"If he comes back, press this." He pointed to a quarter-sized red button on the inside of the drawer pedestal. "Or this one." A matching button was mounted inside the desk's other wing. "Hit it with your knee, and it won't be obvious."

"Trust me, I know how to do discreet."

The doctor's mouth pinched in either displeasure or disbelief. "I'm sure. However, Jackson is fast. Use what advantage you can."

David glanced at the boy. If Dr. Kendrick had patients—*excuse me,* clients—that were so dangerous, should he be treating little kids when their appointments overlapped this way? He remembered the incredible hulks outside the door. Hmmm. *Guess this particular kid carries his own protection.*

"Very well." He looked up, past the cliff of the doctor's chest, and met his glare. "Did Vanessa ever use the panic button?"

Dr. Kendrick's scowl deepened, and his gaze veered to a spot over David's left shoulder, in the vicinity of the paper clip holder. *Aaannd wait for it—here comes the lie.*

"Vanessa had her own methods of self-defense."

"Really? What? I might want to invest in some training myself."

The fierce gaze, more intense under the jut of the overhanging brow ridges, slid to the right. *Uh-huh. Let's hear it, Dr. Liar.*

"Krav Maga."

And I'm the love child of Princess Leia and Jabba the Hutt. "Interesting."

Dr. Kendrick's gaze flicked from the Tomlinsons back to David, but he didn't retreat from behind the desk. This close to him, David could detect the wild fragrances of mint and lemon and almond, reminiscent of one of his aunt's home-crafted body washes. God, if he closed his eyes and just smelled the man and listened to him when he wasn't barking orders—which admittedly was infrequent to the point of nonexistent—Dr. Kendrick could be his dream lover.

"We have a problem."

Oops. David's eyes snapped open. Heat infused his neck and crept up his cheeks until he probably looked parboiled. He needed to control his little trips to fantasy land, because him and the doctor? *Never gonna happen.* Not when the man couldn't look at him without disgust twisting his features even further.

Since that expression hadn't yet left his face, he probably never looked any happier. David had a sudden urge to pat the man on the arm or rub his back to see if he could release the tension in those broad shoulders.

"Ordinarily," Dr. Kendrick said, "Vanessa entertains Benjamin for fifteen minutes while I speak with his mother alone, but—"

"No problem. I can handle it."

The man snorted, heavy brows lowering further.

Okay. Maybe he didn't feel sorry for the guy. It wasn't as if he was trying to overcome his monster-of-the-week look with a kinder, gentler attitude. It was almost as if he embraced the beast persona, reveled in it. Or at least didn't bother to counteract the impression.

But poor little Benjamin deserved better than to sit in the office while the doctor and his mother talked about him as if he weren't there. David had had more than enough of that crap in foster care. Kids paid more attention than adults realized.

"Believe me, Dr. Kendrick, I can be very entertaining." David kept his gaze fixed on the doctor, but he wiggled his ears, just once, and was rewarded with Benjamin's muffled giggle.

"Doctor," Mrs. Tomlinson said in perfectly round tones, "I'm sure this young man will be more than adequate. May we begin?"

Well, that high praise put Dr. Doubt in his place, now didn't it? Mrs. Tomlinson progressed into the office with the doctor as her retinue. When David turned back after the door had closed, Benjamin was standing in front of him, his chin just clearing the top of the desk.

"Well, hello there. Escaped your chair, did you?"

He nodded. "You can wiggle your ears."

"Yup." David did it again, carding his fingers through his shaggy hair to reveal his ears in all their protuberant glory. Yeah, there was a reason he wore this style. Years of remarks about jug ears had seen to that, but Benjamin was at the right age to appreciate them for their raw entertainment value. "Can you?"

"Yes." He screwed up his face and then raised his eyebrows to their limit, which succeeded in moving his scalp, but left his ears stationary.

"Excellent." David pointed to the crest on Benjamin's blazer. "What's that on your jacket?"

He looked down, his chin bumping his chest. "Dragon."

"Really? That's awesome. My school mascot was the hornets." The boy screwed up his face and stuck out his tongue. "I know. Lousy, right? Dragons are much cooler."

"What's those?" He pointed to the pastilles mounded in the candy dish.

"Candies. Would you like one?"

"I'm not allowed."

"Not even one?" Seriously, what kid could resist sneaking a candy when the adults turned their backs? "You're not diabetic, are you?"

His forehead wrinkled in thought. "I don't think so."

"Just in case, we'll wait until we ask your mom."

He sighed and nodded. "What's those?" He pointed to the line of action figures under David's monitor.

"These guys? This one's Legolas. He's an elf."

Benjamin shot him a suspicious glare. "No, he's not. He's only little. Elves are tall."

"Well, he's a toy. A miniature that's supposed to look like the big elf."

"You mean a doll?" His voice dripped with little-boy scorn.

"Not a doll. An action figure. See?" David picked up Chewbacca and faced him off against Legolas on the desktop. "Grrr. Rawr."

"Who's that one?"

"Chewbacca? He's a Wookiee."

"No, he's not." From the disappointed downturn of Benjamin's mouth, David had lost all of his ear-wiggling points. "Wookiees are baseball players what aren't very good yet."

David laughed. "Right. Well then, he's a big furry guy who knows how to fly a spaceship and fight bad guys."

Benjamin nodded solemnly. "Like Vanessa's husband. He flies planes for the Naby. She told me."

Vanessa was married to a Navy pilot, huh? David hoped her husband wasn't stationed overseas while she was pregnant. He held out the little plastic Chewbacca. "Here. He's yours."

The little boy's eyes widened, the overhead lights glinting in their depths, and his mouth puckered in a soft *Oooh*. He took the toy in both hands almost reverently.

"I don't have no toys like this. I can keep him? Really?"

No candy and no toys? Maybe being the corporate equivalent of a little prince had its drawbacks. "Absolutely. In fact . . ." He scooted Legolas across the desk. "Would you like the elf too?"

Benjamin shook his head, cradling Chewbacca against his chest. "No. Only one."

"You sure?" He wiggled Legolas back and forth. "They could have battles or go on adventures to hunt some orcs."

Benjamin stepped back. "No. I don't like elves. Only Dr. Alun."

Why would Benjamin associate elves with Dr. Kendrick? Unless it was the orc reference. Oh well. Nobody did non sequiturs like six-year-olds. "All righty, then. I'll bring a couple of different ones next time, okay?"

A grin split the boy's face, and he nodded vigorously. "Next time."

"You got it."

Benjamin slid Chewbacca into the pocket of his blazer and retreated to his chair, his hand hovering over the pocket as if he were afraid to touch, yet didn't quite believe the toy was there.

David wished it was as easy to make Dr. Kendrick happy.

A strange half-familiar tingle skated under Alun's skin as he tried to focus his attention on Teresa Tomlinson. He couldn't write it off as residual adrenaline from Jackson's odd aggression against David— it didn't have the unpleasant tang of danger. More an awareness. Potentiality, with a flavor of long-ago yearning. He almost had it, but when Teresa took a firm grip on her pearls and sat forward in the love seat, it vanished.

"I'm at the end of my tether, doctor. I've tried everything. Gold. Silver. Platinum. Gemstones of all colors. Every time, he gives them away."

Alun kept his hands folded in his lap, in full view. With dragon shifters, you had to make it very clear that you had no designs on their possessions. "He's still young."

"When I was his age, I had a closet full of treasure."

"But you're female. Females mature sooner than males."

"Yes, but still . . ." She stopped playing with her pearls and twisted one of her rings, a four-carat diamond, pulling it above the knuckle and pushing it back. Classic behavior—display the riches and test whether you'll take advantage of an apparent opportunity. "I can't have my son be the only dragon in the history of the race who doesn't have a decent hoard when he comes of age."

"Teresa, you know I'll continue to see Benjamin as long as you wish, but I believe you'd be better served by waiting another year or two. The hoarding instinct may kick in naturally."

She raised her worried gaze to his face, her eyes the color of opals. "I'm . . ." She sighed, shoulders slumping. "What if this is a symptom? He's the first dragon shifter child born in over fifty years. Our council warns us constantly that our race is threatened, our evolution twisted by the loss of our traditional hunting grounds and the absence of tribute."

Alun relaxed his features into what passed for a reassuring—or at least less threatening—expression. "I think every supe council has said the same thing for the past century. Yes, things are changing. Yes, we all need to adapt. But the world moves rapidly these days, and evolution isn't swift."

She smiled wanly. "Especially for dragons. I think we're more hidebound than even the fae." She jerked one hand to her mouth. "Oh. I'm sorry, Doctor. I didn't mean—"

"No, it's perfectly true. My race is notoriously resistant to progress." Alun uncrossed his legs and leaned forward, his palms out and open to show he was hiding nothing, attempting to take nothing. "But I think you need to give Benjamin more time."

She nodded, sighing. "It's been so long since we had a child among us, we've forgotten what it's like. May we still come for our sessions? Even if you don't treat Benjamin, I feel better after our talks."

"Then by all means, we'll continue. As often as you like." Alun rose and gestured toward the door, knowing better than to offer to help her rise. She'd construe it as an attempt to relieve her of her jewels.

When he escorted her into the lobby, that skitter of nerves returned, like sparks under his skin. He scanned the room for threats. The clinic door was still closed tightly, but even with his diminished abilities, he sensed the presence of the two dragon shifter guards in the corridor. Good. Jackson hadn't returned. He'd share a few sharp words with the Clackamas alpha if the unwarranted aggression didn't abate.

David was sitting at his keyboard in his shirtsleeves. Benjamin was perched in his usual chair, although he was sporting a secretive smile new in Alun's experience with the boy.

He glanced sharply at David, but the man simply hummed under his breath and continued typing. He paused when he noticed Teresa and smiled at her with that deadly human charm.

"Mrs. Tomlinson," he said, his voice low enough not to carry across the room to the boy, "would you object if Benjamin had a pastille? One of my aunt's friends makes them. I promise you, they're very good, and excellent for the digestion. She owns a confectionery in the Hawthorne District, and these are a best seller."

"Well . . ." She glanced at her son.

"Here." He pushed the jewel-bright dish toward her. "Try one. Please."

She selected one of the pastel candies with the same care that she'd use selecting a new emerald. When the pastille hit her tongue, her opalescent eyes widened and swirled with a dragon shifter's avarice response. Alun glanced at David, but he didn't seem to notice anything unusual. Perhaps the man wasn't very observant or sensitive. He'd certainly not had the standard human response to Alun's wreck of a face.

"It's not overly sweet." Teresa reached for another. "May I?" David nodded, and she picked a different color. "Mint and . . . is that . . ."

"Allspice. Cardamom. With an apple cider base."

She closed her eyes. "Lovely."

"So?" David nodded at Benjamin. "Legal for your son?"

She smiled at him with the full force and graciousness of a queen—which was exactly what she was. Queen of the entire dragon shifter race. "Absolutely."

David beckoned to Benjamin, who scooted out of his chair and bounded across the room with more animation than Alun had ever seen from him.

"Mom says it's okay, Benjy. Take your pick."

As the boy made his own careful selection, the feeling under Alun's skin peaked, as if his blood had turned to nuclear champagne. What in the hells was this?

The odd excitement coursed through him—a combination of awareness and promise, with a darker thread of threat. It had been years since he'd been in this close a proximity to any man he found sexually attractive. Perhaps the effect was only the result of his long abstinence, unrelated to David's race.

But if this was the seductive lure of a human? He controlled a shiver. Goddess, no wonder some fae became addicted, so much so that they'd stoop to kidnapping and rape. Not that it excused their behavior, but it might explain the compulsion.

Whatever it was, though, it had to stop, and if getting rid of David Evans was what it took, he'd make bloody damned sure Sandra Fischer lived up to her agreement and replaced him with a nice safe werewolf. Immediately.

CHAPTER ✥ 7

Despite the late hour he arrived home from work, all six of the "girls"—David's honorary aunts—were gathered in the living room, waiting to hear about his first day on the job. As he'd expected, when he told them the sorry state of the gray lobby, they were horrified. As a result, they all showed up the next morning toting their own offerings to the cause, like benevolent fairies at a christening.

So he wasn't allowed to open the blinds. Whatever. He now had three boxes of goodies that would brighten the place like indoor sunshine. He dared even kill-joy Dr. Kendrick to object.

He set the last box on his desk and flexed his hand. His burn was virtually nonexistent today, thanks to Aunt Cassie's miraculous salve. He'd begged, cajoled, and wheedled—and when the bills were looming especially high, he'd downright demanded—that she give him the formula so they could build their own cottage industry. She'd always refused, which sent his temper spiraling. He was sure that if she agreed to market that stuff, their financial woes would be over—she'd be rich.

But she still wouldn't be well. David swallowed against a lump in his throat the size of his heart. *Don't think about that. You've got a job to do.*

He lifted three of Brigid's gorgeous vases out of the first box—one a swirl of dark green, indigo, and violet; the second a starburst of red, orange, and yellow; the last an ombre, fading from magenta at the base to pale peach at the lip, like a tequila sunrise.

The wonderful thing about Brigid's vases was that they were beautiful on their own; they didn't need flowers to complete them. He dropped a handful of Aunt Cassie's potpourri—the one she called

Soothe the Savage Beast—into each vase, adding a little pat to his favorite, the green-indigo-violet one. In a way, it reminded him of Dr. Kendrick. Dark, but with depth. If you held it up to the light, you could see surprising nodes of gold hidden in the darker whorls.

In this cave of an office, those would never show up, but David knew they were there, and that's what counted.

He hummed as he set out magazines the girls had donated— Elinor's *Rock & Gem*, Peggy's *Fine Cooking*, Nola's *Woodcarving Illustrated,* and a half-dozen different quilting magazines from Lorraine. He topped off the collection with a couple of gossip rags and a tabloid or two he'd picked up from the check-out stand, just for fun. He kept the Star Wars graphic novels in his desk drawer. Those were for Benjy.

As David was about to toss all the blow-in advertising cards into the recycling bin, he noticed that the cleaning service hadn't emptied it, or the trash either. The procedures manual had been quite specific about office cleanliness standards. This was a clear infraction. Was it intentional? Could Dr. Kendrick have slipped the service something under the table to give him another excuse to fire David for dereliction of duty?

As soon as the thought occurred to him, he dismissed it. Dr. Kendrick might be the surliest psychologist in the history of the world, but sneaky? Never. David would bet his bow ties on it.

No, this was a simple case of sub-par service delivery, number one on the list of David's unforgivable sins, and he refused to put up with it. He picked up the phone, ready to speed-dial the cleaning company. *Hold on. Get the whole story first, Evans.*

Could they have skimped on the inner sanctum too? He shuddered when he imagined Dr. Kendrick's reaction to that. He knocked cautiously, just in case the doctor had hibernated in his office overnight. When he got no answer, he entered.

"Just wonderful," he muttered, hands on his hips. Both wire-mesh trashcans were half-full. They'd vacuumed the gray carpet, but hadn't bothered with any horizontal surface higher than that. Cup rings marred the coffee table, and Dr. Kendrick's used mug was on his desk.

Right, then. First thing on the docket after he fixed this? Call the clueless service and threaten them with the Wrath of Kendrick. That ought to scare them out of their Lemon Pledge withdrawal stupor.

He grabbed a bin in each hand and stalked back to the lobby. When he shook the first load into his own can, something rattled against the metal. He peered into the nest of crumpled paper and used tissues. One corner of a CD case was poking out of the mess, shrink wrap still intact.

David fished it out with careful fingers. One side of the case was blank, but two words on the other side shifted his heartbeat into high gear.

"Holy cats. Gareth Kendrick?" How stupid could David be? Dr. Kendrick must be related to Gareth, whose band, Hunter's Moon, had swept the Grammys last year. You couldn't beg, borrow, or scalp a ticket for their upcoming concert at the Moda Center, as David knew all too well. He'd tried all three methods.

He had every one of the band's albums. He hadn't heard a scrap of a rumor about solo work from any of them, so this was new, possibly underground. David had never been a dumpster-diver, but for an unreleased Gareth Kendrick CD, he'd make an exception.

He wiped the CD case off and tucked it in his desk drawer. If the doctor had tossed it, it was totally fair game, right? If David couldn't catch the concert, he'd at least have some new music to compensate.

As he closed the drawer, he compared Gareth's fallen angel beauty—soulful blue eyes, tousled brown-gold curls, a full mouth that broke your heart even when he smiled—against Mal's biker bad-boy good looks. Jeez, poor Dr. Kendrick had grown up comparing himself to both of them? Even if the guy was a crabby unapologetic dictator, maybe David should cut him a little slack.

Alun stomped down the stairs, damning the F1W2 with each step. He still hadn't been able to reach Sandra Fischer for a replacement. Her assistant had been apologetic but firm. David was the only qualified temp on their roster who wasn't either committed to a long-term assignment or down with the flu.

Last night, he'd been desperate enough to contact Vanessa's father-in-law and try to convince him that as a werewolf, she'd be in no danger if she returned to work.

That went as well as he'd expected.

He stood in the corridor outside the door to his offices, his palm damp on the handle of his briefcase. His previous reaction to the human was surely an anomaly. A combination of surprise and the dormant battle reflexes that had surfaced when Jackson had accosted David.

He'd spent two hours last night in deep meditation, reinforcing the control he'd perfected in decades of denying his fae roots. Since he felt none of the unsettling prickle beneath his skin that had troubled him yesterday, he'd succeeded.

So why was he standing in the corridor? This was his office, damn it, his practice, something he'd worked for years to accomplish, despite opposition from the Queen and initial resistance from the supe communities. But they needed him. They needed his work. Supe genes came with a price, which often manifested in mental instability. He'd made it his mission to develop treatments to help them.

It was the only way he knew to atone for his transgressions.

He straightened his shoulders, steeling himself for a recurrence of his inexplicable response, and opened the door.

David wasn't at his desk, but by the clinks and gurgles issuing from the kitchenette, he must be brewing another pot of his extraordinary coffee.

Alun sniffed experimentally. Instead of the David-scent that had driven him to distraction yesterday, another smell invaded his senses. Not disagreeable or unsettling. Almost . . . comforting. He closed his eyes and breathed in the subtle fragrance. Mint. Meadowsweet. Vervain. The aroma of coffee infused the air as well, mixing pleasantly with the herbal scents.

He inhaled deeply, and his nerves settled in a way that made him realize exactly how on edge he'd been. Although keenly aware of how resistant to change his race was, he thought he'd learned to adapt by necessity. Perhaps he was just as set in his ways as any throwback Seelie courtier.

He opened his eyes and scanned the room, his attention immediately caught by a scatter of periodicals on the table nearest the door. The damning inches-tall headline of one of those despicable tabloids screamed at him from the top of the pile.

Bigfoot Sighted in Oregon Coast Range!

The blurry photograph of a shambling, fur-covered figure that accompanied the story was all too familiar—Ted Farnsworth, one of his past clients, a bear shifter with an exhibitionist kink who'd gotten into trouble with his elders for exposing their existence to humans.

Damn and blast. He'd thought Ted had his compulsions under control. Alun snatched the foul thing off the table. He'd make a discreet call to the bear council. Perhaps this was an old photo, recycled by the paper for lack of any new sensation.

Another tabloid, this one with a picture of a fanged human face with vastly elongated ears, lay under the first one.

Batboy Found in Cave Under Mount Hood!

Shite. How had the photographer captured a vampire fledgling mid-shift? The flash must have blinded the poor thing for months.

A growl rumbling in his chest, he seized the second paper and stalked down the hallway, rolled-up tabloids held in his hand like a newsprint cudgel. Tonight was his PTSD group—humans who'd had traumatic encounters with a supe. The last thing those people needed was something like this—they'd think they were being mocked, their experiences trivialized.

He parked himself in the doorway of the kitchenette. "What is the meaning of this shite?"

David glanced up from pouring coffee into the urn and grinned. "Just a little silliness. Something to help folks pass the time."

"I have clients who would be not just offended by this, but possibly traumatized."

"Seriously? By a bogus Bigfoot article and Batboy?" David looked contrite for about two seconds, and then his lips firmed in a stubborn line and he exhaled through his nose like a dragon shifter attempting to light up. "I'm sorry for that, Dr. Kendrick, but perhaps if I had access to at least some of the clients' chart information, I'd have a better notion of appropriate reading material."

"No."

"No, I wouldn't have a better notion?" David asked in an overly sweet tone, with a flutter of his ridiculously long eyelashes.

"No, you can't have access to the client charts."

"Then maybe you could share some of your secret rules with me so I don't violate them by accident."

"There's no reason. You won't be here long enough for it to matter."

Hurt skittered across David's face and for a moment, Alun regretted his words, but facts were facts. A human had no place in a psychology practice that catered to the supernatural. He pushed his inappropriate remorse away. "You've turned my waiting room into a circus."

"I wasn't aware that a dozen magazines, a few knickknacks, and a handful of potpourri constituted a circus. Clearly I attended the wrong shows."

"I like my office uncluttered. Soothing."

"Fine. Keep it that way. But the lobby isn't for you. It's for your clients, and their ideas of soothing may not be the same as yours." He dried his hands and binned the crumpled paper towel. "Have you ever waited in your own waiting room? It's boring. Your clients need something to occupy themselves while they wait their turn to be glowered at by you."

"I don't glower at my clients."

"Really?" David hoisted the coffee dispenser. "Lucky them." He walked toward the door, but Alun refused to budge. "Excuse me."

"I don't. Glower. At anybody."

David held up the shiny chrome urn so it reflected Alun's face, a convex image even more distorted than reality. "Take a look, Doctor. That's the definition of glower. Please move. You haven't replaced me yet, and I have work to do."

Alun moved aside and watched David's stiff-backed walk down the hall. Did he really do that? Glower? David didn't understand. This was just the way his face looked now. It didn't matter what kind of expression he wore, he always looked like a monster about to attack.

Didn't he?

He ducked into the restroom at the end of the hall and switched on the light. David had set a handful of potpourri on the counter in a blown-glass vase. Alun breathed in the scent and forced himself to look at his face in the mirror above the sink.

After two hundred years, his facial deformities still shocked him. What would he look like to someone who wasn't accustomed to seeing it? He knew. *Monster. Demon. Beast.*

He tried to unclench his heavy jaw, unbunch his overhanging brow ridges, unsquint his narrowed eyes. He pushed the corners of his mouth up with his index fingers, forcing a smile.

Shite. That was scarier than the alleged glower. He flicked off the light before he gave himself nightmares and strode down the hallway and into his office, closing the door without another word to David.

David kept his back toward Dr. Kendrick until the door to his office closed behind him. Why in the world had he said that? He might have once visited Planet Tact, but he was not a native. Probably one of the reasons he was so relentlessly boyfriendless.

Should he apologize? Clear away the magazines, pack the vases up, stow everything in his car? As much as he hated to admit it, Dr. Kendrick was right—David had no authority to change anything. He was only a temp. A very temporary temp, if the doctor had his way, which he definitely would if David weren't a tad more conciliatory.

He sighed and started gathering magazines, but put them down again when the first clients arrived, a middle-aged couple holding hands like a pair of teenagers. By the time he'd checked them in and gotten them both coffee, the woman was settled in with one of Lorraine's quilting magazines, the man with the latest *Fine Cooking*.

Okaaay. Dr. Kendrick's OCD commitment to bare surfaces would have to suffer. If the clients liked the magazines, they stayed, every last one of them. Well, not the tabloids, but those had been an impulse buy anyway, a kind of an in-joke because the blurry photo of Bigfoot had reminded him of the way Dr. Kendrick stalked around the office as if he were on a search-and-destroy mission.

Stop it, David. Remember—cut the poor guy some slack and maybe, just maybe, you'll keep this job for more than two days.

CHAPTER ⚜ 8

Alun avoided speaking to David for the rest of the day. He knew he was being petty, but damn and blast, he hated to admit there was anything to David's accusations. Each of his clients, though, had been reading one of those ridiculous magazines when he'd called them in from the lobby. Half of them had asked him if he was wearing a new tie, or had gotten a haircut, obviously noticing something different about him, but not able to identify what it was.

The only difference was that he was intentionally trying to keep his expression benign—if such a thing was possible given what he had to work with.

He had one last client before his human PTSD group—Kristof Czardos, the oldest vampire on the planet. He held tremendous status within the vampire community and had been head of their council since he'd emigrated from Hungary in the late 1890s.

Unfortunately, he was starving to death.

Not because his abilities had faded—he could still heal a bite with ease and cloud the minds of those he fed from without breaking an undead sweat, and his control was so complete that he hadn't killed a donor since before the fall of Constantinople. But he'd developed an aversion to the taste of blood.

When you had only a single nutritional option, if you couldn't consume it without gagging, you tended to lose weight quickly.

Even the scent of human blood under the skin sickened Kristof these days, and Alun purposely scheduled his appointments before the PTSD group, so he'd have the chance to desensitize himself against the nausea. He'd made some progress—enough to walk through a reception room full of humans without retching now—but he was still unable to feed.

Shite. *David.*

Alun's heart kicked into a gallop, and he thrust himself out of his chair. How would Kristof react when forced to interact with a human, not just hurry by him? Considering how resistant David was to minding his own business, he'd strain Kristof's icy restraint to the breaking point.

He crossed the office in four giant strides and tore open the door. Kristof was standing in front of David's desk as the man offered him that thrice-damned blood-colored dish full of candy. David cut a glance at Alun, but didn't take his attention away from Kristof.

"What did I tell you?" David said. "They're awesome for an upset stomach. Have another."

What in all the bloody hells?

Kristof, to Alun's stunned amazement, took one of the pastilles and popped it in his mouth with no hint of fang. He nodded. "You are right. I haven't felt this well in eons."

David beamed at him. "Would you like me to package some up for you? You can take them with you when you go."

Kristof executed a formal half bow. "I would be honored. Thank you." He turned and nodded at Alun. "Dr. Kendrick. You have a most accomplished young man here. I commend you."

"Yes. Well." Alun cleared his throat, avoiding David's gaze, and gestured for Kristof to enter the office. "Shall we?"

If he didn't think he'd scare the dickens out of the two women who'd arrived early for the eight o'clock group session, David would have leaped out of his chair and danced around the room. Of course, given his negative talent, they might expire from laughter instead, but *holy smoking crap.*

Mr. Czardos had complimented him to Dr. Kendrick. Ha! Maybe the doctor would see there were other ways of caring for patients— Gah! *Clients.* That David could be an asset to the office, one worth keeping.

If all the stars aligned and he was able to hold on to this job until Vanessa returned from maternity leave, he'd be able to save enough to get Aunt Cassie out of the soggy Pacific Northwest for a few weeks in the middle of winter, when she was most likely to succumb to pneumonia. Someplace sunny and decadent, maybe a cruise in the Mediterranean, like the one they'd always talked about.

The one he'd lost hope they'd ever take together.

He ignored a tiny sting in his heart. So what if he couldn't go along? As much as he wanted to spend the time with his aunt, see her pampered and relaxed, he wanted her healthy more. If that meant sending one of the girls in his place so he could keep working, he'd suck it up and deal.

Even if Dr. Kendrick continued to be a gold-medal contender in the World Cantankerous Championships.

Throughout the next hour, another dozen people, both men and women, ranging in age from late teens to middle age, arrived for the group. David gave himself a mental high-five when all of them consumed a minimum of one cup of coffee and leafed through one or more magazines.

Miraculously, he had one pertinent piece of information besides name for each of these clients—their intake date. They'd all been in this group for at least six months, yet none of them spoke to each other. They sat scattered around the room, always keeping a chair or two between them. As if half-fearful, they glanced at others in the room and then away, not meeting David's gaze, exhibiting a whole range of avoidance body language.

Jeez, if this was what they were like before the group even started, the actual session must be torture.

What this room needs is a little music to loosen things up. He tapped his fingers on his knee, contemplating the closed office door. Dr. Kendrick had another ten minutes with Mr. Czardos. David slid his contraband CD out of his desk drawer and unwrapped it, the crinkling cellophane sounding as loud as a string of firecrackers in the silent room.

He'd have preferred his first hearing of a brand-new Gareth Kendrick album to be piped through better speakers than the ones on his computer monitor, but if anyone needed the stroke of that velvet voice, compelling yet plaintive, it was this bunch tonight. Though David had to admit that as much as he loved Hunter's Moon's music, and Gareth's vocals as its front man, his voice had never stirred him the way Dr. Kendrick's did.

Awkward.

He inserted the disk into the optical drive of his computer and cued up the first track. An acoustic stringed instrument played an intro—not a guitar, for all that Gareth was the lead guitarist for his band. It almost sounded like a lute or a harp.

Whatever.

The melody, even without lyrics, caused a catch in his throat and a prickle in the corner of his eyes. All the clients in the waiting room raised their heads, the longing on their faces probably matching the expression on his own.

Gareth's voice slipped in, twining around the harp like a long-lost lover, the language unrecognizable until David caught the word *cariad*—Welsh for *darling*. He closed his eyes and clutched the edge of his desk. God, if he didn't move, he'd start to weep, and even though his dancing was enough to bring tears to others' eyes— and not in a good way—he didn't think collapsing into a sodden mess was his best professional choice.

The clients must have felt the same because all of them were swaying in their seats in time to the music. One of the women stood and began to dance. Another joined her. Then another.

Oh what the hell.

David launched himself out of his chair, sashayed around his desk, and joined the gyrating group in the middle of the room.

CHAPTER ❖ 9

Alun tried very hard not to be annoyed by Kristof's gushing praise of David, but with every new compliment, his formerly relaxed jaw tightened and his previously lifted brow ridges lowered.

No doubt his eyes had narrowed to slits as well. Even without an unforgiving reflective surface to confirm it, he could tell—he was glowering.

Kristof, either not noticing or counting it business as usual, continued on in his melodic old-world accent. "I had never considered whether a simple stomach remedy might palliate the symptoms."

"Won't a non-hemoglobin-based food adversely affect your constitution?"

He waved one long, paper-white hand. "Not anything that trivial." He stilled, as motionless in thought as the corpse he'd never been. "An apple cider base, I believe. Some magic practitioners use cider as a blood substitute in modern rituals. Perhaps that is why I found it so agreeable."

"I doubt the candies possess any magical properties." Shite, could he sound any more like a sulky schoolboy?

Kristof's lips thinned in a wintery smile. "Clearly you haven't tasted one."

"David isn't a supe, Kristof. He's only a man. A human man."

"I noticed." His bland tone was its own comment.

Alun remembered that the vampire was bi and tamped down a surge of fae territoriality. David's presence in his office didn't make him Alun's property, especially since he'd be gone as soon as Sandra Fischer stopped sneezing partial panther shifts.

"Right." He forced his hands to relax on the arms of the chair. Whatever his personal issues with David, this was Kristof's treatment session, not his own. "So do you think you'll be able to feed?"

"No. The thought of blood is . . ." A ripple of distaste crossed Kristof's narrow face, the equivalent of a silent scream in a vampire of his age. "No."

"Then why don't we discuss—"

Kristof held up one index finger. "Hold." He cocked his head a fraction of an inch, gaze unfocused. "Do you hear that?"

Alun listened, hands slowly tightening again on the arms of the chair until his nails broke through the brocade. *Shite.* Gareth's voice. Gareth's harp. The thrice-damned CD. The soft rhythmic thumping that Alun had attributed to nearby construction work took on a different meaning, and he catapulted himself out of the chair. "Wait here."

He yanked open the door.

His entire human PTSD group was snaking around the waiting room like Maypole dancers in search of pole and ribbons, caught in the snare of Gareth's music.

Oak and thorn, had his brother run mad? He was the last of the fae bards. He knew the effect of his music when it wasn't buffered by his non-fae band-mates and the electronic interference of modern musical equipment.

Yet he'd recorded himself playing Gwydion's blasted harp, the most powerful instrument in all of Welsh lore. Anyone who heard this would literally dance until they dropped, unable to escape the spell within any defined circle.

A circle like the ring of furniture in his lobby.

The line made another circuit of the room while Alun hovered in stunned disbelief, and he realized David was in the lead. While everyone else, from the nineteen-year-old victim of an obsessed werewolf stalker to the fifty-nine-year-old witness to the transformation of an entire pack of swan maidens, danced in perfect time to the music, their arms waving with the lyrical grace that a true fae bard always inspired in his audience, David moved like a victim of a different kind of dance entirely.

St. Vitus's.

David jerked and twitched without regard to the beat of the song, punching the air randomly, and occasionally pausing to shake his perfect arse or indulge in arcane movements with his arms, as if he were shaping letters.

If that was his intent, he was as poor a speller as he was a dancer, because the letters resembled an *A*, a *Y*, an *M*, and a *C*.

David pranced past Alun. "Woo woo woo!" he called, flapping like a spastic owl, and the rest of the group hooted in response.

"Interesting," Kristof murmured at Alun's shoulder. "I hadn't realized you'd added dance therapy to your repertoire."

"I didn't realize vampires made jokes."

"It's a privilege reserved for the highest rank."

"Good to know." Alun strode behind David's desk and killed the CD playback.

Immediately, all the erstwhile dancers blinked at one another, ducking their heads in well-deserved embarrassment. Goddess preserve him, this could set them all back months. Here, in the place where they should be safe, they'd been exposed to another supernatural phenomenon.

David stood in the middle of the room, his arms still raised overhead, the tails of his jacket flaring out like wings, his gaze riveted on Alun. One of the clients, the appliance technician who'd encountered a nest of teenaged vampires while repairing a furnace, slapped David on the shoulder on his way to his seat.

A peculiar feeling swirled in Alun's belly, attempting to climb up his ribs. He clenched his fists, fighting for control, unable to identify the sensation. Goddess, what horrifying remnant of his past had David conjured up now?

Alun glanced around, searching for an escape route, but Kristof was waiting in his office, and one of the clients was occupying the restroom. The whatever-it-was clawed past his chest to the base of his throat.

David lowered his arms and crossed them over his stomach, swallowing convulsively. "Dr. Kendrick. I . . ."

Shite. He couldn't open his mouth or it would erupt. He couldn't let it loose in front of this group, adding yet another trauma to what they'd already suffered.

He turned away from the curious gazes of his clients, from David's flush-reddened cheeks, strode down the hallway as if the entire pack of the *Cwn Annwn* were baying at his heels, and barricaded himself in the copy room. The space was barely a closet, housing office equipment and a shelf or two of supplies. He braced his hands on either corner of the copier, drawing in huge breaths in an attempt to dispel whatever this was that threatened to burst out of him.

Oak and thorn, he was about to explode. He squeezed his eyes shut as pressure rolled up from his belly through his chest, up his throat and out his mouth in an uncontrolled shout.

Laughter.

Rusty and overwhelming and nearly unrecognizable laughter. He hadn't been tempted to so much as chuckle since the night of his curse. No wonder he hadn't recognized the feeling, but Gwydion's bollocks, it was bloody brilliant.

So he surrendered to it. Completely.

He chortled. He guffawed. He roared. He ran through the entire menu of laughter, gorging on it as if at a feast. Finally, he was reduced to a breathless wheeze.

David.

This was all his doing. Stubborn, impudent, maddening, *human* David, with his wildly colorful office accessories, constant challenges, and the worst dancing Alun had seen in over two millennia.

Goddess strike him blind, but the man was bloody wonderful.

Now what in all the hells was Alun supposed to do about him?

My stars, the look on Dr. Kendrick's face. David had *so* stepped over the line this time. *Jeez, Evans, you think?* Over the line and straight into a pile of crap of his own making.

He cast a sidelong glance at the closed door of the copy closet. He should apologize. Grovel. Abase himself. Throw himself on the doctor's nonexistent mercy.

Definitely on his must-do list for the evening. But for now? He stalled, wanting to savor his last few minutes of employment before Dr. Kendrick canned his ass. What the heck had come over him? He'd been seized with the uncontrollable desire to shake his pathetic booty. He'd never fallen that far off the professional wagon on a job before, not even when the furniture and office supplies had been flying about his head.

He checked the coffee urn, but it was still half-full. He couldn't use making a fresh pot as an excuse to delay the inevitable, and he doubted even Aunt Cassie's special blend would save him now. He gathered the pastilles he'd bundled up for Mr. Czardos and handed them to the man, who was standing in the doorway of the office, as still as if he'd been turned to stone by the horror of David's dancing.

"I doubt I'll be here for your next appointment, but you can get these at Ash Grove Confectionery on Hawthorne."

Mr. Czardos accepted the little packet with a gracious inclination of his head. "You are very kind. But I expect I shall see you again nevertheless."

David forced a smile. "I'm just a temp."

"Even so." He nodded again and glided through the waiting room and out the door with a gait so swift and smooth that he was gone almost before David could blink.

Time to face the music. Gah! Music was the problem. He should never have given in to the temptation to scavenge that CD. Unbecoming conduct aside, if Dr. Kendrick wanted to get technical about it, he had grounds to fire David for theft alone. Even though the CD had never left the premises, it certainly wasn't where the doctor had put it.

David crept down the hallway, the low murmur of the clients' conversation at his back. But no matter how he slowed his steps, the dang hallway wasn't that long. He arrived at the door of the supply closet far too quickly.

He took a deep breath. Tugged his jacket straight. Straightened his bow tie. He tapped three times with one knuckle and cracked the door open. "Dr. Kendrick?" When he received no answering roar, he slipped inside.

The doctor was standing in front of the copier, his back to the room, his hands gripping the corners of the machine. His knuckles were white and his shoulders were shaking, probably with suppressed rage.

"Dr. Kendrick." David's voice was little more than a croak. "I apologize. I realize that I—"

Dr. Kendrick whirled and lunged forward. David clenched his eyes shut, his arms flying up to protect his head. He braced for a blow, but it didn't come. He could feel the heat from Dr. Kendrick's body, that massive chest inches from his face.

"David."

"Nnnnng?"

"Look at me."

He cracked one eye open and peeked at the doctor, whose arms were hanging loose at his sides. His fists weren't clenched, his teeth weren't bared, and he wasn't wielding any blunt instruments.

That was a good sign, right?

David dropped his arms and raised his chin. "Whatever you want to say, I deserve it. Fire me. Get me banned for life from Fischer Temps. Just don't . . ." His voice failed and he swallowed. "Don't hurt me."

Dr. Kendrick recoiled—not much, just a tiny flinch, but as close as they were, and as small as the room was, it was obvious. "You really believe I would injure you?"

His voice was low, almost a whisper, and that look in his eyes— was Dr. Juggernaut actually *disappointed*? David tugged on his bow tie, suddenly afraid he'd misread more than one situation today. "I don't know you very well, and you looked so angry, and—"

"I don't have any desire to hurt you, but if you'll permit, I do want to do something else."

"What?"

"Goddess forgive me," he murmured. "This." Dr. Kendrick framed David's face in his enormous hands and lowered his head until his mouth was a hairsbreadth away from David's. "Do you permit?"

He couldn't breathe, he couldn't think. The hair on his arms stood at attention at the whisper of Dr. Kendrick's—*Alun's*—breath against his cheek.

David shut his eyes and moaned, "Oh yes. Please," and Alun closed that last tiny distance and kissed him.

Warm. Gentle. Soft. The man looked like a goblin berserker, but he had the mouth of an angel. David was so startled by the sweetness of the kiss that he almost forgot to participate. *Must correct* that *heinous error.* He clutched Alun's shirt and parted his lips in invitation—*I'm open to suggestions, big guy*—but Alun didn't take the bait. Where David expected fierce and possessive, befitting a man with Alun's hot temper, the kiss was thorough but almost shy.

Alun drew back, his thumbs brushing David's cheekbones. David teetered forward, breath ragged, off-balance in more ways than one. He gazed up at Alun, and somehow, whether it was the dimness of the room, or David's overactive imagination projecting what he expected to see based on that incredible kiss, Alun's face didn't look as monstrous. His eyes—*so beautiful.* Hazel, swirling brown and amber, pupils wide. The brow ridges weren't as pronounced, the jaw not as heavy, maybe because the man was smiling.

Smiling, for the first time since David had walked in the door.

"Your face . . ."

Instantly, Alun shut down. He backed off and turned away. "I'm sorry. I overstepped the bounds. I should have known. Someone as beautiful as you would never—"

"Hey!" David crowded close and poked Alun on the shoulder until he faced David again. "I make my own choices, thank you very much."

He grabbed Alun's head and pulled it down, carding his fingers through the surprisingly soft hair, prepared to kiss the holy freaking crap out of the man.

A giggle echoed down the hallway. *Clients. Work. Dang.*

With one last stroke down Alun's chest—which, yes, felt just as awesome under his hands as he'd imagined—David stepped back. "The group. They're waiting."

Alun's eyes, nearly all pupil now, showed only a narrow rim of amber. David shivered at the heat and intent. "Damn the group."

"Alun. No. They need you."

"Bloody hells." Alun shook his head like a dog shedding water. "What was I thinking? You're—you're—"

"An employee? I don't care if you don't."

"What does it say about me that I never considered that?" He ran a shaking hand over his rumpled shirt and glanced down past his waist, where a very impressive bulge interfered with his excellent tailoring. "Leave me, please? I can't face them like this."

David's gaze was still riveted on the front of Alun's pants. "Uh. Right." He cleared a throat gone dry. "I'd get the clients settled in your office, but . . ." He gestured at his own groin. "I'm not suitable for family viewing either. I'll duck into the kitchen."

"As you wish."

Alun turned, hunching over the copier again. David told himself the little twinge of hurt at the abrupt dismissal was unreasonable. They were at work. Clients awaited them a few yards away. The least he could do was attempt a graceful retreat and allow Alun the same.

Unfortunately for both of them, David might as well have had *klutz* tattooed on his butt at birth. For Alun's sake, though, he'd give it his best shot.

CHAPTER ✤ 10

As Alun escorted his PTSD group into the office, the taste of David's kiss lingered on his tongue—coffee, mint, and a subtle wild flavor like water from a Faerie lake. His fingers tingled as if he were still trailing them over David's face. His skin still prickled where David had touched him, his senses alight in a way he hadn't experienced since Owain.

Yet Owain had been *achubydd*. David was human. Was this how it always was when human joined with nonhuman?

Never before had he been tempted to challenge his fate. Of course, not once since his curse had any man viewed him with less than abject horror, blatant disgust, or stultifying pity.

Of everyone in both realms, his own brothers included, David was the only man who'd ever looked at him with something as simple as annoyance, and just now—he crossed his legs against the tightening in his groin, so very inappropriate in this setting—with undeniable lust.

For the first time since he'd begun his practice, Alun felt a thread of empathy toward offending supes who dared risk everything for the sake of a human. And Goddess help him, he was tempted to take exactly that risk.

Even as the group waited for his opening remarks, he remained hyperaware of David. He could distinguish his scent among a dozen other people, sense his every movement beyond the closed office door—every shift in his chair, every rustle of his crisp cotton shirt, every trip he made across the lobby.

Nearly giddy with the sensations, alive as he hadn't been since the day of his curse, Alun had to force himself to pay attention to his job, to listen and respond to the group.

But as the hour passed, as each client recounted some halting memory of a personal nightmare, Alun's residual thrill diminished. Every story illustrated how ill-equipped humans were to face the supernatural world, how necessary the Secrecy Pact was for the safety of all.

By the end of the session, the last pitiful spark of his earlier elation had vanished.

If he chose to pursue a relationship with David, as curious and obstinate as the man was, Alun held no illusions that he could continue to conceal the details of his nature, or that of most of his clients. David seemed resilient, but no more so than the broken people in this room had once been.

The notion that he might shatter David's bright spirit sent his heart into a death-drop to his toes.

Yet David wasn't the only one who'd face catastrophic loss. For human victims, the damage, whether physical or psychological, was personal. Confined to the individual. But if the evil or unscrupulous or just plain ignorant learned of these hidden communities, the risk to the otherworldly races was far greater, up to and including genocide.

The purpose of the pact, the reason the penalty for violations was so severe, was to prevent just such tragedy. Was he reckless enough to chance a punishment greater than his curse? Selfish enough to put his own desires ahead of the welfare of every other supernatural being? Heartless enough to gamble with David's sanity?

Goddess help him, the choice was not as easy as his conscience demanded.

As if Alun's kiss had turbocharged his blood, David couldn't sit still. He pinged around the office, inventing ways to occupy himself, to keep his mind off Alun and his hands and his chest and, God, his *mouth*.

He washed all the cups by hand instead of loading them in the dishwasher. Arranged the magazines in perfect fans on each end table. Refilled the coffee supplies and stacked the coasters in strict color-spectrum order.

But no matter how slowly he tried to do each task, when he finished, he'd swear no time had passed at all, as if he'd acquired an unfortunate hyper-speed superpower.

He actually changed the battery on the digital clock, certain it had slowed to a complete halt.

What was up with that?

He nearly put Gareth's forbidden CD back on, if only to give himself something to do.

At long last, the office door opened, and the group straggled out. Each of them offered him a smile—probably remembering what a spaz he'd been in their earlier dance party—and some of them chatted among themselves, which was a definite change from when they'd all arrived.

Maybe this group therapy stuff really worked.

When the last of the clients finally left, David locked up and stalked across the waiting room toward Alun's door with a single item on his agenda.

Kissing. Lots of it.

For that, the love seat in Alun's office held way more promise than the freaking supply closet. But as he passed his desk, the emergency line lit on his phone. With an inward curse, he picked up the call.

"Dr. Kendrick's office. This is David. How may I help you?"

"Give me Kendrick." The man's voice put Alun's best growl to shame.

"May I tell him who's calling?"

"No. Put me through. Now."

Instead of using the intercom, David walked inside. Alun was standing at his window, the blinds open, his face a reflected smear in the black glass.

Drat. David had wanted to see if that heat was still in Alun's gaze, if he could steal a caress from those big hands or cadge another kiss before duty called again.

"Someone on the emergency line for you. He wouldn't give his name."

Alun's shoulders rose and fell once. He glanced back and met David's gaze. There. Was that a teensy spark?

"Thank you." He lowered himself into his chair, the leather sighing under his weight. "You needn't wait. I expect to be engaged for some time."

David swallowed against a lump in his throat the size of the geode on the corner of the desk. Had he misunderstood? Did Alun regret what had happened? Crap, did David need to revert to thinking of him as *Dr. Kendrick* again?

If only the man would look at him, give him a smile, a word, a single freaking clue that the kiss had been as life-changing for him as it had been for David.

But he only sat, his hand on the phone, his gaze fixed on a point above David's head.

"Right. I'll leave you to it, then." He backed out and closed the door as the last of the fizz died in his veins, turning him back into his ordinary screw-up self.

He perched on the edge of his chair, thumbing his worry stone, talking himself down off the mental ledge. *It's only professional courtesy, Evans. Doctor-client confidentiality. Naturally he couldn't let you stand around and eavesdrop on the call.*

Huddling behind the desk, he willed the emergency line light to go dark. *One more word, that's all I need. Just one.*

Oh, who the heck was he kidding? He needed *way* more—more of what they'd started with that kiss—but he'd settle for a word, if only that rotten growly caller would shut up and get off the phone.

After a tedious half hour of sorting paper clips, testing pens, and sharpening already pointy pencils, the light flickered, and he surged out of his chair. But before he made it past the edge of his desk, it lit again. Dang it. He sighed and looped the strap of his messenger bag over his shoulder.

Give it up, Evans. You'll have to wait until tomorrow to find out what—if anything—this meant.

Coward. That's what he was. A thrice-damned, gods-forsaken, bloody-minded coward.

His "emergency" call—the usual follow-up by the Clackamas alpha, venting about Jackson's lack of progress—lasted its standard two minutes. When the man hung up, Alun kept his phone off the hook so he'd appear occupied.

Avoiding the consequences of his actions. Avoiding his inevitable choice. Avoiding David.

He dropped his head into his hands, his fingers splayed around his oversized skull. He had no doubt that if his group hadn't been waiting, he'd have taken David right here in the office, on any convenient surface.

Had he stooped to the entitled conduct of the Sidhe lords of old? He wasn't that bad, surely. He'd never spirit the man away from his friends and family, behind the gates of Faerie to be trapped by time. And as long as Alun retained the face of the beast, he couldn't pass the threshold in any case.

But if he were no longer cursed, if he could convince David to come with him into Faerie, install him in the stone cottage in the willow grove by the lake, present him to the Seelie Court as consort, would Alun be tempted to take that step?

Goddess, he talked about other people's feelings for a living, but if he expected this to go any further, he'd have to face his own.

But how? For all his age, for his degrees and training, he had no experience with this particular conundrum.

He straightened in his chair, his head lifting as he realized he knew someone who had experience to spare. Mal never had any difficulty finding more partners than was reasonable for one man, although Mal didn't look like the last refugee from the Demon Wars, either.

He snorted as he punched the emergency line again, the irony not lost on him that he, the psychologist, should have to depend on relationship advice from his irresponsible man-whore of a brother.

Mal picked up on the first ring. "What's wrong?" The rhythmic thump of overloud club music didn't mask the sharpness in his tone.

"I can call you for something other than trouble."

"You can, but you never have." Another voice, lifted in question, cut in behind Mal's. Even though he couldn't make out the words, Alun recognized the speaker. The recorded version of that voice had lit the fuse for his own personal explosion not two hours ago.

Before that, this evidence of a brotherly reunion that didn't include him would have pierced his gut like a poorly aimed sword thrust. Now, he brushed it aside as irrelevant.

"Can you go somewhere to talk?"

"I can talk here."

Alun ground his molars together. "Fine. Go somewhere I can hear what you say."

The background noise faded almost at once, so the infuriating man had already been on the move. If Alun didn't need his help, he'd have hung up.

"All sorted, brother. Now spill."

After decades as a therapist, Alun considered himself a master of leading up to his true conversational objective by subtle degrees. But all his skill, his years of practice, his professional composure, deserted him, leaving him as awkward as a new-minted page boy.

"I kissed David," he blurted. "In the supply closet."

"Flaming abyss, Alun. I'd no notion your technique was that pathetic."

"Mal . . ." Alun pinched the bridge of his nose, fighting for control.

"Now me, I'd have kissed him someplace else. That delectable mouth, say, or that spot behind his ear, or—"

His vision sparked red, and he slammed his fist on the desk. "You will not. Ever. So much as *glance* at the spot behind his ear."

"Or what?" Mal's voice lost its amused overtone. "You sound like one of the Obsessed."

"It's not that way. It was only a kiss." Or two. More, if he'd had his way. "But he's human. I can't allow it to proceed." He swiped his fist across his lips as if he could wipe away the memory of David's mouth. "Right?"

"Shite, Alun. No matter what propaganda you have to swallow to work with the larger supe community, the fae have never proscribed humans. What's the bloody problem? You want him. Go get him."

"You know why I can't. The last time . . ." Alun had firsthand experience of the risk of giving in to his desires, his consuming passions. The last time he'd succumbed, the result had been Owain's death and the massacre of the last known enclave of *achubyddion*. Genocide.

"Sod it, you're not likely to cause the extinction of the human race because you want to get laid."

"But—"

"You've got some bug up your arse about self-denial, but there's nothing in the Seelie code that says because your lover died, you have to be a damned martyr."

A tiny seedling of hope sprouted beneath Alun's sternum. "So you think it's all right, then?"

"Hells yes. But so you know," Mal lowered his voice, "I'll not mention this to Gareth."

The hope shriveled and died. "Probably wise, although I doubt anything could make him think less of me."

After the abduction of his human lover by Unseelie fae, Gareth had plunged into a depression so wide and deep that even now, centuries later, he had yet to recover. As a side effect, he'd developed an opposition to fae mating outside their race and class, which Alun's betrayal of Owain had solidified into outright fanaticism.

"Alun. You get that I think Gareth's wrong, yeah?"

"I know." Alun wished he believed it as well.

"Then for the sake of the Goddess, stop wasting time and shag the man already. Just don't . . ."

"Don't what?"

Mal's sigh was clearly audible. "Look. I understand the attraction. I liked the lad myself. But don't get . . . attached. He's not like Owain. His human life can be measured in the turn of a single Faerie year."

"No danger of either of us ending up in Faerie. Not while my curse bars the gates."

"It'll be no different in the Outer World. He'll age. You won't. As long as you go into it knowing it'll be short-term . . . well . . ." Mal muttered an unintelligible curse. "I don't want you to get hurt again."

Alun's throat thickened, and the corners of his eyes prickled with heat. "I love you too, brother."

"Oh piss off." Mal's chuckle burred over the line as the music swelled again, signaling his return to the club. "But next time I see David, I expect him to walk like he's had the ride of his life on your Sidhe-lord dick."

He disconnected before Alun could rail at him for disrespect. Damn and blast. He let his head thump against his chair's headrest, unsure if he was any closer to a decision than before Mal's dubious assistance.

He still couldn't quite believe that David was able to ignore his appearance and perceive the man beneath the monster, more so because his behavior had matched his brutish face since the moment David had walked in his door. But it had been so bloody long. He wanted to take this chance, to see if Mal was right and he could claim an island of happiness in the vast dark ocean of his exile.

But how long would David be willing to stay with a beast? He was beautiful. Charming. Young and appealing. Even Kristof had noticed. Why would he settle for anything less in a partner?

Right. Alun would have to work for it, that's all. Back in the days before Owain had blinded him to all other men, he'd known how to woo a lover. Although in the full flower of his fae beauty, with the *glamourie* for insurance, he'd rarely done little more than smile.

He suspected that wooing David—if he had the courage to do it—would take rather more effort, along with a great bloody mountain of luck.

CHAPTER ❁ 11

After a restless night interrupted by enough erotic dreams to make internet porn unnecessary for life, David's attention was as scattered and uncertain as it had been when he'd left the office. While brewing his aunt's tea or watering her forest of houseplants or feeding her finches, he'd flash back on Alun's lips, the warmth and breadth of his chest, the heat in his eyes, and he'd zone out. When he came to, he'd be standing in the middle of the room, his fingers tracing his own lips as he remembered the feel of Alun's kiss.

But when he'd expected a repeat performance . . . *nada*. Then that distance in the way Alun had sent him home. Did that mean he had regrets? That last night had been a one-off, never-to-be-repeated slip off his grouchy pedestal?

What if . . . *Crap*. Heat rushed up his chest and infused his face. Had he done something, sent some dorky mixed signal, to lead Alun on? Maybe not before they'd hit the supply closet, but once inside, he'd practically offered Alun his ass on a Xerox platter. That was *so* not the kind of temp agency he worked for.

When he stopped to consider it logically—yeah, like that ever happened—it made no sense that Alun would be interested in an awkward, wrong-side-of-the-executive-desk temp like him. Disfigured or not, he was still head and amazing shoulders above David. He could do way better.

But David's doubts didn't stop him from taking an extra careful shower as he got ready for work, or shaving super close, or choosing his best-fitting pants and the gray-blue shirt that matched his eyes.

He was debating the merits of his two favorite bow ties when his cell phone rang. His heart gave a sideways bump like one of his worst dance moves, but it wasn't Alun. It was Fischer Temps.

"Hello?"

"David. Sandra Fischer." Her voice sounded as if she'd spent the last week at a hookah bar.

"Ms. Fischer, if you don't mind my saying so, you sound as if you still belong in bed. Cutting your recovery time short can lead to a relapse."

"David. I—"

"My aunt makes this amazing throat tonic. I'll bring some by for you. In fact, I could do it today on my way in to Al—Dr. Kendrick's office."

"David. That's what we need to discuss."

David's stomach tried to duck and cover. "We do? Look, I know you said you didn't think I was ready for another office job, but it's turned out fine, right?"

"No."

So Alun had had second thoughts after all. David sank down on the edge of his bed, his bow ties limp in his hand. "No?"

"Dr. Kendrick has asked that we replace you at once."

"But there isn't anybody. That's why Tracy—"

"Tracy is no longer with the agency."

"What?" David croaked, as if he were the one with the flu.

"Her lapse in judgment resulted in offending one of our most influential clients. What do you expect?"

"Please. Don't take it out on Tracy. She was totally slammed with you and so many others out sick." He tightened his hand around the silk of his ties. Why hadn't he considered that his sin-by-omission could affect Tracy too? But he'd thought only of himself. *Selfish selfish selfish.* "The mistake is totally on me. I didn't mention your opinion to her about my . . . my unsuitability for office positions. She was doing the best she could."

"Exactly."

"All right." He swallowed hard and laid his ties over his knee, attempting to smooth out the wrinkles left by his damp fist. The poor things would never be the same. "When I bring your tonic by, we can talk about another assignment." He'd make another pitch for poor Tracy at the same time.

"David." Did she sound a little apologetic? Not Sandra. She never did conciliatory. Must be the lingering effects of her illness. "There won't be another assignment. I'm terminating our agreement with you."

"But—but I need the job. My aunt—"

"I'm sorry, David. I like you, I really do. But you've been a disruptive influence in every office placement. I think it's time for you to rethink your career objectives."

He curled forward, arm across his belly, cell phone pressed so hard to his ear that the back of his earring cut into his skin. "Please, Sandra. I need the flexibility of the temp agency. With Aunt Cassie's health so uncertain—"

"I'm afraid my decision is final. I wish you luck."

Why couldn't he think? His mind was as dark and empty as a club after hours. "I . . . There are a few of my personal belongings at the office."

"Please retrieve them this morning, before Dr. Kendrick arrives for the day. The security guard will accompany you, and you can leave your card key with him when you're done."

A hot beam of anger cut through his mental shadows. "You think I'd steal from him?"

"It's company policy, David. Nothing personal."

"Of course not." *Because we wouldn't want anything personal to interfere with the perfectly pristine offices of Dr. Alun Kendrick.*

The need to see David, to seek him out this very instant, had Alun pacing his apartment, unable to concentrate on any of his usual pastimes, this single morning stretching longer than half his life.

Oak and bloody thorn, two hundred years of perfect control, and he'd lost it because of a human who didn't back away from his face? No doubt about it, this wooing shite would be the death of him.

It had been easier when he'd simply paid for the privilege in a discreet brothel in Regency London. Or in San Francisco during the Gold Rush, lured by the downcast gaze of Chinese immigrants who considered him no more monstrous than any non-Asian.

Or in the endless Yukon nights when darkness was his refuge and men were willing to ignore pleasantries in exchange for a winter's worth of venison.

But now? Here? He hadn't the least notion of how to proceed, of what constituted a proper lover's offering. According to the mawkish web pages devoted to romance, flowers were a traditional choice, so he'd frantically called florist after florist until he'd found one willing to do a rush delivery to his apartment.

He eyed the resulting massive bouquet, the blooms bright and exotically fragrant. Nothing as pedestrian as carnations nor as obvious as roses. Chaotic, yet harmonious, like David himself, and like the feelings that crowded Alun's chest when he thought of the man.

He checked his watch for the fifteenth time. Was it too soon to go downstairs? Alun had been ashamed to realize he'd never made an effort to find out when David arrived, nor how much time he spent outside office hours adding all those personal touches and tweaks aimed at comfort for either his clients or himself.

Awkwardly juggling the flowers with his briefcase, he opened the door to his apartment, taking the stairs slowly, reciting the ogham alphabet in his head to calm his libido.

Birch, rowan, alder, willow . . . David had been as tender and pliant in his arms as a willow branch— *Stop it. Ash, hawthorn, oak, holly, hazel, apple* . . . He'd tasted faintly of apple too, from those ridiculous candies he kept in the flame-hearted dish on his desk.

Shite. Next time, he'd stick to the *DSM-5*. The list of obsessive-compulsive disorders. At this rate, he'd present half of the diagnoses himself.

He reached his clinic and stood in the corridor, the tissue wrapping the bouquet crinkling in his fist, his other hand locked on the handle of his briefcase.

You're a two-thousand-year-old Sidhe warrior, not a stripling at his first fete. Open the thrice-damned door and face the man.

Tucking his briefcase under one arm, he turned the doorknob.

Locked.

Alun frowned. David was always early. *Always?* It had only been three days. Alun blinked in surprise when he realized exactly how quickly he'd succumbed to temptation. What did that say about his character? All he needed was the correct leverage, and his vaunted ethics toppled like a stone down the hillside.

With his briefcase still clamped under his elbow, his other hand full of flowers, Alun fished for his card key in the inner pocket of his jacket. Damn and blast, where was the bloody thing? *Aha—got it.*

He opened the door, his gaze snapping immediately to David's chair. Empty. The skin prickled along Alun's spine, and his hair lifted on his neck. *Wrong. Something was wrong.* What was it?

The desk was bare except for the telephone and the computer workstation. No brilliant-crimson candy dish. No row of tiny figures marching in the shadow of the monitor. No cobalt mug in pride of place on the credenza.

Alun's briefcase slipped from his lax fingers and landed on the carpet with a muted thump. He turned slowly, surveying the room. The handblown vases were gone. The magazines cleared from the tables. The stack of woven rainbow-hued coasters missing from the sideboard.

The office was exactly as it had been before David had arrived. Exactly as Alun had told David he preferred. David might never have been here at all, save for the whisper of potpourri vanishing under the heavy lemon scent of the cleaners' furniture polish, and the pathetic bouquet Alun was still clutching in his fist.

He trudged into his office, disappointment riding him like a banshee on the wind.

How could David leave without a word? Didn't Alun deserve the courtesy of a reason? Even Owain had given him that, however little Alun had wanted to hear the truth.

He glared at the ridiculous flowers and flung them in the trash.

David hadn't struck him as a coward, had never avoided a confrontation, so why hide now? Was it his face? That he could understand at least, but it hadn't deterred David last night. Alun needed the man to look him in the eye and give him reasons.

Then he'd try like all the hells to get him to change his mind.

Alun checked his schedule. Nothing until four thirty. He had time.

He strode through the office, locked the front door, and barreled down the stairs to the underground parking facility two at a time.

Thank the gods for the heavily tinted windows of his Land Rover that allowed him to drive in full daylight without causing mass hysteria on the roads. But when he climbed into the driver's seat, it dawned on him that he had no idea what David's address was.

He let his oversized forehead drop onto the steering wheel. Bloody fool. But as he was about to give up and go back inside, his long-dormant tracking sense lit up like a sunrise, revealing David's location as clearly as if the man were standing on the top of a hill in a single beam of moonlight.

When he pulled out of the parking garage, though, he realized the instincts that had served him so well in Faerie—leading him in the shortest, straightest path to his quarry—had significant drawbacks in the Outer World. Here he had to contend with traffic and one-way streets and thrice-damned freeways. By the time he pulled up in the shade of a tree outside a pristine Sellwood bungalow, a persistent growl was rumbling in his chest and his teeth ached from clenching them in his battle grimace.

David was here, his presence bright as the flame of a torch. Alun shouldn't feel this connection, not with a human. *How do you know? You've never kissed one before.* For all he knew, this happened with everyone. He made a mental note to ask Mal about it the next time he saw him.

The sidewalks were empty, but he donned a wide-brimmed hat to shield his face from anyone watching from curtained windows, and hurried up the walk to the wide front porch.

He knocked on the door with the pent-up anger of the frustrating drive, with the disappointment of discovering that David cared as little for him as the shallowest of fae courtiers. Had David kissed back only to keep his job?

If that was the case, why leave?

The light shuffle of footsteps on the other side of the door was his only warning before it swung open to reveal a bird-frail old woman leaning on a whimsically carved cane, her head swathed in a handwoven head scarf the color of new leaves.

She looked up into his eyes, and when their gazes locked, he staggered back a step, although she held her ground.

A druid.

Here. In Portland. *In David's house.* Not just any druid either. Gwydion's bollocks, the last time he'd seen an aura that large, with that many colors, it had been on the Arch-Druid of Salisbury Plain before Julius Caesar and his bloody Romans first set foot in Britain.

She drew herself up to her full height—not more than five feet at a guess. "Lord Cynwrig. I never thought to see you in the light of day. Have you done with hiding away in the dark, then?"

Alun drew in a sharp breath at her use of his title and his Welsh name, although he shouldn't have been shocked. She was a druid. It was her job to know everything *about* everything. Druids lived nearly as long as the Sidhe, although from the way her aura was wavering at the edges, this one's end-of-days was near.

"I am Dr. Kendrick in this life, Elder."

Her sloe-black eyes narrowed. "Kendrick. You are the man who dismissed my Davey."

"*Your* Davey?" Impossible. If David were a druid, Alun would have been able to tell.

"My nephew, but he is as a son to me."

"I never tagged him as a druid. Your shielding spells must be formidable."

She folded both her hands on the head of her cane, shaped like a smooth-capped acorn. "He is not a druid and is unaware of our ways. I would prefer . . ." she fixed him with an imperturbable stare ". . . that he remain so."

Alun inclined his head. "As you wish." Only an idiot fae crossed a druid unless he had the full might of the Sidhe host at his back. Even then, the outcome wasn't assured. "I could ask the same courtesy."

A smile quivered on her thin lips and glimmered in her eyes. "You may ask. I will consider. But Davey's safety shall always drive my purpose."

"Understood. May I speak with him?"

"Why?" Her voice held a hint of steel under the quaver of the elderly. "You wish to make him even more unhappy?"

Goddess, he *had* upset David last night. But that still didn't give David the right to scarper off with no reason given. "I wish to understand why he chose to leave. Surely if we speak of courtesy—"

"Auntie. What are you doing out here? You should be resting."

Alun's head snapped to the left at the sound of David's voice. Goddess, he was even more beautiful in this sun-filled room than in the dim order of the office. He was wearing a sky-colored Henley and faded jeans that looked softer than well-worn leather. Alun's mouth went dry with the desire to fold him in his arms. But clearly David didn't want that, or he'd not have left.

David crossed his arms over his chest, a frown wrinkling his brow. "What are you doing here?"

"I think you owe me an explanation."

"For what? For not clearing out fast enough to suit you? Did I leave a nongray item in the office to offend you? Forget to close the blinds and allow a stray beam of sunlight to break in and wreak havoc?"

Alun scowled, off-balance again as he always was with David. "You know very well that's not it. If you objected to my—to me, you should have said so. I would have respected your wish." *Although I'd have tried my damnedest to change your mind.*

"My wish?" David clenched his hands at his sides and stalked, stiff-legged, into the room. "My *wish* was to keep my job."

"Then why did you leave?"

"I didn't leave, Dr. Clueless. I was fired."

"Fired?"

"With extreme prejudice." David glared at him, his lips pressed in a flat line, but Alan caught the telltale tremor nonetheless. "The freaking security guard had to escort me back to collect my stuff."

"But—"

"Do you know how humiliating that was? You could have at least asked me. Warned me that I was out of line, that you didn't—"

Alun grabbed him by the shoulders because, at this rate, the man might never shut up. "What are you talking about? I didn't fire you."

"You're not technically my employer, remember? I got the ax this morning from Sandra Fischer herself, thanks to your eloquent complaints about my inappropriateness for the job."

Goddess, all those messages he'd left for Sandra. They'd slipped his mind, chased away by the taste of David's mouth and the scent of his skin. He'd intended to call back, to rescind his request for replacement, but he never thought she'd be back on the job so soon, not after a bout with F1W2.

"Sandra took you off the assignment?"

"You must have been exceptionally persuasive, because she did better than that. She terminated me from the agency. I'm officially unemployed, so I'd appreciate it if you would leave so I can wallow in my self-pity."

Alun's hands tightened on David's shoulders. "Listen to me. First, I don't believe for one instant that you intend to waste a minute on self-pity. That's not your style."

"That's all you know." He sniffed and lifted his chin, nose in the air. "For your information, I've been positively wretched. No Oreo is safe when I'm in the throes of whinging."

A smile tugged at Alun's lips, but he fought it off. "What do you know about whinging?"

"I'm an expert. Ask anyone."

Alun met those lake-storm eyes, noted the stubborn set of the pointed chin, the dip of those slanted brows over the narrow nose. He'd have to work for this one.

He held David's gaze and pulled out his cell phone, keying in Sandra's number from memory. She answered on the first ring.

Of course she did. Even cursed and banished, he was a gods-forsaken Sidhe lord. She was a third-level panther shifter from the worker class. He outranked her.

"Dr. Kendrick. I expected your call. Naomi said the office was locked. Should she locate building security?"

"Who's Naomi?"

"She's your new office manager. A coyote shifter from the Umatilla tribe. She comes very highly recommended by the Wiccan Health Collective."

"I don't need an office manager." David's brows dipped lower and his lips curled downward, but he didn't drop his gaze from Alun's. "I already have one."

"Oh. I didn't realize Vanessa had returned to work."

"Not Vanessa. David Evans."

"But . . ." She coughed, a sound that morphed into a throaty yowl. Apparently she wasn't entirely over the F1W2 virus.

Why couldn't the woman have stayed in her cave until he'd had a chance to sort out his own tangled feelings? He hated having his hand forced.

"I expect you to correct this. Reinstate David with your agency. Immediately. Reactivate his assignment as my office manager."

"Tracy," David murmured, a definite challenge in his eyes. Alun raised his eyebrows. "She needs to rehire Tracy too."

"The reactivation order extends to your assistant as well, who was astute enough to place David in my clinic. Please see to it at once. Otherwise, our arrangement is terminated, and you'll find all the clients I've referred to you will likewise seek other staffing resources." He hung up on another tortured yowl and took a step toward David. "There. You see? Proof."

David put his hands behind his back and retreated, keeping the same distance between them. "Being a therapist must be difficult for you."

"What do you mean?"

"You can't just order your clients to get better."

Alun scowled and paced forward. "I don't . . . What else can I do? I've given you your wish. I've given you proof."

"I don't want proof, you stupid man." David's backpedaling brought him up against the wall. "I want explanations."

Alun reached out with a tentative hand and brushed his thumb over David's clavicle, feeling distress vibrate in the elegant bones. "How about this? Any message Sandra received from me was from before last night." He gazed into David's eyes, willing him to believe, but unwilling to get any more specific under the knowing gaze of the druid. "Before. Understand?"

"No. I don't understand why you complained about me in the first place, let alone why you changed your mind."

"He objected to you because you're human."

The air shivered with the truth of the druid's statement, reverberating in Alun's brain like the call of Herne's horn. Damn and blast. He should have remembered. Druids, because their job was to know everything, weren't bound by the Secrecy Pact. They could reveal information when they deemed it necessary. Since he'd agreed to her request for secrecy, his word bound him. Her reply hadn't been so explicit.

Trust a druid to hedge her bets.

David hustled over to her and took her by the elbow, leading her gently to a tall-backed rocking chair padded with patchwork cushions in shades of blue and green. Alun had assumed David's fondness for rainbow-hued objects had been a statement about his sexual orientation, but no. He'd been raised by a druid. They always surrounded themselves with the most vibrant colors of nature.

"Auntie, that's like saying he objected to me because I'm breathing. Everyone's human."

She clutched his arm, her gaze riveted to Alun's face. "No, Davey. Not everyone." She nodded at Alun. "And most assuredly not him."

CHAPTER ✤ 12

Disappointment washed like ice water through David's belly. Bad enough that Alun was glowering—yes, glowering, no matter what the big doofus said—at him, dominating the room with his height and chest and alpha-hole attitude. His aunt had just made the first insensitive comment he'd ever heard from her.

No matter how controlling Alun was, he didn't deserve that.

"Auntie." He couldn't keep the censure out of his tone. "It's not fair to blame him for an accident of birth or the result of illness. He can't help the way he looks." He glanced over his shoulder. "Although he needs to work a little on the way he acts."

"Don't use that tone with me, Davey. I'm not talking about his appearance, although . . ." she peered at Alun through narrowed eyes, "I judge it to be entirely his fault."

"Aunt Cassie." David couldn't help it. He spoke sharply to her, the way he'd been tempted to lash out at every past sacrifice. But Alun? No, he couldn't let her drive Alun away. "I can't believe you—"

"She's right." Alun's voice was weary. Resigned. "On both counts."

His aunt leaned forward, her hands resting atop the head of her cane. "Consider what you say, Alun Cynwrig. No doom can fall on me from such revelations. The same cannot be said for you."

David stood up and propped his hands on his hips. "'Doom'? 'Revelations'? Have we wandered into the latest Cluster Realms adventure?"

"Davey." She took his hand and drew him down to sit on the floor at her feet, as she'd done when he was a boy fresh out of foster care. "The world is wider than it seems, and not all of it is visible to the human eye."

He forced himself to get down off his self-righteous high horse and back into cajoling mode, little as he wanted to. "Is this one of your new age-y woo-woo talks, Auntie? Do I need to break out the pyramid hat?"

A smile glimmered in her eyes, although her face was solemn. "This is no joke, Davey *bach*. All those fantasy stories you're so fond of, they're not so far from the truth." She nodded at Alun. "Your Dr. Kendrick is Lord Alun Cynwrig, formerly first among *y Tylwyth Teg*, later a high lord of the Seelie Court from the realm of Faerie."

"Shite," Alun muttered.

A chill wafted through the room, lifting the hair at the base of David's skull, but heat surged up from his belly until he felt like a kettle about to boil. He had to clamp his teeth together so he wouldn't shriek in frustration—because seriously? *This* was how they'd decided to treat his distress? As a *joke*?

"I'm not a child anymore. You can't distract me with tall tales or—"

"Davey, I speak the truth. Lord Cynwrig was not born of this world."

His aunt's tone was infused with the no-nonsense steel he recognized from his troubled youth, and his gaze darted between her and his erstwhile boss. *Holy cats. She really means it.* "Get *out*. Alun's an elf?"

"An elf." Alun rolled his eyes. "Goddess give me strength."

"A . . . fairy?"

This time, Alun growled, baring his teeth. "No one calls me that and lives."

"Well then, what?"

"He is a Sidhe warrior, *cariad*. A famous one at that, one of three brothers from the Welsh fae who dominated the Seelie Court after the Celtic Unification."

"Three . . ." David's jaw dropped. Holy cats. No wonder Mal and Gareth were so hot. Unable to sit still, he jumped to his feet. "You're not messing with me? Magic is real? Really, really *real*? Like unicorns? Centaurs? Mermaids?"

She chuckled. "Don't get carried away. There are many uncanny species, yes, but also many folk with active imaginations. Not all you've heard is false, but not all you've heard is true."

"I don't care." Hugging himself, he bounced on his toes. "Even a little of it is more than I'd ever hoped—" He stilled, squinting at Alun. "Is that why you didn't want me to work for you? Because I'm not like you? Not a supernatural demigod?"

Alun snorted. "Hardly godlike, demi or otherwise."

Aunt Cassie squeezed David's hand. "I suspect his clients are all members of the supe community."

"'Supe'?"

"Supernatural."

"You mean they're here? In Portland?"

Her mouth quirked. "They're everywhere. But it is in their best interests to remain . . . discreet."

"Wait. How exactly do you know all this?"

She twinkled at him. "The woo-woo shit is more useful than you've ever given me credit for." She held up a finger. "But just as not all things are false, not all things are good."

"Sure. I get it. Still. So. Freaking. Cool." He glanced at Alun. "But you said Alun— I mean Dr. Kendrick—"

"Alun," he said. "To you, I am Alun."

David smiled, warmth spreading through his chest. "Alun. Why is your appearance your own fault?"

He hesitated, and David's stomach plummeted. *He still doesn't trust me.*

"Go ahead, Lord Cynwrig. He's aware of the wider world through no agency of yours. You're free to share."

David held up a hand. "Whoa, whoa, whoa. You mean as long as someone else lets Hello Kitty out of the bag, everybody can spill?"

Alun shrugged. "More or less."

"So your face . . . Do you look this way because of this *Tylwyth Teg* thing you are?"

"Were. I'm Sidhe now. Technically. No, I was . . . cursed."

"It could be worse, I suppose. At least you're not a vampire or something."

"No. That would be Kristof."

"Shut up. Vampires are real?"

Alun nodded.

"Werewolves?"

"Vanessa."

"Your office manager is a werewolf. So that means . . ." David dropped onto the sofa. "And little Benjy? Surely he's not a vampire."

"Dragon shifter."

His mouth dropped open. *Dragons? Seriously?* How über-freaking-cool was that? "What about that poser guy? Jackson. What's he? Demon? Troll? Were-jackal?"

"Worse." Alun's voice dropped to a husky whisper. "Lawyer."

David gulped. "Now that . . . is *scary.*"

Alun braced himself for a barrage of questions—and judging by the way David stalked toward him, dodging the more personal ones would be challenging. David placed a hand on Alun's arm.

"So, what do you—"

"Davey." Cassie's voice wobbled, and she drooped over her cane.

He closed his eyes for an instant and took a deep breath before hurrying to her side. "Auntie, you've overdone it again. The doctor warned you about too much exertion."

"Bah. I'm fine." Her white-knuckled grip on the cane belied the words.

"Come along, Madame Stubborn. You need to rest. Do you need me to carry you to the sun porch?"

Perhaps years of exposure to her had inured David to the full force of the druid glare, because *shite.* The look she directed at him would have frozen any ten Sidhe in their tracks. David only chuckled and helped her to her feet, wrapping an arm around her waist.

He gave Alun the stink-eye over her head. "We're not done with this conversation Dr. Ken— Alun. There's *lots* more I want to know. About this curse, for one thing."

Alun sighed and nodded, but Cassie rapped David's wrist with her knuckles. "Davey. Curses are not taken lightly, nor are they easy to discuss. Perhaps you should grant Dr. Kendrick some privacy."

"Privacy-schmivacy. Secrets are a deal breaker." He escorted her across the room, toward a sunny, screened-in porch. "That goes for you too, little missy. Full disclosure."

Secrets. He had too many to count—although thanks to David's druid aunt, he had fewer of them than an hour ago. But what could he afford to share? Not his curse—the truth of it could send David running, and Alun wouldn't blame him.

Alun stood in the middle of the room, shoulders back, chin up, as if he were awaiting the Queen's own sentence, while David settled his aunt onto a chaise and spread a bright coverlet over her legs. *Share enough to keep him, but not too much.*

After fussing with his aunt's blanket for several minutes, David returned, pausing just inside the arch, his expression somber. Goddess, he was beautiful. *Too beautiful for you.*

"So." Alun's voice came out rusty. He cleared his throat. "You'll return to the office, then."

David tilted his head, peering up at Alun from under his thatch of shiny hair. The moment drew out, David making no comment, and Alun's palms began to sweat.

"Are you *telling* me or *asking* me?"

"I—" Alun swallowed the rest of his retort. If David came back to work, but not to Alun's arms, would it be worse than not having him near at all? Alun wasn't sure. "I hope you would choose to return."

"Why?"

Alun scowled, his brow ridges shading his eyes from the bright sunlight. "I told you."

"No. You asked me why I *left*. Now I'm asking you why you want me back."

"Because I need . . ."

David made a let's-get-on-with-it motion with his hand. "Yes?"

"Your help?"

"Nice try." David took a step closer. "Is closer sex in the future?"

"Maybe."

"Why?"

Alun retreated, blinking his burning eyes. Of course. Why would David, so perfectly beautiful, as bright as the midsummer sun, want to cower in the shadows with Alun? "I'm sorry. Never mind."

"Not so fast, Dr. Gloom. I've never been in the closet, and I'm not starting now, not even for you. Are you ashamed of me?"

"What? No. But—" He gestured to his face. "You can do better."

David snorted. "Uh-huh. Because I'm so good at that."

"David. You must understand. To draw attention to myself is to put the supe communities in danger. I must remain as inconspicuous as possible, and if I put myself on display by going out in public, that becomes impossible."

David's expression turned troubled. "So you're saying we can never go anywhere together?"

Alun heaved a sigh. "Sadly, no."

"We can't exactly hang out here. Dang it." He bit his lip, glancing at the sun porch, where Cassie's head scarf was visible over the back of her chaise. "I wish I could have my own apartment, someplace we could be alone, but— What about your place? I could make dinner for you. Or, you know, we could do . . ." he waggled his eyebrows ". . . other things."

For a moment, at the idea of David in his home and—please the Goddess—in his bed, Alun's heart—and his cock—lifted.

Except . . . *human*. Alun ground his teeth together. When he'd moved into his flat with all his distinctly *non*-earthly possessions, he'd had it bespelled against human incursions by a witch's collective for whom he'd done a sensitivity retreat. The charm was intended to protect the Secrecy Pact—it wasn't nuanced enough to admit a human who already *knew* all the secrets.

He shook his head. "I'm sorry, but that's not possible."

"Why?"

"It's . . . complicated."

"No kidding," David muttered. "But there must be somewhere you're willing to go with me. Someplace other than the copy closet."

Shite. If Alun wanted a real chance with David, he'd have to come up with some solution. But in the meantime . . .

He leaned forward and murmured into David's ear, "What do you wager that I can make the closet worth your while, at least in the short term?"

David's breath hitched. "What do I get if I win?"

"What makes you think I'll allow that?" David moaned as Alun drew back, grinning. "Can I expect you at the office in time for my first appointment?"

"Is that a challenge? What do you bet I get there before you?"

CHAPTER ✲ 13

Finally being allowed full access to the client records was *awesome*. Whenever Alun had a break, David bopped into his office with a new list of questions about supes. And Alun answered them. Every freaking one—and some of them were pretty far out on the *freaky* scale too—but it was such a rush not to be so stinking *clueless* anymore. For the first time in any job ever, he felt like part of the team.

Even so, it was more than a week—including a freaking long, boring, *lonely* weekend—before Alun strode past David's desk after the last client of the day with a terse remark about inventorying the office supplies.

Sproing. David's brain whited out and his briefs got several orders of magnitude more binding. He blinked stupidly at his monitor for a full thirty seconds, until he heard the *snick* of the closet latch.

He hurriedly put the phones on night answer and stumbled down the hall in Alun's wake, his heart beating in a dance more awkward than any move he'd ever laid down in a club. When he opened the door, darkness greeted him. He reached for the light switch.

"No." Alun's voice rumbled like the promise of thunder, and a shiver chased down David's spine, lifting his already interested cock to attention.

With a whisper of movement, the door shut behind him, leaving the darkness complete except for the blinking green LED lights on the printer. Silent except for the muted hum of the sleeping copier, the rasp of Alun's breath, and the staccato patter of his own heartbeat in his ears.

Alun's hands on David's shoulders drew him forward, turning him gently until the warmth of his massive chest pressed against David's back, the hard length of his cock resting in the cleft of David's ass.

Warmth ghosted across his neck, lifting the hair on his nape, and then Alun kissed him there, at the top of his spine, just above his collar. David sucked in a desperate breath, blinking in the cocoon of darkness.

"I've watched you all day." Alun spoke against his neck, his lips so soft, his voice a dark, suggestive rasp. "Do you know that when you answer the phone, you tilt your head and your hair lifts, so I can see this spot right here." Alun kissed the skin behind David's right ear, tongue teasing the post of his earring.

"Alun," David moaned. "Please. Let me touch you."

"No."

"Then keep talking to me. I love your voice. From the first time I heard it, doing transcription for you. The way you said 'Twenty-nine-year-old male presents with—'"

"David." His chuckle vibrated through David's entire body. "Nobody gets turned on by chart notes."

"It wasn't what you said. It was how you said it. Your tone. Like beat poetry recited by really kinky angels."

"I'll remember that. If I should see you squirming a bit as you type, with a naughty tilt to this beautiful mouth." Alun traced the line of David's top lip, and David captured that teasing finger, sucked on it until Alun growled deep in his throat.

David couldn't stand it another second. He'd never been a passive lover, and he wasn't about to start now. He released Alun's finger with a decisive *pop*, then ducked away from his grasp.

"What are you doing?" Alun's voice held an undertone of laughter that David had never heard before, and his cock got even harder.

"Leveling the playing field." He lurched away, bumping his hip bone against the copier and hitting something with his elbow that gave way in a bright metallic clatter.

"What was that?"

"I think it was paper clips. Never mind."

"You are a force of nature." A smile in his voice. David wanted to see that smile. Feel it under his lips.

"That's the nicest thing anyone's ever said about me. Usually they call me a vortex of disaster." *Ah. There.* He ran his hands up the crisp cotton of Alun's shirt until he found the knot of his necktie and yanked, bringing Alun's head within reach. "But for you, I'll try to keep the near-death experiences to a minimum."

"Do your worst. I'm not afraid."

He lifted a trembling hand and stroked Alun's cheek. Despite the distorted bone structure, his skin was amazingly soft. "No stubble. How does that work?"

"High fae are all beardless."

"But Mal has scruff. What—"

"Fae *glamourie*, an illusion. Our only hair is on our heads and our . . . nethers."

"Really? Can't wait to see that." David pressed his parted lips against Alun's mouth, and there it was. The smile. His knees tried to buckle and his breath caught, but Alun breathed for him, kissing him with a hunger David had only dreamed of.

David pulled back and tried to remember how his lungs worked while Alun scattered soft-as-air kisses across his cheek, his temple, the slope of his stupid diagonal eyebrow.

Skin. He needed more skin. If Alun's lips felt that good, imagine what the rest of him would feel like, naked and hot and hard against David.

He fumbled with the knot of Alun's tie. "Don't strangle me, Dafydd. Things are just getting interesting."

"What did you call me?" Ha! Tie undone. David dropped it on the floor where it could commune with the paper clips.

"Dafydd," Alun said against David's jaw. "The Welsh version of your name." He nibbled along David's jaw until he returned to his starting place under David's ear. David had to steady himself by holding on to Alun's shoulders with both hands and a prayer for strength. "If you don't like it—"

"No. I mean, yes, I like it." David wrestled with the buttons on Alun's shirt. It had been so long since he'd undressed another man, and dealing with the placket backward was almost more than his sex-obsessed brain could handle. "It's actually my real name, but . . ." Success! David pushed the shirt off Alun's shoulders and down his arms, where it got stuck on his wrists. Shoot. He'd forgotten about the cuffs.

"Easy, *cariad*. I've got them." A rustle of fabric, and Alun's hands were between them, making short work of his cuff buttons. "But what?"

Without the shirt, the scent of Alun's skin overwhelmed David, soap and the sharp tang of male sweat at the end of the day, overlaid by a half-familiar wild scent and the unmistakable musk of his arousal.

David closed his eyes—*so what if it's stupid in the dark?*—and breathed it in.

"But what?" Alun's voice was laced with amusement.

"What what?"

"What about your name?"

"Oh." Another deep breath. *Mmm. I could live on that smell.* "The American version was easier for people to say." David leaned forward and nuzzled Alun's chest, sampling the skin of his solid pectoral with the tip of his tongue. The flavor was just . . . *wow*. Salty, with a hint of spice and an almost effervescent edge. *He tastes like adventure.*

David let his lips and tongue continue their exploration. Nipple. Yes! He suckled there until Alun moaned and laced his fingers through David's hair.

"Dafydd. Oak and thorn, I want you."

"Excellent," David murmured, and trailed kisses across the acre of chest, aiming for the other nipple.

But halfway there, he encountered a different texture under his lips and pulled back, tracing the spot with gentle fingers. The ridge of scar tissue had to be over an inch across, and it extended from Alun's clavicle all the way down to his waistband, possibly beyond, although considering the length and solidity of the cock that had been riding David's hip bone moments ago, he wasn't incapacitated.

"What . . . Alun, what is this?" David pulled away and reached for the light switch, but Alun grabbed him.

"Don't."

"What happened to you?"

Alun released him, and one bare shoulder brushed David's wrist as he bent down and, judging by the sound of rustling fabric, retrieved his shirt. "The curse. It's all part of the curse."

"Let me—"

"No!" Alun's growl rivaled his tone on the first day they met. "It's bad enough you have to look at my face during the day. You don't need—"

"Wait a minute. So the dark closet wasn't just kinky sexy fun times? You don't want me to *see* you?" Heat of a different sort replaced David's earlier lust. "Screw that, Alun." David groped for the light switch and flipped it on.

Alun blinked furiously in the sudden brightness and turned, hunching his shoulders as he buttoned his shirt.

"You don't have to hide from me." David laid his hand on Alun's shoulder and pulled him around, which was damned hard to do, considering the man was six foot bazillion and solid muscle. But David was nothing if not persistent, and Alun finally sighed and gave in.

He kept his head bowed, his arms crossed over his partially buttoned shirt. David unfolded those arms and unbuttoned that shirt. The scar was as wide and long as he had imagined, the angry red of a recently healed wound rather than the faded track of one as old as this must be.

David touched the scar, gently tracing its length from Alun's collar bone to below his navel, where it disappeared behind his trousers. Alun clenched his eyes shut, and David could practically hear his teeth grinding.

"Does it still hurt?"

"Only when you do that."

David snatched his hand away. "Shoot, I'm sorry—"

Alun's eyes snapped open, and he grabbed David's shoulders. "Not your touch. Your gaze. It hurts when you see how truly ugly I am. I want—" He swallowed, and his hands flexed on David's shoulders. "I wish I were still beautiful. For you."

"But you are. You have lips." David kissed him to prove it. "Amazing lips. You have the most gorgeous, soulful hazel eyes on the planet." He planted a trail of kisses from one of Alun's eyelids, across the bridge of his nose to the other. "And your heart. The way you want to help people, protect them. That's incredible. Everything else? Incidental."

"Everything?" Alun flexed his hips, pressing their groins together.

David grinned. "Well, I've got to admit that's a huge attraction." He ground back, their erections tight behind their trousers. "Really huge. But beauty isn't just in the skin. It's inside too. Think of Mr. Hoffenberg."

Alun scowled, and on his misshapen features, to someone who didn't know him as well as David did, the expression was fricking scary. "You think he's hot?"

"Sweetheart, everyone, including him, thinks he's hot, but I wouldn't touch him with a cattle prod. I may be a sex-starved boyfriend-repellent klutz, but I'm not *that* desperate."

Alun grunted and rolled up his sleeves. "No. Only desperate enough to consort with a monster."

"Hey. None of that."

"I can't help it. I'm—" Alun sighed as he buttoned his shirt. "Grant me a little grace, David. I've been a beast for many times your lifetime. It will take an effort to get used to this."

Reluctantly, David set his own clothes to rights. "Don't take too long."

"Why? Are you— Do you want to leave me?"

"No. *Heck* no. But I may expire of sexual frustration if we can't get any further than *closetus interruptus*."

Alun followed David into the reception lobby, head down as he retied his tie. Oak and thorn, what a disaster. After two centuries with his own shame as a constant companion, it had taken him over a week to work up the courage for this encounter. Yet despite David's apparent enthusiasm, not to mention the desire coursing through his own veins, Alun couldn't bear to face a lover in the light—especially David, whom he wanted so desperately to impress. How could he, though, if David were able to see every imperfection, every mark of Alun's failure, imprinted on his skin and in the misshapen bones of his face?

David claimed that Alun's ugliness didn't matter, but how long would that last?

"Hello, Mr. Kendrick." Alun's head snapped up at David's overbright greeting. Mal was lounging in David's chair, his feet propped on the desk, ankles crossed. "We weren't expecting to see you today."

Mal's gaze flicked from David's face to Alun's, and he smirked, damn the man. "Clearly. But then, nothing pleases me more than making a nuisance of myself."

Alun felt his habitual scowl settle into place at the way his brother scoped out David, at the urge to push himself in front of David, blocking Mal's view of something he considered his territory—further evidence that his curse hadn't eradicated his possessive fae nature or his Sidhe battle instincts.

"Mal. I thought you were going to call." Alun insinuated himself between David and his brother, allowing his arm to graze David's chest, his hand to dangle by his side, directly in front of David's groin. Mal's shrewd gaze didn't miss that message: *Back off. He's mine.*

Judging by an exasperated sigh from David, he hadn't missed it either. *Shite.*

"I was in the neighborhood. Besides." Mal dropped his feet to the floor and stood up, all the sly mischief draining from his expression, leaving his face tense and bleak. "We need to talk."

David stepped out from behind Alun. "Shall I bring coffee for you both?"

"No," Alun growled at the same time Mal said, "Absolutely."

David patted Alun's arm. "I'll make a fresh pot." He disappeared down the hallway into the kitchenette.

"Let's go, then, and you'll be out of here sooner." Alun stalked into his office and dropped into the wingback chair. "Although if you sent David away for the sake of privacy, you're wasting your effort. He'll just tease the news out of me when you've gone."

Mal tensed with an abortive grab to where his sword hilt would be. "You *told* him about us? About supes? Gwydion's bollocks, man, are you fecking *mental*? I'm the one who'll have to bring you in to face— Wait. Why didn't the alarm sound? Why isn't the Queen already on my arse to arrest you?"

"Because I didn't break the Pact, obviously."

"You want me to believe yon boyo figured it out on his own? He's sharp, I'll grant you, but fae living in the Outer World isn't an ordinary leap of logic."

"His aunt is a druid. She did it."

"Bloody hell," Mal muttered, dropping onto the sofa. "She's got to have an ulterior motive. Druids. There's—"

"Always a catch. Yes, I'm aware. But, in this case, I believe her reasons are pure."

"A druid? Not likely. They're as canny as a whole pack of foxes and as twisty as the path to the hells—and they *never* have only a single objective."

Alun shook his head. "Her love for David is clear. I believe her to be motivated only by her care for him."

"Did she get what she wanted?"

Alun sat back, considering the question as a thread of doubt burrowed into his belly. Druid ways were mysterious even to the fae, but they had similar ties to nature and the power sleeping deep within the earth. Perhaps the changes in the Outer World, the same ones that affected the fae and the other supe races, interfered with their rituals as well.

David was once more ensconced here in the office, with greater access to secrets about the most disturbed members of the supe community. Could Cassie want David here as a spy? It was the druids' job to know everything—could this be how they achieved their apparent omniscience? Not through arcane divination, but through a vast network of informants?

He scowled. Whatever Cassie's reasons, he refused to believe David would divulge details about any client. The man was too serious about his job, too competent.

"Enough. Say your piece."

"You look better than last time. I think your jaw may have shrunk a couple of centimeters."

"If that's all you've come to say, you can leave now." Alun started to rise, but Mal waved him down.

"Don't be so bloody touchy. You're worse than a molting gryphon. Have you made your decision about the Revels?"

"No decision to make. Looking like this, I couldn't get past the portal if I wanted to."

"Say there was a way. Would you consider it?"

Alun's brows drew together, and he searched his brother's face for signs of a trick. Goddess knew it wouldn't be the first time Mal had tried to take the piss out of him. "Why?"

Mal leaned forward, elbows on his knees, and laced his fingers together. "There's going to be a ceremony."

Alun rolled his eyes. "If you're trying to entice me, you're going about it the wrong way. I avoided ceremonies when I was part of the Court. Why would I want to go to this one?"

"Because it's different. I told you about the shift in Court politics, the unrest by some of the disenfranchised groups, the power play by the Daoine Sidhe."

"So? They've been jockeying for position since the Unification. They never thought that the Welsh or the Bretons should have been allowed in, let alone the Manx or the Cornish. I'm not sure they don't consider the Scots beneath them, for all that the Queen is a Scot."

"The Queen wants to put an end to it. She's demanding an oath of fealty from all members of the Court. Individually."

Alun snorted. "One at a time? She won't be able to do that at the Revels. It is the shortest night of the year, after all."

"Only the highest ranking courtiers will swear the oath at the Revels. She's been making the rounds of all the lower orders for weeks. By the solstice, the only ones left will be the high lords."

"Sounds like a nightmare. Enjoy yourself."

Mal punched his palm with his fist and swore under his breath. "You have to be there, Alun, we all do. Gareth's making an appearance."

Alun's teeth clenched. *Serious then.* Gareth hadn't willingly set foot in Faerie since his own lover had been kidnapped by Unseelie fae. "Quite the occasion. Sorry I'll miss it."

"You can't. Anyone who fails to take the oath will be exiled from Faerie permanently."

"I can't be more permanently exiled than I already am."

"Not only that, you'll be declared an enemy of the Court and a fugitive from the Queen's justice. With a price on your head, literally. Any fae, Seelie or Unseelie, who brings in an unsworn will be rewarded." Mal glared at Alun. "The head does not have to be attached to the body."

The idea of the Unseelie hordes and the stray ambitious Seelie lordling on his arse didn't worry Alun overmuch on his own account. However, collateral damage in fae feuds could be cataclysmic, and he now had David to consider.

"Can't I take the oath by proxy?"

Mal shook his head. "No. In person, on bended knee, head bowed to receive the Queen's beneficence. You know the drill. Of course, there's a little twist this time. The oath is not just to the Queen herself, it's to the Unified Seelie Court—and the Consort."

Alun's head snapped back in shock. "An oath to the Consort? Why in all the hells—"

"He's Daoine Sidhe. It's the Queen's way of placating their faction, and you have to admit, they're formidable."

Alun thrust himself out of the chair and strode to the window behind his desk, the blinds now open to reveal the flickering lights of the street below. "Blast. You can wager anything you like that this plot is of the Consort's making. He's had it in for me since I bested him in that ridiculous archery tournament." *Three bloody centuries ago.* The fae could hold a grudge forever.

"No, brother." Mal's voice took on a softer note, conciliatory, something Alun had heard perhaps twice in his life. "He's aware that the Queen nearly chose you as Consort."

"She didn't."

"But she discussed it with you."

"I refused the honor." He'd already met Owain by then. Even if her suggestion hadn't been purely political, as opposed to physical or romantic, there had been no question. "And it was a private meeting."

"You think any meeting in Faerie is truly private? Shite, man, even the trees are as likely to be sentient as not."

"Trees aren't gossips."

"No, but their dryad companions are."

"I hardly think—"

"It doesn't matter how he found out. He knows. And he considers you the biggest threat to his authority."

"He has nothing to fear from me. Even if I wanted his place, which I don't and never did, I'm barred from Faerie. I can't even pass the bloody threshold." Alun's breath stuttered to a halt, then released in a rush. "That's his plan, isn't it? I won't be able to take the oath, and he'll be able to kill me with impunity."

"That's my theory anyway."

"So if I manage to crash this thrice-damned party—"

"A party?" David said from the door, the coffee tray jiggling as he bounced on his toes. "What kind of party? Are we all going?"

Mal met Alun's glare, and his mouth curled up in the wicked grin that presaged every scrape he'd embroiled Alun in since they were striplings. "A once-in-a-lifetime party, boyo. The Midsummer Revels, in the very heart of Faerie."

David's eyes widened, making him look more than ever like a wood sprite. "Get *out*. Really?"

"Really and truly. Interested?"

"Are you kidding? Of course. Can I—"

"We're not going," Alun growled.

"We're not? Oh." David blinked, the bright joy of his expression fading to uncertainty. "Is it because you don't want to be seen with me?"

"Shite, no. I'd be proud to be seen with you, but—"

"Is it . . . is it because I'm a man?"

Mal took his cup from David's tray. "Nah. In Faerie, gender is . . ." Mal waggled his hand back and forth ". . . optional. It's because my brother won't put himself out. Afraid of a little effort and a little pain." Mal took a sip of coffee. "All right, a lot of pain."

Pain. If anyone could handle pain, Alun could—he'd lived with it every day for over two hundred years. If a little more were the only cost, Alun would gladly pay—to see admiration in David's eyes just this once. To have a chance to make love to him without worrying about repulsing him with every touch.

"All right. You win, provided you're not blowing smoke out your arse," Alun said, snatching his own cup off the tray. "Tell me your plan, but wipe that damned smug smile off your face before you do."

If anything, Mal's grin widened. "Well, then. Get ready for an epic celebration, David *bach*, because in a few days' time, you'll be partying with the fae."

CHAPTER ✦ 14

On the solstice, Alun scheduled his last patient at seven so he'd have time to prepare for crossing into Faerie with whatever alchemy Mal had conjured up.

David had almost vibrated with excitement all day, charming all the clients—including surly Jackson Hoffenberg—even more than usual. Charming Alun more than usual too, if he wanted to admit the truth.

He bounded into Alun's office at eight fifteen, as Alun finished dictating the last chart notes for Benjamin Tomlinson. He had exchanged his office attire—which was distracting enough—for a pair of brown leather pants so tight that Alun's mouth went dry, a collarless white shirt open at the throat, and a suede vest with gold trim.

"What do you think?" He raised his arms and turned in a slow circle. "Will this pass muster at a fae jamboree? You told me only natural fibers or skins. Nothing synthetic, and no base metal." He traced the stitching on his vest. "Gold is all right though, isn't it? And stones?" He touched his onyx earring.

"Yes." Alun laid down his recorder and growled, "Come here."

David grinned and shook his head. The track lighting glinted on the highlights in his hair, and Alun had never wanted anyone, even Owain, more than he wanted David in this moment.

"No, sir. I don't want to risk being late. It's our first date outside the supply closet. I want it to be perfect."

A date. Is that how he saw this? Alun blinked, and a slow smile stretched his lips. Yes. It was a date, in that he'd have the chance to spend time with David in a social setting, maybe arrange some alone time in one of his favorite spots in Faerie, the grotto on the other side of the hill from the ceilidh glade, a place he hadn't visited in two hundred years.

Of course, any visit to Faerie, especially for a human, was fraught with the possibility of disaster. Alun would have to be absolutely certain they left before dawn, or David could return to a world he no longer recognized.

Now if only Mal would get here so they could get moving. The sooner the formalities of the evening were taken care of—his blasted oath of fealty to the Queen and her smarmy Consort—the sooner he could spend some quality time with David, preferably with clothing optional.

On cue, Mal sauntered in, dressed in his Court finery, which wasn't that different from David's outfit, although Mal never deviated from black leather and white linen. His broadsword was hanging in a scabbard slung across his back, and Alun raised his eyebrows.

"That's not a ceremonial weapon. You're going into the Queen's presence battle-armed?"

Mal flicked the hilt where it extended above his left shoulder. "It's obligatory for me, remember—Enforcer and bloody acting Champion. It's my job to make sure none of the supplicants attempt to stage a coup."

"I don't give a rat's arse for any coup, but I need to know how you plan to fool the gate into letting me through."

David frowned, his gaze darting between Alun and Mal. "Fool the gate? What do you mean? I thought you were required to attend?"

Mal pulled a small linen-wrapped bundle out of the pouch at his waist. "Let me guess. My tight-lipped, tight-arsed brother hasn't told you anything about the tenets of the Seelie Court, am I right?"

"Um . . ." David glanced at Alun, obviously not wanting to agree if it would upset him.

Alun spared him the distress, and stripped Mal of the satisfaction of announcing everything himself. "The Seelie Court has four primary mandates, and they're non-negotiable. The first is honor, which we're expected to defend to the death."

"Okaaay. Not planning on killing anyone, although Mal's sword is a little alarming." David glanced at Mal from under his lashes. "Hot too."

Mal grinned, the bloody bastard. "The second is looove. Want to test that one out with me, boy *bach*?"

David laughed. "No. thanks, but I appreciate the offer." He turned back to Alun. "So far, I don't see the problem."

"Then there's beauty." Alun rubbed his misshapen jaw. "I don't fit the requirements anymore."

"So you need to get special dispensation? Bribe the bouncer? What?"

"Not so easy." Mal set a tiny brown bottle on Alun's desk. "Faerie isn't a place as physical as this room, or this town, or even this country. It's a magical construct, and as such, it has rules that are enforced by the spell that created it. If you don't fit the standards of beauty encapsulated in the spell, you can't get in. Period. Faerie simply will not exist for you, regardless of how many times you've been there before."

David scowled, rivaling Alun's most disgruntled expressions. "That sucks."

"True. But it's a fact we must deal with." Mal pointed to the bottle. "There's your ticket, brother. Drink up."

Alun picked up the little vial between his thumb and forefinger. "What should I expect from this?"

Mal shrugged. "Not sure exactly. I got it from a druid I know. She swears it'll make it possible for you to pass, but it's only good for twelve hours. Since it's the solstice, and night's only eight hours long, that's plenty of time for you to show up, abase yourself, raise a glass of mead or two, and scarper before somebody decides they need a piece of you."

"Druids," Alun muttered. "Of course it would be druids." He uncorked the bottle and tossed back the contents, nearly gagging as the bitter brew seared his tongue and bit the back of his throat. "Gwydion's bollocks, would it kill them to make it taste less like hell hound piss?"

Mal shrugged. "I imagine they don't think the clientele who need this kind of potion deserve any extra effort. No need to tempt the palate."

Alun tossed the empty bottle in the recycling bin. "Now what?"

Mal shrugged again and tucked the square of linen back in his pouch. "Guess we go. You're not wearing that, are you?"

Alun glanced down at his dress shirt, tie, and summer-weight wool slacks. "Of course not. But I just finished work."

"Then go change." Mal smiled and swaggered toward David, who'd been watching the whole show with wide anxious eyes. "I'm sure David and I can find some way to occupy ourselves. You needn't rush."

"Wait." David took a step back, one hand coming up as if to ward Mal off. "You said there were four tenets. What's the last one?"

"Oh that." Mal flicked his fingers as if brushing away a persistent insect. "Equilibrium. Or as I like to call it—payback."

That's when the cramps hit Alun's belly and his head exploded in a burst of pain.

"Alun!" David started forward when Alun clutched his head and doubled over, but Mal caught his shoulder, holding him back. He struggled in Mal's hold as Alun face-planted on his stupid gray carpeting. "Let go, damn it. He needs help."

"You can't do anything. This is the druid spell, doing what it's supposed to. We can only wait until it's done."

Alun's back arched, and he jerked, his limbs flopping as if he were seizing.

"Can't we—" David swallowed as Alun curled into a fetal position, his body shuddering and jerking as if from invisible body blows. "This can't be worth it. There had to have been some other way."

"Trust me, if I could have found a way around this without involving druid magic, I'd have found it. With druids, there's always a catch—some shite about cosmic balance. Besides, fae and druids? No love lost there."

"Why?" Alun jackknifed, stiff-limbed, then curled again, tighter than before. God, David hated to see someone in this much pain, yet be unable to help.

Mal slung an arm across his shoulders, but it didn't feel like a come-on. It felt like comfort from a companion in adversity. "The ways of our people, David *bach*. Who's to say how the feud began, but since we dearly love a good feud, no one feels the urge to uncover the truth."

"Then how can you ever fix it?" David leaned in to the embrace, counting the seconds in his head, determined to call 911, regardless of what Mal said, if this went on longer than another minute. "Equilibrium does *not* equal payback, no matter what you think. Once people start down that path, nothing *ever* evens out, because everyone on both sides is always convinced *their* loss is greater than the other person's. So if you ask me, you've *all* broken a Seelie tenet. Why punish Alun and not everybody else? It's so unfair."

"Shite." Mal rubbed his other hand over his face. "You've got a point."

Alun groaned, his limbs jerking, and David pressed his fist against his mouth until he cut the inside of his lip against his teeth, tasting the metallic salt of his own blood. *This has gone on long enough.*

But as he ducked out from under Mal's arm to grab the desk phone, Alun took a giant shuddering breath, and the tension went out of his back and shoulders.

He rolled to his hands and knees and shook his head heavily. "Damn druids. Always with the pain." He pushed himself to his haunches and stood as if he were unfurling from a chrysalis.

When he lifted his head and blinked at them, David's mouth fell open and his eyes threatened to leap out of their sockets. Was *this* what Alun looked like before the curse? He'd thought Mal was gorgeous, but Alun beat him to hell in a go-cart.

Dark, silky hair fell across a smooth forehead and framed cheekbones that would make any Abercrombie model weep. His nose, no longer fleshy, was straight and sculpted, his jaw strong and square, with the same cleft—although without the magical stubble—that his brother sported. His eyes were the same luminous hazel, but they were no longer shadowed by the oversized brow ridges. His lips—well, those hadn't changed. *Thank goodness.*

"Mother of us all," breathed Mal. "That witch really knows her craft."

"What?" Alun's chest still heaved in the aftermath of the transformation. "Is something—" He touched his face, and shock chased the weariness from his eyes. He swept his hands across his forehead, down his cheeks, over his jawline. "Shite." He yanked his tie off and ripped open his shirt, scattering a handful of white buttons on the carpet like snowflakes.

His chest was smooth, unmarred, hairless. He looked up, mouth working as if he couldn't form any words.

"If you're done messing about, brother," Mal drawled, "you'd best get ready to go. We can't be late to the party—that's just rude."

CHAPTER ❧ 15

David had expected a longer trip to the gates of Faerie—or at least something a little less prosaic than pulling into the Audubon Society parking lot and hiking down a trail in Forest Park. *I shouldn't be surprised, I suppose—after all, if vampires and shape-shifters show up for regular psychotherapy sessions, anything is possible.*

Even so, as he followed Alun and Mal down the path, he wished he hadn't left his worry stone at home. He was still off-kilter. Watching Alun's agony had been horrible, yes, but ever since he'd been revealed in all his jaw-dropping glory, he'd been different. Distant.

David could understand why. Why would anyone who looked like that—a lord of the freaking Sidhe, for goodness sake—want anything to do with dorky David Evans, temporary office manager and full-time screw-up?

The two hulking figures ahead of him stopped next to a shoulder-high boulder. Well, shoulder-high to them. It topped David by a good two inches. Why hadn't Alun seemed this tall before? Had he actually grown during the transformation?

No, when he'd stood next to Mal that first day, David had noticed they were exactly the same height. Maybe the double dose of excessive male beauty just made him feel extra-small.

Alun turned toward him, the moonlight that filtered through the trees dappling his more-than-perfect face. "We leave the path here, Dafydd. Can you see well enough?"

He was still calling David by the name he'd first uttered in their second abortive closet encounter. That had to count for something. "Sure." *I'll just follow the glow of your skin.*

"Take my hand." Alun extended his palm, the full sleeve of his poet's shirt billowing in the breeze. "Mal, you follow behind."

"No worries there. Nice pants, David."

Alun scowled. "On second thought, you lead."

"Spoilsport." But Mal grinned and struck off uphill through the trees.

Although David could have sworn the dense woods would inflict serious damage on their party clothes, Mal somehow led them down a path with plenty of clearance for his double-wide shoulders.

For all I know, the trees moved aside for him.

Mal paused by a narrow stream. "This is where we see if that potion is worth what I paid for it. Are you ready, brother?"

"As I'll ever be." Alun took a deep breath and blew it out, then turned to David. "You must do exactly as we say from now on, understand? You don't know the ways of Faerie, and you might do something—"

"I—"

Alun stopped David's protest by laying a finger across his lips. "—*inadvertently* to put yourself or the two of us in danger."

A fair point. David had no idea what to expect. "Okay."

"As we cross the water, watch my feet and only my feet. Follow in my steps exactly. We'll know if we've succeeded when we reach the other side."

David eyed the stream. Mal and Alun could probably cross it with a single stride, although David would have to take a running leap. Were Alun and Mal pulling an elaborate prank on him? But Alun's agony had been real, and his altered appearance was one heck of a persuader. "I'm ready."

Instead of stepping across to the other bank, Alun placed one foot on a flat rock in the stream that David hadn't noticed before. He kept his gaze riveted on Alun's boots, as per instructions, and followed. One rock. Two. Three. *Wait just a fricking minute.* Four? Five? They could have crossed the silly little brook and back three times by now, but Alun kept going—another ten stones before he finally stepped out onto a grassy bank.

When David joined him, Alun was shaking, a sheen of sweat on his forehead. Mal slapped him on the shoulder.

"See? No problem at all."

"Speak for yourself," Alun growled, but the expression on his face as he gazed around—*And holy cats, where did that giant freaking hill come from?*—was full of wonder.

Mal nudged David's ribs. "Not much farther now, boy *bach*. Up the tor, through the woods, and we'll reach the ceilidh glade before you know it."

David peered up the steep, rocky slope to its distant crown of trees. "How many miles would you say?"

"Distance is relative in Faerie, but we'll never get there if we don't start walking."

With every step up the tor and through the woods, Alun's connection to the One Tree grew stronger. Power infused him, as if he were absorbing it through his skin, through the breath in his lungs. *I'd forgotten. After so many years away, I'd forgotten the sheer intoxication of it.*

When they arrived at the ceilidh glade, already packed with the cream of Faerie, he faltered. After two centuries in exile, what kind of welcome could he expect, especially given the reason for his exile? He nearly turned around, but then David took his hand, his eyes wide and shining as he took in the throng.

"Wow. It's like the Waterfront Blues Festival crossed with Fashion Week and a little *Game of Thrones* thrown in for the cosplay." He stood on his tiptoes, peering through the crowd to the dais on the other side of the clearing. "Hey, is that your brother? The Hunter's Moon Facebook page said the band was playing at some festival in LA this afternoon."

"They were."

"How did he get here so fast?"

Alun smiled down at David. "Magic. Do you imagine the way we arrived is the only path to Faerie?"

"Cool," David breathed.

Mal bumped Alun's shoulder with his own. "Don't stand here like a bloody wallflower. Mingle. You'll be less conspicuous that way."

Ah. Good point. Alun kept a tight hold of David's hand and ventured out from under the trees. The glade was twice the size it had been the last time he'd been here—it expanded and contracted to fit the occasion. However, given how crowded it was, and how many fae, both high and lesser, managed to nearly run David over, Alun suspected tonight's event might be challenging its limits.

David pressed against his side, his hand bunching Alun's sleeve. "Don't look now," he murmured, jerking his chin at a point beyond Alun's shoulder, "but that guy in the overdecorated suit is glaring at you."

Alun snapped his head around, following the direction of David's gaze. The Consort. He bared his teeth in a battle grimace that could pass for a smile—barely.

David punched his biceps. "Way to be subtle. What part of 'Don't look now' don't you get?"

He gazed down at David and stroked his cheek with the back of his fingers. "Haven't you learned, *cariad*, that the surest way to get someone to look is to tell them not to? Besides, in this company, it's always wisest to face trouble before it ambushes you in the shadows."

David leaned into the caress. "Fine. So who is he?"

"The Consort."

"*The Consort?* What kind of a name is that?"

"It's not his name, it's what he is. The consort to the Queen."

"If everyone refers to him by his function rather than his name, no wonder he looks so pissy. Does he at least *have* a name?"

Alun frowned, trying to remember the last time he'd heard the Consort's true name. "Rodric. Rodric Luchullain."

"No wonder he prefers 'the Consort,'" David muttered.

The Consort turned away with one last stony look at them, and Alun's frown deepened as he tracked the man through the crowd. "I remember him being shorter. And less . . . blond."

Mal squinted at the Consort's retreating back. "From your former exalted position, everyone looked shorter. That's what an inflated head does for you." He shrugged. "The blondness I can't answer for. Maybe your color sense was blunted by . . ." *By Owain's radiant fairness* hung in the air between them as if Mal had said the words. His habitual cocky grin faded, and he turned away, muttering "Shite. Sorry."

Alun waited for the gut-punch that followed any thought of Owain, but it didn't come. *Should I feel guilty that I feel less guilty?* He'd think about it later—for now, he had David to consider.

The fifth time David had to dodge a reveler, he tugged on Alun's hand. "Is this just because I'm human? They think I ought to step aside for them without even an 'excuse me'?"

Alun pulled David behind him before a bejeweled courtier could knock him over. "No. This is unusual, but perhaps it's because you're with me. Often, when a fae is exiled, other fae aren't required to observe the usual Court protocols. Sometimes that extends to ignoring the outcast completely."

"Like shunning?"

"A little, although it's more similar to the 'cut direct' in Regency England—they're free to behave like supercilious arseholes, and the disgraced person has no choice but to swallow it." Alun seethed at the unfairness. David had done nothing to warrant such rudeness. "I fear you're being tarred with my unfortunate brush. I'm sorry."

"They're dissing you because of the curse? You're the one who has to deal with it, not them. Why would they care?"

Mal scratched his chin—bare of his Outer World scruff since *glamourie* would be nullified in the Queen's presence anyway. "You haven't told him the story?"

"No."

"Bloody hells, brother. Isn't it time?"

"I—"

Suddenly Gareth appeared in front of them, his mouth twisted with the same disgust he'd heaped on Alun since Owain's death. "I wonder how you dare to show your face."

Right then. What's a party without a family brawl? "Me? What about that latest CD of yours? If the Queen finds out you recorded Gwydion's bloody harp, you'll—"

"I'll what? Be condemned to exile? I'd welcome it, never to return to this thrice-blasted place."

"Exile might be the least of it. She could condemn you to death."

Gareth's eyes, vacant as the day his lover had been taken by the Unseelie fae, held no fear. "That I'd welcome too."

"If you care nothing for yourself, consider this: if your sentence is death, as Queen's Enforcer, Mal would be your executioner. If you care nothing for yourself, you might at least think of him."

"Oi. Leave me out of it."

Gareth ignored Mal and leaned in. Alun clenched his fists, willing Gareth to take the first swing, but David suddenly pushed between them and grabbed Gareth's hand, pumping it with unabashed enthusiasm.

"Gareth. Wow, I'm a huge fan, you've no idea." Gareth blinked, and David let go, a blush creeping up his throat. "Well, of course you have no idea. You don't know me from Lady Gaga. I'm David Evans. I'm . . . well . . . I'm temping for your brother. It's such a thrill to meet you and . . ." He trailed off, grimacing, as Gareth continued to stare at him. "Sorry. Too over the top?"

If Gareth is foul to David, I'll throw the first punch myself.

But to Alun's surprise, Gareth grinned, and his eyes lost their deadness. "Not in the least. I'm always happy to meet a fan."

A tall thin fae Alun didn't recognize sauntered over, casting a contemptuous glance over Alun and his brothers—although he ignored David. "Well, if it isn't the three Welsh fairies."

The three of them drew themselves up, the disdain in the stranger's tone uniting them when blood connection could not. They stared him down until he backed off, strolling away in the company of half a dozen other courtiers, all of them laughing.

David tugged on Alun's sleeve. "I thought you said no one called you fairies."

"No one with any elegance of mind."

"Or who doesn't want to find his hand tucked under his pillow without benefit of his arm," Mal muttered.

"So what is his problem?"

"He's Irish," Alun said.

"So?"

"He doesn't consider us true Sidhe." Gareth's earlier smile had disappeared behind the grim face he'd worn when he'd first faced Alun. "Before Unification, he wouldn't have bothered to spit on us."

"And that's a disadvantage? What, his spit is a collector's item?" David glared after the jerk, his fists planted on his hips. "I'll bet you can buy that crap by the bucket on eBay."

Mal snorted, and a smile teased Gareth's mouth for a moment before he caught Alun's gaze.

"A pleasure to meet you, David." Gareth nodded once at Mal, but glared at Alun. "You will take him home before dawn. I'll be watching." He turned on his heel and strode to the dais.

Mal ran a hand through his hair and whistled. "Look at it this way. At least he spoke to you."

"True." Alun tracked Gareth as he took his guitar out of its case. *No harp tonight. At least he's not a total idiot.* "I'm not certain whether that's good or bad."

CHAPTER ❈ 16

M al slung an arm across David's shoulder. "How about a drink, boyo? These parties never stint on the mead, thank the Goddess."

"Um . . ." David glanced from Alun's glower to Mal's smirk. "I—"

"Mal, don't you need to see a man about a horse?"

Mal laughed. "You could have come up with a better line than that, brother, but I can take a hint. Have fun." He disappeared into the crowd.

"Dafydd." Alun's voice was wine and chocolate and velvet darkness. David shivered, tempted to close his eyes and let it wash over him, but he didn't want to waste a single second, nor squander a single glimpse of Alun's face, gorgeous enough to match the voice. "Come with me. We've time before the ceremony. I want to show you something."

"Tell me it's a supply closet."

The burr of Alun's low chuckle went straight to David's balls. "No. But you might like it better."

David grabbed his hand. "In that case, let's go."

Alun unlaced their fingers, and David opened his mouth to protest, but when he wrapped his arm around David's shoulders, tucking David's arm around his own waist . . . Well. That was much better, wasn't it?

The rest of Hunter's Moon had joined Gareth onstage, and they struck up their first tune as Alun led David around the edge of the crowd.

"Where are we going? Is it far? Because if it's more of Mal's 'relative distance' crap—"

"So impatient."

"You know how I hate secrets. Tell me."

"You see that path beyond the dais? There's a place there where we can be alone."

"Will there be kissing?"

"Assuredly."

"Skin?"

"Without a doubt."

"Sex?"

Alun leaned closer, his lips brushing David's ear. "Depend on it."

"What are we waiting for?" He pulled Alun in a ninety-degree turn and aimed for the path in a straight shot through the crowd of dancers who'd already begun swaying to the music.

"Hold, Dafydd." Alun drew him back. "See the circle of stones?"

David looked at the ground where smooth white stones gleamed in the moonlight, nearly overgrown with moss and framed with tiny white flowers. "Yes."

"That is a faerie circle. If you venture inside while a true bard plays, you must stay and dance until the music stops."

"I take it your brother is a true bard."

"The last one in Faerie."

"As much as I love his music, I've got another agenda tonight." He let Alun lead him back to their original path. "Wait. Is that why—at the office—when I played his CD?" Alun nodded, his teeth glinting in a wicked smile. "Holy crap. I've been ensorcelled, and I didn't even know it."

"Does that bother you?"

David scanned the dancers inside the circle. They didn't look distressed or annoyed. In fact, they seemed well on the way to totally blissed-out. "Little bit. I'd prefer to choose to dance rather than be forced to do it."

"Trust me, *cariad*, anyone who has ever seen you dance would prefer that your choice take you in another direction entirely."

David sighed. "I know. Pathetic isn't it?"

"Yet I wouldn't have it any other way. Your dancing is what broke through and allowed me to *see* you."

Once past the dancing circle, Alun led David through a tunnel of flowering vines, mixed honeysuckle and wisteria. They emerged on the shore of a lake. The moon hung low over the water, its reflection turning the surface as silver as a newly minted coin.

"Whoa. The moon is *huge*, as if it's closer to Earth."

"Technically, we're not on Earth. We're in Faerie."

"Is it the same moon?"

"More or less. But in Faerie, the objects are affected more by their importance, their relevance to our customs and heritage."

"So objects may be smaller than they appear?"

"Or larger, so it's best to make no assumptions about size."

David shot a sly glance at Alun. "Is that a warning or an apology?"

Alun laughed, the sound echoing across the water. "Neither, you cheeky boy. Now come. This way."

The gurgle and chime of water over stone filled the air. A tumble of rocks formed a natural stair next to a brook, and Alun led David up the rough steps until they topped out into a pocket meadow, encircled by shoulder-high boulders. On the far side, two trees were twined together, their trunks fused, and their branches laced overhead like living rope.

As Alun drew him under the tree, David glanced up into the thick leaves, their scent like sage and bay. The spot seemed totally isolated, but after Alun's warning, he couldn't take privacy for granted.

"I'm not going to look up and see a woodland creature staring down at me like River Tam spying on Simon and Kaylee in the bowels of *Serenity,* am I? Because that would be creepy."

Alun pulled David forward, his smile glimmering in the dappled moonlight, his eyes hot and dark. "You are quite safe here, Dafydd *bach*. Safe from everyone but me."

David looped his arms around Alun's neck, threading his fingers through the silky hair that tumbled over his shirt's collarless neckband. He smelled better than the forest, yet part of it. "Good thing I don't want to be rescued, then, isn't it?"

He tugged on Alun's hair, urging him to lower his head. The infuriating man knew what David wanted, and he teased, standing up straight so David was forced onto his toes to keep his hands clasped behind Alun's neck.

Hmmm. Two could win at this game. David laced his fingers together and jumped, wrapping his legs around Alun's hips. Yay! For once he managed not to fall prey to the God of Awkward, possibly because Alun caught him, his lovely large hands cradling David's ass, holding him tight, their groins pressed together behind the double layer of leather.

On the one hand, the leather molded over interesting parts of the male anatomy very nicely. On the other, it was thicker than cloth and it didn't breathe worth a crap.

Therefore, it had to go.

But first, kissing.

Trusting Alun to hold him steady and keep their cocks rocking together in a slow, maddening grind, David let go of Alun's neck and trailed his fingers over the square jaw. He nibbled a line of toothy kisses from the cleft in Alun's chin to the hinge of his jaw just beneath his ear, Alun's rumbling groan adding a delicious vibration to the friction of their mated erections.

Why can't time freeze right freaking now—with Alun's curse left behind on the other side of the threshold, and the two of them alone in this enchanted space? It wasn't just his beauty that made this so hot, although that was zero hardship, but for the first time, Alun wasn't letting his guilt come between them. *He's finally letting me in.*

On the other hand, if time froze, they'd never get to the naked part of the evening—and David wouldn't miss that for all the mead in Faerie.

Although David wasn't a supe, his mouth was one hundred percent high magic, judging from the resonance thrumming through Alun's veins from his kisses. When David pulled back, Alun nearly growled.

"Easy there, tiger." David grinned as he slid down Alun's body. "More kissing is on the agenda, but it's time to get more skin in the game." He took a step back, giving Alun a once-over. "I mean, the whole young-Hugh-Jackman-in-Mr.-Darcy-dishabille look totally works on you, but I want what's underneath, and I don't just mean the clothes."

Unable to speak, Alun nodded. He hadn't truly bared himself—either figuratively or literally—since his last time with Owain, and that had been tainted with furtiveness, secrecy, and Alun's own resentment. This time, all he had to overcome was the fear that David, having seen Alun's unblemished body, would shun him when he was once more a beast.

He reached for David, his hands trembling as he parted David's vest. David caught his wrist and petted him as Alun would gentle a spooked stallion.

"Are you okay? I know I can be a bit much, but you want this too, right?"

Alun forced a smile. "Never doubt it. However, it's been rather a long time for me, copy closets notwithstanding."

"Me too." David laced his fingers with Alun's and pressed a kiss to the back of his hand. "How long?"

"A hundred years, give or take."

David's eyes widened, and he burst out laughing. "Yeah okay. Compared to that, I guess eight months isn't too bad. If I'm gonna date an immortal, I better get used to the difference in timescale."

"We're not immortal, Dafydd. Very long-lived, true, but we die. We age eventually, although we hold the years more easily than humans do. We can be killed, if it's handled correctly."

"You know what? Death talk is kind of a buzzkill. I don't even want to *think* about you dying. I'd rather think about how to get you out of those pants, because if I don't manage that in the next sixty seconds, *I* might perish from a case of terminal blue balls."

Human. Alun clutched David's hands. *His life will be over in the blink of the Goddess's eye.* Could Alun handle that? For the first time in his own indecently long existence, he could understand the impulse to hold a human lover in Faerie, where they wouldn't age so quickly. *And be trapped here, away from home and family, at the mercy of the notoriously fickle fae whim.*

He was almost glad he didn't have the option, not when his own tenure was measured in the length of a druid potion. *If I were reinstated, if the curse were broken, would I have the strength to take him home before dawn?* Oak and thorn, Gareth was right to mistrust him, to mistrust them all.

But for now, tonight, Alun could pretend he was whole and strong and deserving.

He eased David's vest off his shoulders and let it drop onto the moss at their feet. David reached for Alun's jerkin, but Alun brushed his hands away. "Not me. Not yet."

David canted an eyebrow. "Is this one of those instructions I'm supposed to follow on pain of untold disaster?"

"No, but we will never have another first time, Dafydd. I wish to unwrap you slowly, so I have many moments to remember."

David blinked and favored Alun with his beautiful smile. "When you put it like that—" He held his arms out to the side. "Do carry on."

"Excellent."

Under Alun's questing hands, David shivered. "That voice. I might come just from hearing you talk."

"In that case, I'll be silent."

David groaned. "Sadist."

Alun grinned and turned his attention to David's shirt. As he undid each button, he followed with a kiss—to David's cheek, one eyebrow, the glorious spot behind his ear, the smooth column of his throat. With each taste, David's breath hitched, firing Alun's senses until he feared he'd be the one to shoot early.

When David moaned and reached for him, Alun caught his wrists. "Not yet."

"Please. When do I get a turn?"

"When I say." Alun skimmed the shirt over David's head and tossed it aside. *Goddess, how the moonlight caresses his skin.* Alun was jealous of its touch—therefore, it needed to share.

He trailed his fingers over David's chest, brushing his copper nipples, skimming his rib cage, his body like poetry made flesh. *He fits so perfectly in my hands.*

Alun dropped to his knees and kissed the shadow beneath David's hip bone as he unfastened the leather trousers. The way they hugged David's arse made them nigh on impossible to remove, so Alun whispered a word, calling on the One Tree to ease his way, and—

"Goddess bless. You're not wearing underdrawers."

David laughed breathlessly. "Not much room for them in these pants."

Alun grinned up at him. "I'm not complaining." He had even less desire to do so when David's cock sprang free, inches from Alun's lips. "Ah, *cariad*. How beautiful you are." He pressed a reverent kiss to the head, and was rewarded with the quick intake of David's breath.

"Alun, you— I— Ooohhh."

Alun nuzzled the soft curls at David's groin. *Thank the Goddess I needn't fear he'll be disappointed by my body.* At any rate, his previous lovers had been appreciative—but nothing about David was remotely predictable. What if he—

"Alun." David stroked the hair off Alun's forehead. "You're thinking too much. I can tell."

He hid his face against David's taut belly. "You're exquisite. How can I hope to—"

"Hey. Don't make my decisions for me, okay? Just—" He wiggled his hips, setting his cock bouncing in a way that made Alun want to laugh. And how long had it been since lovemaking was filled with that kind of joy? *Too long. I can't wait anymore.*

He took David's cock into his mouth and sucked as he skinned those tantalizing leather trousers down to the ground, using another touch of magic to dispose of David's boots as well as his own. *Footwear can be so inconvenient.* Then he cupped David's arse and pulled him closer, taking him all the way to the root.

"Holy—" David's fingers tightened in Alun's hair. "Please— I need..."

Alun drew off slowly, hollowing his cheeks, savoring David's taste, so wild and sweet. With one last swipe of his tongue, he looked up. "You need what, *cariad*?"

David sucked in a breath and exhaled in a whoosh. "I need you naked and I need you *now*. No way am I coming alone. That's *my* first-time requirement."

"Very well." Alun rose as he stripped off his shirt. When he would have unbuttoned his waistband, David batted his hands away.

"Uh-uh. I've been dreaming about this since I met you." He busied himself with the buttons.

The sight of David—naked and glorious, kneeling before him—nearly took Alun over the edge. "That long?" he croaked.

"Shut up. You have your dreams and I— *Oh.*" His breath wafted over Alun's cock until he had to call on the One Tree for strength. "And I thought your *voice* was amazing." David peeked up from under his bangs. "May I taste?"

Alun nodded, clenching his jaw to keep from begging. Then—the heat of David's mouth. *Goddess. And I thought his kisses were magic.*

Luckily for Alun's self-control—although not perhaps for his libido—David didn't linger. Instead, he tugged Alun's pants all the way off. Once they were both free of clothing, Alun dropped to his knees again so they were chest to chest. Oak and thorn, the beat of David's heart against his own, nothing between them but skin . . .

He cradled David's head in one hand and captured his mouth in a greedy kiss as he circled both their cocks with his other hand, slicking them both with another breath of magic. His own groan matched David's at the slide of silken flesh, their thrusts growing as frantic as their kisses.

David clutched Alun's arse with one hand, his other tweaking Alun's nipple until—

Alun tore his mouth away, gasping as he came in ropes between their chests, until he thought his heart would follow, to be laid at David's feet. David whimpered, nuzzling Alun's chest as he stiffened and shot.

Still shuddering, Alun rested his head on David's shoulder, his forehead damp against salty skin. He planted an openmouthed kiss there, at the base of David's neck. It would leave a mark.

Good. Because he's mine.

CHAPTER ❧ 17

Afterward—with David held close in the circle of his arm—was the most at peace Alun been since before Owain had chosen the *achubydd* path. The brook sang to them, a soothing burble, and the breeze feathered David's hair against Alun's chin until he chuckled from simple contentment. Then David sighed and kissed the spot in the center of his chest, running a teasing finger from nipple to nipple, and Alun decided contentment was overrated.

"No scar," David murmured against his skin.

"No. It's part of the curse, so the druid's potion dealt with that too."

David shifted, rolling until his pointed chin dug into Alun's pectoral. Alun felt his gaze as if it were a shaft of Faerie fire. "What did it feel like?"

"The potion, you mean? As if someone had cracked me open like an egg and put me back together with the shell inside."

David scrambled to a sitting position. "Does it still hurt?" He ran his hands over Alun's torso, from neck to groin. "Where? What can I do?"

Alun captured those wandering hands and moved them lower, over his cock and bollocks. "One or two things come to mind."

"Don't change the subject." David's voice took on the tart tone he used when he thought Alun was being obtuse, although he didn't move his hands, and began a slow stroke that woke Alun's nerves like lightning under his skin. "I mean do you still feel any residual pain from the change?"

"I'm feeling much better."

David sat back and lifted his hands in the air, fingers spread. "No more cock therapy until you tell me the truth."

Alun sighed. "Very well. But I need incentive. Come here." He pulled David down against his chest again, capturing one of his hands, and pressed it flat against his belly, just below his rib cage. "Right here, this is where the curse waits, like a demon moth in a cocoon." One whose legs were made of knives, its wings of sharded glass, but David didn't need to know about that. Alun had had two centuries of dealing with pain. He could hide this one for long enough to prolong this precious time with David.

"So it'll hatch out again, like the freaking alien out of John Hurt's chest?"

"Who is John and why is he hurt?"

"We really need to work on your cultural reference points."

David snuggled against him, and Alun forgot about his straining erection in the wave of contentment that washed over him.

"Alun."

"Hmmm?" Alun stroked David's hair, the tender skin behind his ear, his spine like smooth stones under his skin.

"How did it happen? The curse? Will you tell me?"

"It's not a pretty story, *bach*. Why do you want to know?"

"Because it's a huge part of your life."

"Two hundred years out of two thousand. Your idea of huge—"

"I'm talking about its effects on your life, doofus, not percentage."

"Doofus?" Alun lifted his head and stared at David, eyebrows lifted. "You couldn't do better than that?"

David glared back. "I said doofus and I meant doofus. From what you've said about the Court and Faerie, it doesn't change much. It can't because the magic that created it is so old and no one remembers it, right?"

"Yes."

"But you left, Alun. You *changed*. You became something other than an overdressed dilettante with good bone structure and perfect hair. *That's* huge. So won't you please tell me what it was that turned you into you?"

"Well . . ." Alun stroked David's arm. "It was a dark and stormy night . . ."

David smacked him in the ribs. "Shut up. I'm serious."

"So am I."

David's sigh ghosted across Alun's chest, and he could imagine the accompanying eye roll. "Fine. Dark. Stormy. Continue."

"I was a different man then, you're right. Arrogant."

"I don't think that part's changed," David said dryly.

Alun chuckled. "Entitled, then. Overcompensating. It was not long after Unification, and my brothers and I were committed to proving the Welsh fae were the equals of the Irish and the Scots."

Goddess, those days had been both heady and terrifying, when the dwindling number of fae in all six of the Celtic realms had reached a tipping point. Without joining forces, crossing the unspoken class and race lines that had kept the realms separate and borderline hostile, they might all have vanished for good. By the time the Queen had forged the Unification pact with the Daoine Sidhe, the Cornish fae were decimated, the Manx all but extinct, and the Bretons so reclusive that no one, supe or human, had seen one for decades.

Only the Welsh had a large enough host, with strong enough warriors, to demand equal status. Alun and his brothers had literally fought for their place at Court. Their victories—on the battlefield and in the bedchamber—made them overconfident and far too self-important.

"There was a man. His name was Owain. Owain Glenross."

"Was he a Sidhe warrior, like you?"

"No. He was another kind of man entirely. Another race. We called them *achubyddion*. Rescuers." *Saviors.* "They were nomadic, quite secretive, and for good reason. In fact, in the first years after we met and became—" He glanced down where David's head was pillowed on his chest. Would this story change his opinion of Alun? Change his feelings? Would it upset him that he wasn't the first that—

"Lovers?" David's gaze was steady, no accusation in his tone. *Yet.*

"Yes. He would never tell me when or where we would meet next."

It had driven Alun crazy, not knowing the next time—if ever—he'd taste Owain's mouth, feel the velvet skin of Owain's cock against his tongue, watch Owain's eyes glaze with pleasure as Alun moved over him.

Perhaps Owain himself had never known. He hadn't been the leader of his clan, so perhaps their movements had been as secret from him as from Alun.

But Alun had never considered that at the time. He'd only known that the one man he wanted above all others, regardless of the lures cast out to him by dozens at Court, both men and women, hadn't loved him enough to live openly with him, or at the very least, tell him where to find him each night so they'd never have to sleep apart.

In Alun's hubris, in his mistaken estimation of his worth at Court, he'd been certain he could protect Owain from the others who might covet him to further their own plans. Because everyone knew that as heady as draining an *achubydd* to the brink of death could be, it was the moment after death, when the soul flew outward, that was the true prize. Capture an *achubydd's* soul on its flight, and you could do nearly anything, including create life where none had been.

David nudged him. "So what happened?"

"I'd seen Owain only the night before—he'd sent a message to meet him in a spot in the Outer World, at a cottage in the hills near Llithfaen. Somehow—I don't remember how—I discovered his clan's location afterward. They were camped in the mountains not far from the Stone Circle at the heart of Faerie, so I—I decided to deliver an ultimatum."

He only knew that he had an opportunity to be with Owain again after a single day, and that this time, he'd convince Owain to come away with him, to leave the clan and become Alun's consort.

He could swear he'd been as stealthy as any wraith when he stole out of Court that night. He'd left Cadfael in the stables and gone on foot, because the camp wasn't far from the Queen's pavilion, but it was high in the hills, across a rocky escarpment that even the most sure-footed of steeds could not have passed.

Owain objected to what he called Alun's barbarian trappings, so he'd left his sword, longbow, and hunting knife behind, and carried only a belt knife.

Foolish, foolish mistake.

The thunder had rumbled in the distance, the wind whipping his hair across his face as he climbed.

The camp was a dozen tents, no more, all the mottled gray-green of moss-covered boulders. Sturdy mountain ponies grazed in the sparse grass, and several heavy wagons ringed the fire in the center of the clearing.

They were so pitifully few—a race on the verge of extinction—but Alun hadn't thought of that, blinded to everything but his own desires. When he strode into camp, so certain of his welcome, Owain stared at him in horror, gaze darting to the other men, women, and children who milled about the circle of tents.

Goddess, what did he think Alun would do? Murder them all? He didn't even have a weapon.

He held up his hands, palms out. An older man with Owain's eyes, his hair completely white, stepped forward.

"How came you here, Alun Cynwrig?" he said in a voice like steel-edged wind.

"I came alone. On foot."

The old man canted his head. "That is not my meaning."

"I don't know." He glanced at Owain's face, at the stark terror there. "I heard it, that you were camped here, from somewhere. A rumor."

"Yet rumors rarely have a truth so crystal clear that one can follow them like a hawk to his aerie." He turned to Owain, his face implacable. "Perhaps you heard more than a rumor."

"Grandfather, I swear to you—"

The old man held up one hand, and Owain dropped his gaze, staring at the ground at his feet, his fingers twisted together. "I need no oath, my son. But look to your own resolve. I fear you may have lost your path." He turned to the onlookers. "Come. Let us leave Owain and Lord Cynwrig to their farewell."

Alun clenched his teeth, hands gripping his belt, a heavy molten weight in his belly. Farewell? Not bloody likely. Surely Owain loved him enough that he wouldn't sever all contact.

"Alun." His voice was low and urgent, and he glanced over his shoulder to make sure they were alone. "You shouldn't have come."

"What did he mean by our 'farewell'? I know I shouldn't have come with no warning, but I had to see you again."

Owain shook his head, blond hair brushing the shoulders of his leather jerkin. "You knew when we began this that our time was brief." He sighed. "I fear you've only made it briefer. My grandfather doesn't countenance outsider knowledge of our clan."

Alun strode forward and captured Owain's face between his palms. "Then come away with me. I can protect you. Once I've claimed you as consort, no fae can touch you."

"You assume too much, Alun. You assume I want to leave my family. That I want to have no one but you at my back."

Alun's fingers went cold. "But you love me. I know you do. Why wouldn't you want me to claim you as consort?"

"Think of the history of my people. What would that be but another form of enslavement. For what is enslavement but the total absence of choice?"

"It's not the same. I love you. I wouldn't treat you like a slave."

"What of when you grow tired of me? Your race is notoriously fickle."

"I'm not like that."

"You're fae. You can't help but be like that." Owain turned his head and pressed one kiss into Alun's palm. "No, Alun. I can't go with you."

Alun felt as if he'd been ripped open from throat to groin, his soul laid bare to the elements. "You'd choose them over me? What has this been, then? A mere fancy of yours? Revenge against the race that's wronged yours?"

"Not a fancy, *cariad*. Never that." Owain's voice was sad, resigned. "But I was selfish. I thought only of you and of myself—not of my people, my clan, or my family. I had hoped . . ." His gaze drifted to the surrounding trees and rocks, and he sighed. "No matter. We should have known that any love born of the blood of an innocent would never prosper." He stepped back, out of Alun's reach. "Good-bye, Alun."

"That's it? Your grandfather decrees it, and you fall in line, surrender without a fight?"

"I surrender because he is right."

Fury burned in Alun's gut, swirled in his chest, clouded his vision. "Then damn you. Damn you and all your kind."

Turning on his heel, he strode blindly out of the camp and into the maze of rocks and trees, tears prickling the corners of his eyes. He paused before the final descent onto the meadow in back of the royal pavilion, eyes stinging worse than ever. Goddess, he couldn't walk back into Court looking as if his heart had been cut out, even if it was the truth.

Although he swiped at his eyes with a shaking hand, they watered still. The inside of his nose burned with the acrid smell of smoke. *But the* achubyddion's *fire had been unobtrusive, low and banked.*

He whirled and stared at the smoke roiling over the crest of the hill, exactly at the point where the camp had been.

"Goddess, no." He took off at a run, heedless of the stones sharp under his hands as he clawed his way up the rocky hillside, ignoring the frigid water seeping into his boots when he splashed across a stream without benefit of the stepping stones.

The storm that had threatened all day overtook him, wind lashing the rain across his face. By the time he crashed through the trees surrounding the clearing, the smoke was choking him, burning his lungs, his eyes, and flakes of ash seared his skin.

The camp was nothing but sullen embers, the tents and the wagons reduced to ash. And the people. *Goddess, the people.* Alun dropped to his knees next to the body of a child, a little girl no more than six or seven. He closed her sightless eyes with gentle fingers, commending her to the Goddess.

The rain poured down in sheets, quenching the fires. Alun stumbled from one body to the next, each with the same rictus expression. Owain's grandfather's body lay beneath a rowan tree at the head of a path that led farther up the mountain, his arm flung out as if to point the way his murderers had gone.

Goddess, had his parting curse brought this down on the heads of every man, woman, and child in the camp? "I didn't mean it so. Goddess forgive me, I didn't."

Owain was nowhere in the ruins of the camp. "Owain!" he bellowed, but heard nothing but the howl of the wind. He followed the path pointed out by Owain's dead grandfather, staggering through a tunnel of ivy-choked juniper, until he emerged onto the Stone Circle plateau.

The altar at the power point of the circle wasn't empty. Owain lay there, his hands and feet bound. He turned his head.

"Alun." His voice was a thread, and Alun saw the livid bruises on his throat.

Alun rushed across the grass as thunder boomed overhead. He fumbled with the ropes binding Owain's wrists, but the rain had soaked the knots, rendered them slippery. "Goddess. I'm sorry. I'm so sorry."

"You . . . did not . . ." he struggled to swallow ". . . but fae . . . curse . . . can't . . . escape."

"I swear I didn't mean this. If I could take it back, I would." Shite. He pulled out his belt knife and sawed at the ropes, careful not to cut Owain's abraded wrists. "I'll make it up to you. Somehow. Anything you want."

Owain's dull gaze shifted beyond Alun's shoulder, and his eyes widened. "No," he croaked.

Then pain exploded at the back of Alun's head.

"When I woke up, Owain was . . ." Alun shuddered, clenching his eyes shut, the image still as fresh and raw as it had been that day. This time, though, David held him, stroking his face, his arms, his neck. Comfort, not seduction. "I never saw who did it. The instant I saw he was dead, the curse struck."

"I see where this is going," David murmured, rising on his elbows to look down into Alun's face. "You blame yourself, don't you?"

"The worst part was that as soon as I'd become the beast, turned as hideous outside as I was inside, I was effectively banished from Faerie. Not only did I bring it on him, but I couldn't avenge him."

"Is that what breaks the curse? From what you've said about Owain, vengeance doesn't sound like his kind of gig."

"Not him, perhaps. But his grandfather was the Elder of the entire *achubydd* race. It wasn't just a massacre of one roving band of *achubyddion* that night. It was a genocide. The last enclave. All their lore was oral, so everything about their race, their history, their traditions, their existence, was wiped out in a single night. All because of my carelessness in allowing myself to be observed, and my stupidity for allowing my hurt pride to leave them unprotected."

David shook his head. "You realize that—" A horn sounded in the glen, loud and bright, reverberating as if the player were only yards away. David startled and glanced around wildly. "What—"

"It's time for the ceremony." *Perhaps it's just as well, before David thinks of more questions to ask—questions that I don't wish to answer.* Alun pushed his guilt aside for a little while longer, long enough to enjoy the rest of the night as a man whose hideous appearance wouldn't drive his lover away. "We must return to the ceilidh glade."

"All right." David sat up, but held Alun in place with one hand pressed to his sternum. "But don't let this downer conversation ruin what came before." He stroked Alun's face with his other hand. "Holy cats. You are so freaking gorgeous. Do you think we'll have a chance to sneak down here again before we go home?"

A shiver of alarm chased across Alun's skin in the wake of David's touch. Now that he'd experienced true fae beauty, how would he react when the curse distorted Alun's features again, when his scar once again bisected his chest?

"Perhaps, if you're still willing after what's bound to be an interminable ceremony. Although you have as much reason to be ashamed of me here, with my history, as you do at home with my appearance."

"Hey. None of that. We are *not* ruining this moment." David kissed him, hot and sweet, then stood up, the moonlight gilding his skin. He ran his fingers across his semen-spattered belly. "How good is moss for post-sex cleanup?"

"Unsatisfactory. But unnecessary." Alun captured a drop of spray from the brook on his finger and blew on it.

David glanced down at his now-clean skin. "Magical wipes? Nice trick. Now where the heck are my pants? I've gotta say, all this rustic bucolia is scenic as all get-out, but give me a bank of sixty-watts and a full-length mirror when it comes time to get dressed."

Alun rolled to his knees and captured David's hands, pulling him close enough to kiss his belly, the cut of his hip. "Mirrors are overrated." He skimmed his hands up David's body, from his ankles to his chest, and his clothes were once again in place.

David glanced down. "Uh . . . oookaaay. That's . . . um . . . useful." He cocked an eyebrow at Alun. "You're still naked though. Not that I object, but it could make for a very interesting ceremony."

Alun grinned. By the time he'd gained his feet, his clothes were in place and as pristine as they'd been when he'd first donned them at his apartment.

David propped his fists on his hips and glared at him. "If you can do *this*, why did it take you forever to get our pants off earlier?"

"That way was more fun."

"Humph." David fingered Alun's sleeve. "Must save a lot of time in bar hookups."

"I haven't hooked up with anyone in a hundred years, remember. Besides, with my curse active, I can't access the power of Faerie." He held out a hand. "Come. Royalty gets testy if you keep them waiting."

CHAPTER ✤ 18

D avid's skin still tingled from Alun's touch and the pressure of his hand in the small of David's back as they threaded their way through the throng of fae, whose diversity rivaled a hundred Kellogg's variety packs. The dais at the far end of the clearing, where Gareth and his band had performed earlier, was bathed in a golden glow that didn't come from any lights that David could see.

Magic. *Hunh. That crap must save a ton of infrastructure work.*

Alun stopped about two-thirds of the way through the crowd, next to an attenuated fae who looked like a cross between RuPaul and Dennis Rodman.

"Wait here. I don't want you too close to the ceremony."

David tried not to feel hurt. Did Alun want to hide their . . . whatever it was? Relationship? If so, he needn't bother, considering the way the rest of the crowd continued to ignore David's existence. David wished again that these pants had a pocket for his worry stone, because if ever he needed to focus his calm, it was while Alun walked away from him and mounted the stage.

"Oi." Mal appeared out of the crowd and handed David a pewter tankard with a stylized dragon handle, full to the brim with a golden drink that smelled of honey and cinnamon. "Drink up. Getting hammered is the only way to make it through one of these damned ceremonies."

"The pellet with the poison's in the flagon with the dragon." David sniffed the brew gingerly, then took an injudiciously large gulp and choked. For something that smelled like punch at a teetotaler convention, this stuff had to be higher proof than Bacardi. Mal pounded him on the back so hard that David lost his grip on the

tankard. It tumbled to the ground, soaking the hem of the lacy gown of the tall fae, who glared at Mal and took one giant step to the side.

Mal chuckled. "Don't mind these yobboes. I'll get you another."

"No. Really," David wheezed. "I'm fine."

"Bollocks." Mal retrieved the cup and buffeted David on the back again. "Facing this shite requires serious self-medication. Don't move or I'll never find you in this lot."

David opened his mouth to beg Mal not to leave him alone, but how pathetic was that? He was standing in the middle of hundreds, each creature more beautiful or fantastical than the last, yet he felt more alone than if he were the only one in the middle of a football stadium. None of them paid the slightest attention to him, as if he were invisible. *I'm not even important enough to rate irritation.* Even his tent-pole neighbor had only responded to the results of David's clumsiness, not to David himself.

Don't take it personally—just imagine it's a cosplay night at a club. No different than me on the dance floor, repelling everyone in sight with my horrific moves.

He sighed as three tall, androgynous fae—and face it, all of them except the waist-high ones were taller than he was—stepped in front of him, blocking his view of the stage. He craned his neck, but gave up. To see around this bunch, he'd need stilts.

White-blond hair that any of the *LOTR* elves would kill for rippled down each slender back in front of him. David ran a self-conscious hand over his boring brown hair. True, he had a rocking cut, but nobody in the whole crowd except Alun and Mal had hair shorter than shoulder length. Even Gareth's soft mop of curls brushed his shoulders.

"See you there?" the one in the middle said. "He returns as though his disgrace were naught."

"Perhaps. Worse has been forgiven, although not by him, the self-righteous Welsh bastard." The one on the right tittered—an honest to goodness titter, but David was suddenly too interested in the conversation to roll his eyes at the incongruity of the sound. "Does his presence mean he chooses to revert to the old ways?"

David willed himself more invisible. *They're talking about Alun. Is this what he meant about his history? What the heck are the "old ways"?*

The one on the left shrugged with a grace that David had only seen on ballet dancers and beauty contestants. "If he takes the oath, he must follow the tenets or be foresworn."

"Think you that will matter? More than a century or two in dreary exile is needed to cure an arse that tight."

"Will he take his place as Favorite again?" Righty, clearly the gossip queen, wasn't about to let go of their through-line.

"Why should he? He's no better than any of the rest of us now."

The one in the middle sighed. "A shame. A Sidhe with morals was so refreshing."

"We have morals."

"Yes, but we're never excessive about it."

They moved on, and David could see the dais again just as Mal returned with his refill.

"*Sláinte*, mate." Mal took a swig out of his own mug, but David gazed into the honey-colored liquid, swirling it until a tiny vortex formed in the center. *The pellet with the poison's in the twink who can't think.*

"Mal, what do any of these people do?"

"You're looking at it."

"Party and gossip? That's it?"

"There's the occasional tournament and jockeying for position, but yeah."

"Is it unusual for one of your kind to bring a—a human to one of these parties?"

Mal lowered his tankard and squinted at David. "Is this a trick question?"

"No. No tricks. But is it?" He peered around. "I don't think I've seen another human here tonight. Only fae."

"Well, there's Gareth's bandmates. They're all shifters."

David goggled at him, then belatedly took a sip—a very *tiny* sip—of his mead so he didn't look like a clueless hick. "Really?"

"Two werewolves, a jaguar, and a kangaroo."

"Kangaroo shifters? Seriously?"

"Well, he's Australian. They had a totally different evolution down under." He took another swig of mead and grinned. "Makes for interesting business meetings."

David narrowed his eyes and poked Mal in the shoulder. "I think you're dodging the question. Come on. What's the deal with humans?"

"Well . . ." Mal carded the fingers of his free hand through his hair. "Sure you don't want another drink?"

"Mal. Give it up or I'll never make coffee for you again."

"All right, all right. No need to get extreme. The thing is, we fae have a history of . . . well . . . stealing humans who take our fancy."

"Steal them how?"

"Take 'em across into Faerie and keep 'em until we—not that I've ever done it, mind you—get bored."

"Then what?"

"Then we chuck them out. Problem with that is that time in Faerie runs differently than time in the Outer World, and you can never predict exactly how. But you don't have to worry about that. As long as we leave before dawn, we're good."

"Is *that* what Gareth meant? About taking me home before dawn? I thought he was playing supernatural chaperone and forbidding Alun to have sex." *Thank goodness Alun hadn't paid attention.*

"Nah. Gareth's got a bug up his arse about that—his own human lover was kidnapped by the Unseelie before Alun was cursed. He's never gotten past it, not really."

Poor Gareth. No wonder so many of his songs are sad. "Does he, you know, resent me because I'm human?"

Mal snorted. "Not bloody likely. He'd turn human himself if he could, or do anything, including call down the Queen's own curse, if it would keep him out of Faerie. But he's the last fae bard. She's not about to let him go."

David took another sip of his drink. "But she let Alun go."

"Aye, well, Alun's not a bard, is he? He may have been her Champion and Enforcer, but he was only a warrior, same as any other Sidhe." Mal scratched his chin—*Where did his scruff go? He had it before we crossed the stream.* "Although she'd likely have tried a little harder to save him if she didn't have a spare in yours truly."

The same as any other? I don't think so. Truth to tell, all this relentless fae perfection got on David's nerves. Mal at least had the bad boy biker attitude going for him. Gareth looked like a postmodern Roger Daltrey. But Alun's beauty beat any of the other Sidhe idling in the crowd because he was the only one who looked as if he had a purpose. Even with his beast-face, he beat them all because he wasn't freaking useless.

Suddenly, David needed to see Alun, to ground himself again, remind himself that this wasn't his life, that the two of them had more waiting for them at home. *Even if I have to whack his stubborn head to convince him.* He edged around another cluster of oblivious fae until he had a clear view of the stage.

Alun was standing to one side of the main group, whether by his own choice or because the others had shifted away from him, David couldn't tell. His feet were planted wide apart, his arms crossed. Apparently two hundred years of grumpy was a hard habit to break, because his forehead was creased in a kinder, gentler version of his habitual scowl; he was the only man on stage who wasn't wearing an expression of bland superiority.

He was also the only one with sex-in-the-forest hair.

The column of his throat gleamed in the golden light, and David caught the slight shadow of one of the love-bites he'd trailed up that perfect torso.

Possessive pride surged through his chest, making him feel six feet tall instead of five ten. *I did that. Me. David the Dork Evans. I had sex with the hottest man in all of freaking Faerie.*

As if Alun could hear his thoughts, his gaze shifted from scanning the other men on the stage and locked with David's across the crowd. His scowl disappeared, and the corner of his mouth lifted in a wry smile.

David's heart lurched, and his skin went cold in spite of the balmy air. *It wasn't just sex. Not for me. I'm falling in love with him.*

But if he stayed with Alun—assuming Alun even wanted him to stay—would it mean effective house arrest for life? If Alun refused to go anywhere that his appearance would cause comment, what did that mean for their relationship? Never to walk hand in hand by the river. Never to take a cruise or a vacation together. Never to do anything as simple as going out for dinner or to a movie.

What about friends? If these were Alun's friends—and given the attitude some of them had thrown when he'd greeted them, David had his doubts—would they accept a human? So far, the supes he'd met—barring Benjy and his mom—had either ignored him completely or tried to get into his pants. Since he had no clue what prompted one behavior over the other, he was at a loss as to what to expect from the nonhuman contingent.

He didn't have a lot of friends himself—especially now that his social life had all but evaporated—but the ones from his club days had bitchy down to an art. They'd no doubt salivate over Mal or Gareth, yet ignore Alun. Or worse, be cruel to him in the way only pretty young twinks could be. He flushed, remembering the times he'd taken the easy path and gone along with their games, regardless of who they hurt. *I'm better off without a social life if that's all it amounts to.*

Could he face the life he'd have if Alun refused to come out of the closet he'd built from the shame of his appearance? David wanted Alun. The twist in his belly and pinch in his chest when he imagined life without him were almost more than he could bear. But he was a social man. Would Alun's company be enough to offset the absence of everyone else?

The expression on his face must have changed from caveman smug to deer-in-the-headlights, because Alun's frown snapped into place again and he took a step forward as if to leap off the stage into the audience.

But at that moment, a golden fanfare rippled through the air, like a symphony's entire brass section, even though the only instruments in sight were Hunter's Moon's drum kit and abandoned guitars.

Guess magic not only saves on infrastructure, it saves on personnel and equipment too.

The crowd parted, shuffling David into close proximity with his mead-splattered neighbor again. He couldn't see what was happening until everyone around them dropped to one knee, leaving him with a clear view of the Consort leading a woman with dark copper hair knotted in an elaborate braid that fell to her hips. Her face was perfect—*whose wasn't, in this crowd?*—like the love child of Charlize Theron and Karen Gillen, with a little Helen Mirren strength of character thrown in around the determined jaw. Her gown was the color of new leaves, and David was interested to note that it was much simpler than the Consort's elaborate outfit, although it was cut to fit her rocking body perfectly.

Her Freaking Fae Majesty, I presume.

"*Hssst.*" Mal dug an elbow into David's thigh. "Down."

David glanced around wildly. He was the only one standing. Gah! Way to be unobtrusive. He dropped and huddled next to Mal. What were the chances no one had noticed his big giant faux pas? He'd been invisible so far.

He sneaked a glance at the irritatingly beautiful faces around them. All of them were focused on the couple proceeding up the impromptu aisle. Thank goodness. Relief washed through him, and his fingers tightened around his mug. When he checked out the royal couple, though, he discovered that one person had definitely noticed. *What a moment for my cloak of invisibility to fail.*

Although the Queen's attention was directed at the stage and the men who awaited her there, the Consort's gimlet glare was focused directly on David, and he didn't break it until he'd have had to turn his head to maintain eye contact.

Not. Creepy. At all.

"You have serial killers in Faerie?" he whispered to Mal out of the side of his mouth.

"Yes, but we call them warriors."

"Outstanding," he muttered.

The Queen and Consort reached the stage, and the audience rose in one graceful wave—except for David, who struggled to his feet in the backwash, always the last to get the freaking memo.

CHAPTER ✤ 19

The base of Alun's skull buzzed with the warning of nearby danger. After two centuries of dormancy, though, he couldn't pinpoint the threat, which might be nothing more than the usual political jockeying, petty jealousies, and vain ambitions that were part of any Court, fae or human.

Trapped on the dais in the eldritch glow of Faerie light, he studied the eddying crowd in their ridiculous finery, searching for the out-of-place, the key to his nagging worry.

Perhaps he was disturbed by the way so few fae paid any attention to David whatsoever, their gaze slipping over him as if he were concealed by the *glamourie* of *not-here*. Considering how David drew Alun's attention like a signal fire on a distant hillside, he found the crowd's inattention odd and alarming.

Standing next to Mal, David was wearing the same self-satisfied smirk as he had in the office, when he'd scored a point off Alun about his magazines or his potpourri or his blasted candy dish. Then, as he stared at Alun in the gathering of the cream of the Daoine Sidhe, his expression fell, nearly panic-stricken.

Had he just realized that come the dawn, Alun would return to his usual hideous form? Now that he'd seen a different face, an unmarred body, would he always compare the beast to the man, and find the beast wanting?

Alun wanted to abandon his place in the line, actually took a step forward, despite the futility of attempting escape after the Faerie light had engulfed the dais. But then the fanfare heralded the Queen's arrival, and he had no choice but to stay put, forcing himself to remain still. The last thing he wanted was to attract attention, to remind the jaded crowd of who he'd been, of how he'd behaved, of what he'd done.

He frowned at the flecks of gold that swirled in the Faerie light. Standing up here in a shower of bloody glitter wasn't exactly the best way to remain unobserved. Why couldn't the Queen conduct her business in her pavilion, the way she'd always done?

As Queen and Consort wended their maddeningly slow way to the dais, Alun's unease increased. The Consort stared at David—*he would be the one who registered David's presence, blast it*—probably because of the implied insult in David's delayed obeisance. The Consort had always been a stickler for demanding the respect he thought was his due.

There's danger here somewhere. I'm sure of it. Alun folded his arms and kept his gaze riveted on David until he lost sight of him when the crowd surged to its feet.

When the Queen mounted the stairs—without the Consort's assistance, although he offered his hand—Alun rapped his chest with his right fist and bowed with the others in the traditional salute. Her cool green gaze swept the line, no doubt cataloging alliances, slights, and political expediency in the brilliant, merciless brain that had engineered the Unification.

She took her place on the wide, intricately carved stool that was all the throne she'd ever allowed, the Consort at her right shoulder, guarding her nondominant hand. In another blare of spectral trumpets, she raised her left index finger, signaling the beginning of the ceremony.

Alan had considered his place carefully. He'd maneuvered himself so he was in the prime spot, three-quarters of the way back in the line of nobles. Not close enough to the front to be a sycophant, not stuck in the mediocre middle, not at the back with the desperate.

He barely listened as each man ahead of him was called forward to kneel before the Queen. He surreptitiously scanned the crowd, looking for any sign that his presence was noted as anything other than routine. As he drew nearer to his turn, he abandoned his scrutiny of the audience and paid closer attention to the Consort.

The man *was* taller, he could swear it. When the two of them had sparred on the practice field, Alun had had at least four inches on the bastard, who'd always tried to overcompensate by wielding a sword that was too long for him.

Now, though, the Consort couldn't lack more than an inch of Alun's six foot six, which meant he was now taller than the Queen, who topped six two in her flat velvet slippers.

Was it *glamourie*? But *glamourie* rarely worked on other Fae, and never in the Queen's presence. As the ritual dragged on, and the closer Alun got to the front of the line, the more he became convinced that something was rotten in Faerie.

Finally, Alun stepped forward and dropped to one knee in front of the Queen, his right fist over his heart, head bowed.

"Lord Cynwrig." She touched his shoulder, permission for him to look up.

"Majesty."

"We are pleased you have returned to our presence." The Queen's low, musical voice called up images of water over stones, or a dawn chorus of birdsong. It set Alun's teeth on edge and sent a spike of dread down his spine.

"No more pleased than I am to be here, Majesty."

The Consort's brow wrinkled in an attempt to figure out whether an insult was intended. *Work for it, Rodric, you wanker. I speak no more than the truth.*

"Are you prepared to swear your fealty to Queen, Consort, and realm?" the Consort growled.

"That is why I've come."

"Lord Alun Cynwrig, first among *y Tylwyth Teg*, Champion of the Seelie Court, do you swear fealty to your Queen?" At the Queen's emphasis on his Welsh origins, the hairs on the back of Alun's exposed neck rose, and he had to force himself not to retreat. Why call that out here, when the purpose of this thrice-blasted ceremony was to test her subjects' commitment to Unification?

Whatever the case, he had no choice but to continue down this path. "Majesty, I so swear, unto and on pain of my death."

He hoped like all the hells she hadn't just painted a target on his Welsh backside, or that his oath would at least prevent open season.

David jostled for a better view and managed to score a gap between two broad-shouldered bruisers by infringing a bit on NBA RuPaul and all their trailing lace in time to hear Alun swear he'd be true blue to the ice queen until death did them part.

"And do you swear allegiance to Faerie, heart's home to your race?" The Queen's lilting voice carried perfectly over the hushed crowd.

"Interesting," Mal murmured in David's ear.

"What?" David whispered back, never taking his gaze off Alun.

"With the other men, the Consort's oath came before the oath to the realm."

David turned his head, batting cobwebby lace out of his face. "You think that's significant?"

"It could be, but—"

NBA RuPaul stepped away from their whispered conversation. They yanked their sleeve, catching their lace in David's earring and clocking him on the cheekbone with the world's boniest elbow.

"Ow." Another yank, and the onyx stud flew off into the moss, its back falling down the neck of David's shirt. He clamped a hand over his stinging earlobe. Thank goodness he didn't wear hoops or he'd have a slice instead of a hole. "Crap."

"Mother of us all . . ." Mingled wonder and dismay roughened Mal's usual breezy tone. "Alun! To me!"

He grabbed David by the arm and shouldered his way through the crowd. Not that he had to try very hard—the fae, who had previously packed the circle like so many Cirque du Soleil sardines, melted away before them. Some looked horrified, some warlike, but all of them looked stunned—as if they'd only just noticed David's presence and were none too pleased about it.

"Mal," David gasped, "what are we doing? What about—" He dug in his heels, trying to spy Alun on the dais, but a sea of taller-than-tall fae blocked his view.

"Shut up." Mal looked over his shoulder. "Shite. Move your sacred ass."

"My ass is hardly sacred. Where's—"

"It is now. Flaming abyss, now we've gone and done it. We've brought an *achubydd* into the midst of a horde of drunken fae."

CHAPTER ✻ 20

When Mal's shout interrupted the Consort's triumphant request for loyalty, Alun sprang to his feet, scanning the crowd. He located Mal immediately because he was illuminated by an opalescent glow he'd never thought to see again, the aura of a high-ranking *achubydd*—an aura that emanated from David, turning him into a veritable bonfire of temptation.

David an *achubydd*? How was that possible? Owain's clan was the last of their race.

"We found another." Mal's words returned to him, the news of the newly discovered enclave. How had they stayed hidden? How had David—

Druids. Of course. How had he been so blind?

Mal grabbed David and hustled him through the crowd, toward the path to the portal. Thank the Goddess for his brother's warrior reflexes. Alun willed them to move faster, trapped as he was within the confining globe of the Faerie fire.

Then David pulled Mal to a stop.

"Damn it, man," Alun growled, "do you want to die?" Not this time. He wouldn't allow it.

But as he pushed against the barrier, willing David to run, willing Mal to protect him, the fire flickered and died. *Thank you, blessed Goddess.* He turned to the Sidhe lord behind him and pulled the man's ceremonial sword from its scabbard. "Your pardon. I'll leave this at the gate for you."

He was breaking protocol in a huge way, leaving the dais before the Queen and without her express permission, but that infraction paled beside the enormity of introducing the temptation of an *achubydd* into the cauldron of ambitious courtiers who'd never imagined a chance like this could befall them.

He leaped off the dais and sprinted through the crowd toward the telltale glow, ignoring the chaos that had erupted behind him.

"Cynwrig!"

The Consort's roar spurred him on. The bastard could wait until Doomsday for his thrice-damned oath.

Alun's loyalty lay elsewhere.

Mal hauled David through the woods at a speed that was probably an easy pace for a six-and-a-half-foot-tall guy built like a tight end, but David's chest heaved in a struggle for breath, a pain like a blade in his side, as he was dragged through underbrush and stumbled over rocks the size of soccer balls.

"Slow down... Mal," he wheezed. "Can't we use the path? Where's the... freaking fire?"

"You're the freaking fire, boy *bach*, and we have to get you out of Faerie before half the Court decides to warm themselves with a piece of you."

"But—"

When the bushes beside them thrashed, Mal whirled, landing in a crouch in front of David. But the wild-eyed man who leaped out at them, his hair full of twigs, carrying a long freaking sword, was Alun.

He grabbed David's other arm. "Go. They're after us."

The two mega-brothers took off again, supporting David between them, his feet touching the ground only every third or fourth step.

"Who's after us? Ow. Guys, put me down."

"No!" they shouted in unison.

"Not that way." Alun pointed left with his sword. "There."

"That's not the quickest route." Mal tugged David's arm in the other direction until David felt like the rope in a tug of war.

"They'll have that route blocked. They'll try to keep us from crossing the portal. If they can keep us here beyond the dawn—"

"Shite," Mal muttered. "Fine. Your way, then."

They picked up the pace—not hard to do since this way was almost straight downhill. David had never been afraid of heights, but his stomach tried to hide behind his spine at the nearly vertical view. Alun and Mal must have been half mountain goat, because they never put a foot wrong.

As they barreled down the slope, David heard the baying of hounds over his own wheezing breath.

"Shite." Mal's grip tightened on David's arm. "They've called out the pack."

"Dogs?" David tried to look over his shoulder, a little hard to do in their headlong rush. "Seriously? They've set dogs on us? What the hell did you do, Alun?"

"I didn't swear an oath to the damned Consort, probably violated six different traditions, and broke protocol by leaving without the Queen's permission, but they're not chasing me."

"Hello? Running? Dogs after us? I think that qualifies as a chase."

"They're not chasing *me*, Dafydd. They're chasing you."

They reached the banks of a river and slowed down enough for David to get a good look behind them. A pack of huge white dogs, their ears dark in the moonlight and their eyes glowing yellow fire, surged over the crest of the hill.

He gulped and held on to Alun's arm with both hands. "Why are you standing here? Let's go. Can they follow us across?"

"Ordinarily no. But it's the solstice, one of their hunting nights. They can cross given the right prey."

"They won't." Mal wasn't even slightly out of breath. "Not without Herne, and he took his oath privately since he's not really a party kind of bloke."

"Then we'd better get across." David glanced wildly up and down the river. "Where's the bridge?"

Alun tossed his sword to Mal, who caught it as easily as if it were a set of car keys. "There is none. We have to wade."

"Can't we cross the same stream as the one we got in by?"

"This *is* the same. This is how it looks from the Faerie side."

"Wonderful. Those dogs owe me a new pair of boots."

Alun gripped Mal's shoulder. "Can you hold them?

"I won't have to if you're not here. Go."

They splashed into the river, which was wide but apparently no more than knee-deep. However, it was snow-melt-cold, numbing David's legs as the water penetrated both suede and leather.

Alun grabbed his arm, and David looked up. His lips moved, but David couldn't hear anything between the baying of the hounds and the rush of the river. Why was it so loud all of a sudden? He stared beyond Alun's shoulder as a two-story wall of water rounded a bend and roared toward them.

His eyes popped wide and his mouth dropped open, but he couldn't make a sound as the impossible tidal wave rushed forward. *Holy cats. Just like* LOTR. Alun cursed loud enough for David to hear and hauled him for the opposite bank through water that seemed as viscous as tar.

Alun's grip on his arm bruised his biceps, but he didn't care. He concentrated on keeping his feet under him as fist-sized rocks shifted under his feet, the roar of the approaching water drowning the sound of the dogs and his own yell.

Three yards. Two yards. One.

Alun grabbed him around the waist and heaved him out onto the grassy bank, then dove after him as the wave boiled past and dissipated, leaving nothing but a gurgling brook, sparkling in the moonlight. The hounds' baying deteriorated into frustrated yelps before dying away entirely.

David lay on his back, gazing up at the full moon, which was once again its regulation distance away. His wheezing breath took on a different tempo, and suddenly he laughed. And kept laughing.

Alun crawled over to him, looking weary beyond belief but still handsome enough to stop an Amtrak train. "Dafydd. What's wrong?"

"Wrong? Are you kidding me? Let's see—pissy elves, demon hounds, and a tidal wave in a knee-high creek, not to mention swords, magic, and sex." He flung his arms wide. "Best. First date. Ever."

CHAPTER ✤ 21

D avid's cheek throbbed and his ear stung—a small price to pay for such an awesome adventure. Faerie vanished, along with any sight of Mal—but no hounds with freakishly glowing eyes burst through the invisible gateway, and the stream continued to burble as if to say, *Who, me? I would* never.

Alun, still drop-dead gorgeous, was apparently also straight-up pissed, although why he should be grumpy after the incredible adrenaline rush of their escape was beyond David. They'd made it, hadn't they? Although David still had no clue why they'd had to run.

He helped David to his feet, but didn't speak a single word to him on the way back to the car, or spare a glance as he burned rubber—okay, scattered gravel—out of the parking lot.

As they drove down I-5, David darted a glance at Alun's profile. His perfect jaw was clenched and he was staring straight ahead at the nonexistent traffic.

"So. Do all these shindigs end like that?"

"Mmmphm."

"Because usually when I'm in the middle of a riot, it doesn't involve dogs, swords, or impromptu tidal waves. So, you know, this was different."

"Mmmphm."

David stared out the window and counted three mileposts before he tamped down his irritation enough to try again. "The fourth time I was abducted by aliens, I managed to hijack the spaceship, drive through Jack in the Box for cheeseburgers, then land in the middle of the cricket pitch at Oxford."

"Mmmphm."

Brother. David gave up. Clearly Alun was not in his happy place. When they pulled up in front of his house, he reached to open the door.

"Don't," Alun barked. "Wait for me."

He flung open the driver's-side door and slammed it behind him. *Just freaking great. Dr. Bossy strikes again.* Someone seriously needed to give the fae some tips on how to win friends and influence people. David slumped in his seat, arms crossed, and waited for Alun to stalk around the car. Then he crowded so close after opening the door that David couldn't climb out.

"Do you mind?"

"Mmmphm."

"Oh, do *not* start that again." David shoved Alun's granite-like chest and managed to thrust him back far enough to slither out of the car. He marched up the front sidewalk with Alun dogging his steps as if they were attached at the hip.

Which, unfortunately, they were not.

He stopped on the porch and turned to face the mountain of surly man in back of him. "Gosh, Dr. Kendrick. Thank you for a *lovely* evening. The sex was great, but maybe next time we should bring some travel games so we'll have something to talk about on the ride home."

"Open the door, David, and let me in."

"Why? Is this some juju like inviting vampires across the threshold?"

"No." A muscle ticked in Alun's cheek. "I need to speak with your aunt."

Not to me. Not "I can't bear to leave without touching you again." Not even a hint that he wanted anything to do with David at all.

"It's four o'clock in the morning. She's not well. What makes you think I'll wake her up to be scowled at by you?"

Alun sighed and ran a hand over his forehead, surprise flickering across his face. *He forgot what he looks like now.* "Let me in. Please. I would like to speak with your aunt, but I would really, really prefer not to be behind the wheel when this potion wears off at dawn."

Crap. The potion. "Right. Sure. Um . . . come on—"

The door swung open. Aunt Cassie was standing there, leaning on her cane, with all of David's honorary aunts gathered in the living room behind her. All of them were wearing identical dark-gray homespun robes. *D'oh—I forgot about* their *solstice party.*

"Please join us, Lord Cynwrig, Davey." She gestured for them to enter. "We need to talk."

Goddess. A full druid circle. After he'd learned Cassie's nature, Alun should have assumed it—druids never worked alone. He ought to have realized that the extraordinary effects of David's candies and coffee and potpourri weren't near-mystical at all—they were real magic.

"Auntie," David bustled inside and wrapped his arm around her shoulders. "What are you doing up at this hour?" He met the somber gaze of each of the other women in turn. "Don't your little parties usually end earlier than this?"

A rawboned woman with a long salt-and-pepper braid stepped forward. "We had to wait until you got home, pumpkin, so we could give you your gifts. Although . . ." She peered more closely at David's face, tracing his cheek with a fingertip, then pinned Alun with the druid equivalent of the evil eye. He barely managed to endure it without retreating out the door. "I sense there are more pressing issues to discuss. How did you come by this bruise?"

A bruise? David was injured? When had that happened? Alun surged forward, only to run into a wall of druid anger when all seven of the women turned on him.

David caught the woman's hand. "I took an accidental elbow to the cheek, totally not Alun's fault. It'll be fine with a little ice and ibuprofen, Aunt Regan, so don't fuss."

David might as well have spoken to an oak grove, because Regan and three others hustled him to the sofa and coerced him into lying down. With the force of the druids' attention aimed at David, Alun was able to breathe again without his lungs feeling like stone. Only Cassie was still regarding him, grim and still, her hands folded on the head of her cane.

Regan tucked a coverlet around David's legs as two women hurried into the kitchen and returned with a bag of frozen peas, a glass of water, and two pills in a porcelain egg cup.

David raised himself on his elbows. "Thank you, aunties, but—"

"Take the pills and lie down," Regan ordered.

He sighed but did as he was told, then accepted the peas and held them against his face.

Cassie rapped her cane on the floor three times. "I declare our gathering at an end."

Regan frowned. "Are you sure, Cassie? With the interrupted ritual, your health—"

"Enough. I must speak privately with Davey and Lord Cynwrig. We'll talk tomorrow. Good night."

After each woman kissed David's forehead, they filed out, glaring at Alun on the way. Regan was second to last in line.

"Don't look so terrified, Lord Cynwrig. We don't cut out people's hearts on stone altars by the light of the full moon anymore."

The next woman, with a platinum bob and a double strand of pearls over her robe, snorted. "That was nothing but Roman propaganda." She slanted a sly glance at Alun on her way out. "The sacrifices took place at twilight. More time for the barbecue that way."

He closed the door behind the last one and gave fervent thanks to the Goddess for their absence. The weight of their druid ire notwithstanding, he had no wish for them to witness his imminent transformation. If he had a choice, he'd spare David and Cassie the sight as well, but the chances of hitting early rush hour traffic and being delayed were too great.

Alun moved to the foot of the sofa where he had an unobstructed view of David. The *achubydd* glow wasn't as obvious here in the Outer World, but Alun could no more tear his gaze away than he could cut out his own heart. *So beautiful, inside and out—and now permanently beyond my reach.* David lifted the peas off his face, and Alun winced at the bruise blooming under his eye. *My fault.*

"Since you both obviously know what's going on—and don't think I missed that all the girls seemed in on the joke too—I think it's time to spill the magic beans. I warned you before—no secrets. Screw the supernatural NDA."

Cassie sighed and sank into a rocking chair next to the head of the sofa. "Davey—"

"So what are you? You and the girls? I take it you're supes too."

"We are more . . . meta-supernatural, I suppose."

"That doesn't tell me squat, Auntie."

"We're—we're druids."

"Seriously? What else have I always believed that turns out is a total fricking lie? You're probably not even my real aunt." Cassie dropped her gaze to her cane, and David slapped the peas over his eyes. "Oh lord. You're not. Perfect. Just. Fricking. Perfect."

She reached for him, laying a hand on his shoulder. "You're as much my family as if our ties were of blood, not affection. The secrecy was for your own protection."

"I *hate* that excuse. I hate it almost as much as *But that's how we've always done it.* Ignorance is never positive. Don't you think I should have the whole story and be allowed to make my own choices?"

"He's right. He deserves the whole story—as do I, if I'm to keep him safe."

She nodded. "Very well. David's parents were killed when he was just a child, barely more than a toddler."

He peeked out from under the peas. "I was four, Auntie."

Alun's sword hand clenched, his instinct to arm himself and seek out the perpetrators. His gaze flicked to Cassie's face. "Was it a fae attack?"

She shook her head, her mouth twisted in a half smile. "Ironically enough, no. A simple car accident—drunk driver, something that would never have occurred if they'd remained in Faerie."

"Are you sure?"

"Positive. We cast a number of divination spells, although we weren't able to do it until two years after their deaths."

"Two years. Not long. The evidence should have still been relatively fresh."

David glared at Alun with his uncovered eye. "Two years in foster care seemed like *eternity* to me. One-third of my life at the time, bouncing from foster home to foster home, waiting for the place to blow up around me."

Alun leaned against the wall, folding his arms so he wouldn't give in to the temptation to hold David. "Did the homes really explode?"

Cassie cut a glance at her nephew. "Davey exaggerates. No actual pyrotechnics were involved, but I can't deny that his presence was enlivening to the human families."

An achubydd *child without a trained caregiver? I should think so.*
He studied the flat line of David's lips, the tense muscles in the side
of his throat. "Why did it take you so long to find him?"

"We had no idea that his family existed. His parents had managed
to stay off the grid for their entire lives. We only discovered them by
accident, after they were already dead, because of some anomalies in
the ley lines. We didn't know of the existence of a child until later,
and it took time to locate him inside the foster system, and longer
to fabricate the credentials to allow me to take custody of him."

"Why did you want me though? I mean, am I supernatural too,
like you and Alun?"

"Yes, *cariad.*"

"Really?" David sat up, letting the peas fall into his lap. "What's
my superpower? Is it something cool? Can I turn invisible? Fly?
Read minds?" He scrunched his nose. "I don't have to drink blood or
anything, do I?"

She chuckled and shook her head. "None of those. You are able to
comfort the sick, aid in healing."

"So what you're saying is . . . I'm a nurse."

"And sometimes," she said, "if you encounter a being motivated by
greed and self-aggrandizement, your superpower is to die."

David fell back into the nest of pillows. "Well, that sucks."

CHAPTER ❧ 22

David scowled, barely listening as Alun and his aunt continued the conversation as if he weren't there—*And that's different from all the rest of my life how?*

"We realized that his parents must have had a good reason for remaining hidden, so we put protective spells in place."

"I didn't realize it was possible to hide an *achubydd* in plain sight." David blinked at Alun. "Bless you."

"It's not, really. The power can't be concealed completely. What we did was put charms in place to . . ." She held out one hand, palm up, and flipped it over. "Invert them."

"You turned him into an anti-*achubydd*?"

Crap—achu-whatsis? Isn't that what Owain was, Alun's great lost love? Jeez, why couldn't I have been a vampire after all?

"More or less. However, lately the charms have lost potency. Some of that latent . . . interference . . . has started to bleed through."

David sat bolt upright. "Wait—what do you mean 'interference'? Is that why I could never hold on to a boyfriend without him starting fights with everyone around us? Why all those riots broke out in every office I tried to work in? It was all me?"

"Not you, *cariad*. A human reaction to your nature, skewed by the charms, which are negations, reversals. An *achubydd's* nature is one of comfort and serenity. So the charms had to counteract that."

"Charms? You mean the worry stone, the earring, the one-of-a-kind personal care products? All of that was to hide me?" *Jeez, they'd put him in a supernatural closet, and not the fun kind with copiers and office sex.* "Don't you think your instructions and spells and what-the-heck-ever would have been more effective if I knew *why* they were so important?"

"I did my best, Davey, but the more I lost control of them, the more they started to project distress and agitation. I tried to hold them. Goddess knows, I poured as much into them as I could, but you're strong. You took more than I had."

David's belly clenched. "What do you mean, took more than you had? You mean because you were ill?"

"Not precisely."

Alun, who had been leaning stone-faced against the wall, stood up straight. "You heard him before—he hates not knowing the truth. You owe him the *entire* truth, including the cost of your actions, because, knowing David, he'll discover it eventually anyway. Do you imagine he'll be able to live with himself knowing that he killed you? Trust me when I tell you that's not something he'll take lightly."

"I'm killing—" All the blood rushed from David's head. "Do you mean what you're doing for me—the charms, the spells, the whatever—*that's* what's wrong with you?"

Aunt Cassie scowled and pulled her shawl closer around her. "Not all of it. I'm still old. We all die, Davey. Even druids. Even the Sidhe. I wanted it to be on my terms, leaving a legacy of my choice."

Screw this—everyone deciding what he could deal with, what prices he was willing to pay. "What about *my* choice, Auntie? My choice to have you with me as long as possible? My choice to be a man and fight my own battles?"

Her face crumpled, but she didn't cry. She never cried. Hell, for all he knew, druids couldn't cry—and that was the point. He didn't *know*. That crap ended right now.

"Maybe if I wasn't swaddled in all this Celtic hocus-pocus, I wouldn't be so awkward. Is this hiding me from myself too?"

She nodded unhappily. "*Achubyddion* . . . they want to give too much, risk their own lives for those they care for. It can be dangerous if they're not cautious, and you had no one to train you, to show you the ways of your kind."

"You mean I'm the last one?"

She nodded.

"Perhaps not." Alun's perfect face was solemn, his arms crossed and feet planted like the fricking Colossus of Portland. "My brother told me of the discovery of an *achubydd* enclave they'd never suspected."

Aunt Cassie sat forward, hands gripping her cane. "Alive?"

Alun frowned, and with that face, even his frown was beautiful. "Not all. But they believe some escaped."

She slumped, shoulders rising with a deep breath. "So they're still in the wind. No chance for Davey to find them, for them to take him away."

"Hey!" David tossed aside the stupid bag of peas. "Stop making decisions for me. Who says I'd want to leave? I like my life the way it is. Well, except for causing riots everywhere I go."

"Doesn't that prove that you're not prepared for this world and that the world is most definitely not prepared for you?" Alun asked. "You should continue to use your aunt's protections."

"Screw that!" David's inner bitch stamped a petulant foot when Alun and Aunt Cassie shared an indulgent glance. He was not a child, damn it. "Didn't you hear her? It's killing her. I'm not signing on for that."

"Dafydd—"

"I don't believe that one person is inherently more valuable than another, not in the grand scheme. We can all accept help and affection, but when it comes to trading life for life? *I* get to decide whether I think my life is worth ending someone else's." He faced his aunt. "Don't you get it? To me, your life is more important than mine."

"Davey, all good parents sacrifice their lives for their children. It may not be as evident as a physical death to prolong the child's life, but no parent's life is the same after a child's birth. Everything you do is bounded by the needs of the child."

David laid his hands atop hers. "But I'm not a child anymore, Auntie. I'm a man. And I get to choose from now on."

She sighed deeply, but nodded. "Very well. You always were a stubborn one, Davey *bach*."

"Good." He patted her hands. "Hey, without all the counteractive spells, does it mean I'll be able to dance now?"

Alun chuckled. "I doubt there's enough magic in the world for that." Then a shaft of sunlight pierced the drapes, and he stiffened, his face contorting in a rictus of pain.

"Oh no. It's the potion. It's wearing off."

"Potion?"

"He drank something, some spell or whatever, to abate his curse for one night so he could go do his Faerie duty."

Aunt Cassie's eyes widened, and she covered her mouth with one fragile hand. "Goddess. Tell me it wasn't a druid potion?"

"His brother said it was."

"You fools, don't you realize the danger?"

"I—" Alun's eyes rolled back in his head, and he collapsed, sprawling on the sunburst area rug like a broken marionette.

David scrambled off the sofa and rushed to his side, pressing a hand to Alun's chest. *His heart is practically galloping. That can't be good.* Alun's fingers twitched, and David quickly laced them with his own.

"Davey. You must leave him be."

Alun's back arched, and his lips pulled back in grimace.

"But I saw what it did to him before. The transformation."

"It is his struggle, and ill-advised or no, it was his choice, not yours."

"Can't I at least hold him?"

"You cannot. He is too large, too strong, and the pain will be too great for him to temper any blows. We can only wait until it is over."

David released Alun's hand and crawled backward until his knees hit the hardwood floor. He sat there tailor-fashion at the edge of the rug while the stubborn, taciturn, annoying, *wonderful* man he loved convulsed in front of him and turned back into a beast.

Oak and thorn, has all my skin been scoured off? The rug under his cheek was like a bed of nettles, the soft linen of his shirt like woven barbwire.

Alun pushed himself onto his hands and knees as he tried to find the strength to hold up a head half again as heavy as it had been less than an hour ago.

"Alun." David's low voice was balm to his soul. But when David rested his palm on Alun's shoulder, Alun gritted his teeth, expecting the pressure to set off a firestorm of agony in his over-sensitized skin, his wracked spine. Instead, the pain eased under the gentle touch.

He took a shuddering breath. *Goddess, no one truly appreciates the absence of pain.* But the spot under David's hand was a blessed island of comfort in a sea of torment.

Wait. There and only there, under David's touch?

Achubydd.

"No!" He knocked David's hand away, forced himself to his haunches, and lumbered to his feet, head reeling.

On the floor at Alun's feet, worry clouded David's beautiful eyes. "I'm sorry. Did I hurt you?"

"You can't touch me." Didn't David realize how dangerous it was? If he'd touched Alun during the transformation, he could have been killed, drained to an empty husk by Alun's own need for relief. The idea of David lying lifeless before him like Owain— *No!*

"I didn't realize . . ." David hugged his knees. "I mean, when you changed before, you could touch me afterwards and it didn't bother you."

"You weren't *achubydd* then."

David's eyebrows snapped down over his nose, and he shot Alun a dirty look. "I was too. You just didn't know it, and before you go off on me about that, remember that I didn't know it either."

Alun sighed. "It's not that I'm angry with you, but you have no idea how to command your abilities. Just now, I could have drained you without knowing."

"Drain me? Um . . ." David glanced at his aunt, who was watching them both with a look of pity.

Goddess, anything but that. Hatred, contempt, revulsion—he could handle all of those, but not pity.

"*Achubyddion,*" she said in a carefully neutral tone, "heal through their own life essence, their own energy. Energy is finite, and so must be replenished."

"You mean I could run out of juice, like a cell phone battery, and have to recharge?"

She smiled. "A bit. While an *achubydd*'s resources are limited by their own constitution, the needs of the other are not necessarily so.

If the recipient requires too much, the *achubydd*'s battery dies for good."

David frowned, hugging his knees tighter, his gaze darting between Alun and his aunt. "I still don't see why—" His eyes widened, brows lifting, as he stared at the base of Alun's throat, where the collar of his shirt gaped open over his chest. "Alun. Your scar."

"My scar?" Alun touched the spot between his collarbones where his scar began, but the skin was smooth, unmarred. He ran his hand down his torso. No thick ridge bisected his chest and belly. He ripped the tail of his shirt out of his pants and lifted it with shaking hands.

His scar was gone—his skin as smooth as when he and David had made love in the glen.

He backed away. "Did you touch me?"

"You know I did. Just now."

"No. When I was transforming. *Did you touch me?*"

"Just once. At the beginning."

"Where?"

David hunched his shoulders. "I . . . held your hand. I touched your chest."

Alun rounded on Cassie. "How could you allow him anywhere near me? He could have been—"

"You forget yourself, Lord Cynwrig," she said in her druid's power voice. "I pulled him back before the change took full hold."

"Then how do you explain this?" Alun thumped his fist against his sternum.

"I need explain nothing to you."

"Hello?" David said testily. "If you two are done playing chicken, could you please tell me what the heck you're talking about?"

"You must have healed me. I've drained you. Goddess, I—"

"Relax." He rose in his usual way that made even simple moves look complicated. "I don't feel drained. I feel fine. Other than my butt is numb from sitting on this damned floor. My face doesn't even hurt anymore. In fact, I've never felt better."

Cassie tilted her head, her brow wrinkled. "Davey may have a point, although it's not something I'd considered before. Aid given freely is always less costly than when it is forced, *achubydd* or no."

"Well, duh. That's true for anything. Who wants to be forced to help? We all feel better when it's our own idea."

Cassie leaned forward with both hands on the head of her cane. "Perhaps, but then, *achubyddion* kept knowledge of their abilities secret even from the druids, which is a formidable feat in itself."

"I don't care." Alun paced the path the sunlight laid on the oak floor. "Without knowing more, we can't risk it. If I'd had any idea of this that first day, or anytime since, I'd never have taken him into Faerie." David blocked his path, and Alun sidestepped so quickly he nearly fell. "Stop that."

"No, *you* stop it. It's not like I deceived you on purpose, unlike— oh, I don't know—*other* people I could name." David split his glare between Alun and Cassie. "I mean, first it's a problem that I'm human, and now it's a problem that I'm not? There's no pleasing you, is there?"

You please me too much—that is the problem. Alun remained a safe double arm's-length away from David. "Stay home. Stay hidden."

David narrowed his eyes and propped his hands on his hips. "Oh no you don't, Dr. Domineering. You are not firing me again. I need that job, and whether you want to admit it or not, you need me in it."

The two of them locked gazes until Alun, Goddess forgive him, surrendered. *So weak when I don't really want to win.*

"Very well. But if you come back to work, you are there only as a temp, nothing more. We cannot touch. Not then. Not ever."

After Alun left in all his stubborn martyred glory, David helped Aunt Cassie get settled in her bed, then wandered into his own room. Why did all his relationships end before they ever really started? Granted, most of his previous breakups didn't involve swords and packs of ravening hounds, not to mention discovering he was the supernatural equivalent of a miracle drug.

Damn it, this wasn't his fault! Why was he any different today than he was yesterday?

Needing something to calm his nerves, he reached for the worry stone on his bureau. As soon as he picked it up, though, a weird itching at the base of his skull startled him into dropping it.

The itch stopped. *What the—*

He touched the stone with a fingertip, and a light buzz started at the top of his spine, as if a dentist had rested a drill too close. When he picked it up, the itch hit full-on, worse than before, making him grit his teeth.

"Swell. Now even my own comfort items are fighting me. Good thing my earring is lost forever in Faerie or my ear would have probably fallen off."

Jeez, if this was what all those grumpy men who'd brawled around him had felt, he didn't blame them for flinging office furniture. David was tempted to do some flinging too—himself at Alun, for instance.

Wait. He plopped down on his bed. *Alun's curse.* He'd been cursed by achu-whatever-ion. *Is that why he doesn't want me anymore? Well, he needs to get over that right freaking now.*

David hadn't imagined it. They'd had a true connection last night, before and after the best sex ever. How could the stupid, stubborn *fairy* leave that behind?

Tomorrow. Well, not tomorrow, seeing as it was Saturday. But come Monday, David would wheedle, cajole, nag, and otherwise coerce Alun into changing his mind. Because he wasn't giving up, and Dr. Alun freaking-fae Kendrick would just have to shut up and deal.

CHAPTER ✤ 23

But on Monday, all of David's Alun-stalking plans had fizzled. Every time he'd attempted to get close enough to Alun to touch him, the infuriating man shied away like a skittish virgin. Only one more appointment before the end of the day, and it couldn't happen soon enough, because this lecherous-seducer stuff was *exhausting*.

Mrs. Tomlinson and Benjy walked in, right on time. She was wearing another understated designer masterpiece in black, and Benjy had on his usual midget-preppy-in-training outfit of blazer, flannel shorts, white shirt, and red tie.

"Good evening." David smiled at them, adding a trace of an ear-wiggle to tease a muffled giggle out of Benjy.

She glanced at her son with a fond smile before turning the wattage on David. "Could I ask you a huge favor, my dear?"

"Name it."

"After Benjamin joins me in Dr. Kendrick's office, could you let Hans and Joachim know?"

"The gentlemen in the hallway?"

"Yes. Joachim has a brief errand to run, although Hans will remain in the hall as usual."

"No problem. Would they care for some coffee?"

"That's sweet of you, but they don't indulge while on duty." She settled Benjamin in his usual chair in the far corner. David winked at him, earning a grin and a wriggle.

When Alun opened his office door to invite Mrs. Tomlinson inside, he avoided David's gaze as usual, the big jerk. David sighed as the door closed, and motioned Benjy over.

The little boy scrambled out of his chair and ran across the room. Gripping the edge of David's desk, he leaned his chin on his fingers.

David didn't try to figure out the reason why those big brown eyes looked as if they were swirling because, hey—they probably were.

See? He was totally getting the hang of this supernatural stuff.

"Did you bring another one?" Benjy whispered with a furtive glance at the closed office door.

"Would I let you down?" David pulled the new action figure out of his drawer and handed it to Benjy, who accepted it in his cupped palms as if it were the Holy Grail. "That's Batman. He's a kick-butt crime fighter with a really cool car that he keeps in a cave under his house."

Benjy touched the pointed bat ears on the hooded cape. "He has pointy ears?"

"No. That's just a costume. Really he looks like a regular dude."

The boy opened the front of his jacket, revealing a decidedly lumpy inside pocket.

"What have you got in there?"

"The other ones. Chewbacca and Mr. Spock." He held the pocket open to display the little plastic faces. "And now I gots Batman. Pretty soon I'll have lots. More than anyone in my class."

"How many kids are in your class?"

"Seven. But the others are all like Vanessa, not me."

"You mean girls?"

He wrinkled his snub nose. "No-ooo. Wolfs."

The office door opened, and Benjy shoved Batman into his pocket with the clumsy stealth of the very young. He put his hands behind his back and attempted to look innocent.

David would have to give him some pointers on that.

Mrs. Tomlinson rested her hand on Benjy's shoulder. "You are not to bother David, my son."

"He's not bothering me. Benjy and I are great friends, right, big guy?"

"It's kind of you to say so, but—" Her smooth brow wrinkled in a slight frown as she studied Benjy's bulging blazer. "What do you have in your pocket?"

Benjy clapped a hand over his lumps. "Nothing."

"Benjamin," she said, in the early-warning tone all mothers reserved for when said kids were trying to pull something.

Benjy cut a glance at David.

"Go on, kiddo. Show her." Not like the kid was smuggling letter bombs or grade school contraband—whatever that might be.

The boy opened his jacket and pulled out the three figures, holding them flat on his extended palms.

"What are these?" Mrs. Tomlinson picked up Chewbacca between two pink-lacquered fingertips, causing Benjy to flinch.

David trotted around his desk to stand next to the boy. "Don't be mad, Mrs. T. They're just action figures from some of my favorite stories. Benjy and me, we've got a deal. Every time he hangs out with me, he gets a new play guy."

"When we get up to ten, David said I could have a Death Star!" Benjy hugged the other two figures to his chest as if he was afraid his mother would take them too.

She watched him, so still it was as if she'd stopped breathing. She held the little plastic figure out, just beyond Benjy's reach, and the boy lunged for it. He snatched it from her fingers and half turned, tucking Chewie back in his pocket.

David was ready to leap to Benjy's defense if his mom gave him grief about being grabby, but she didn't look angry. She pressed one hand to her chest and covered her mouth with the other, her eyes glistening with tears.

"I've tried everything. Tonight I even tried a dragon's breath emerald, but he barely glanced at it."

"He's six. What six-year-old wants a stinky old emerald? Even if it's—" She dug in her purse and pulled out a box, flipping it open to display a stone blazing with green fire. David's eyes popped wide. "Holy crap, it's the size of a freaking tennis ball."

"Exactly. Who wouldn't want such treasure?"

"Treasure is in the eye of the hoarder. He likes action figures, not hot rocks. Wait until he's a teenager and starts collecting girlfriends."

She stowed the emerald and held out both hands to David. "Thank you, my dear. You've no idea of the service you've done, nor what it means to us."

David gave her hands a squeeze. "It was totally my pleasure. Pals look out for each other, right, Benjy?" Benjy nodded enthusiastically. "He's ... uh ... not in trouble, is he?"

"Not in the least." She smoothed her son's dark hair, but a stubborn cowlick popped up at his crown. "I couldn't be more proud of him."

Alun cleared his throat, still not sparing David a single glance. "Shall we continue our conversation inside?"

"Yes, of course."

The three of them headed into Alun's office. Mrs. Tomlinson smiled graciously at David, and Benjy waved—with the hand not clutching his pocket—but Alun kept his attention riveted on the fascinating gray carpet, then closed the door with a final-sounding *click*.

Grrrr. When the Tomlinsons were gone, David was so going to tackle Dr. Avoidance—assuming he strayed within tackle distance for once.

He stalked across the waiting room to give Joachim the okay to leave, then stomped around the waiting room, straightening magazines and refilling the coffee supplies. Even if he was royally pissed at his pigheaded boss, he still had pride in his work, damn it. Finally, with nothing else empty or out of alignment, he plopped into his chair and swiveled to face his monitor. What would it take for Alun to stop acting like David was the supernatural avatar of Nurse Ratched?

David looked up from his moody scowl at an inoffensive Excel spreadsheet, and met Kristof Czardos's reddened eyes. Shoot, he'd been so up in his head, he hadn't heard the office door open.

The man—vampire—and should David be worried about that?—had looked frail and wan last week, but tonight he looked downright cadaverous. Wasn't that bad business for vampires? On the other hand, what the heck did he know about it since *nobody would tell him anything.*

"Mr. Czardos, are you all right?"

"I fear not. May I speak to Dr. Kendrick?"

"He's with another client now." One of the unbreakable rules of the office was never to interrupt a session unasked.

Mr. Czardos closed his eyes, his throat and mouth working in what David's interrupted nurse's training recognized as an attempt not to hurl. "He will understand. Tell him . . ." Despite the convulsive swallowing, his voice was still like a steel wire. "Tell him it is time."

It is time. Was that ever a good thing?

David picked up the handset and buzzed Alun's office on the intercom setting so it would broadcast on speaker instead of ring. "Dr. Kendrick, Mr. Czardos is here and he says it is time."

David hung up just as the bone-thin man—vampire—sheesh, this stuff would take getting used to—swayed on his feet in a way that rivaled David's slickest dance moves. In other words, grotesque and a little frightening.

David jumped up and raced around his desk to put a supporting arm around Mr. Czardos's waist. He was shorter than David by a good two inches, and was about as big around as little Benjy. Didn't vampires have a nutritionist on staff? This man was obviously starving to death.

He led him to a chair and helped him sit. "Would you like another pastille? I've got a brand-new stock."

"Thank you." He patted David's hand. "You are very kind, but I fear it will not help me now."

Alun burst out of his office. "Don't touch him."

David snatched his arm from around Mr. Czardos's back. "I'm sorry. Did I hurt you?"

Mr. Czardos's bloodless lips curved in the corpse of a smile. "I believe he was talking to me."

David shot a disgusted glance at Alun looming in the doorway to his office, his chest heaving and nostrils flaring like a bull about to charge. "Trust me, he was talking to me." He faced Alun, glaring. "Which may be the first time all day, I might add. Jeez, Alun, you seriously need to stop giving yourself this mental wedgie."

"David, now is not the time."

David caught sight of Mrs. Tomlinson and Benjy peering around the office door. *Professional boundaries. Right.* Mr. Czardos was in obvious distress, and whatever *time* it was, it for sure wasn't time to traumatize a six-year-old with adult bitch-fighting.

He stood up and moved a careful three steps away. Alun approached slowly.

"Are you sure, Kristof?"

"I have endured as long as possible, but I am at the last of my strength, and the recidivist faction knows it. It is better if I go at a time of my choosing so I can ensure the transfer of power to the leader who will best serve my people."

Alun nodded, his face somber. "If that's what you want, we'll go to Forest Park to await the sun. Mal will join us as witness."

Mr. Czardos inclined his head, and although David expected a sigh, none came. With a jolt, he realized it was because the vampire wasn't breathing.

"Wait a minute. What are we talking about?" He glanced at the door to Alun's office, where Benjy was still watching with enormous eyes, Batman clutched in his fist.

"Tonight I die, young David."

"But—but why? Surely there's something you could do or that your people could do, other than, you know, sucking the blood out of half of Portland."

He tilted his head a fraction of an inch. "My kind are not able to manufacture our own blood, nor can we breathe to aerate it. Our digestive system evolved to convert ingested blood from other species for what we could not manage ourselves. However, after ten centuries, I can no longer abide the taste, despite all of Alun's therapies." He lifted one shoulder. "It is the same for all species: human, fae, shifter, vampire. If we cannot feed, we die."

David sat in the chair next to him, despite Alun's frown. "There must be another way. You could handle the pastilles fine. Isn't there an alternative food source?"

"The pastilles settled my stomach, but they did not alter my aversion. No other foodstuff can replace the blood in our veins."

"And IV doesn't work?"

Mr. Czardos blinked twice and exchanged a glance with Alun that, on a more demonstrative pair of faces, would have equated to dumbfounded.

"IV?" Mr. Czardos asked.

"You know, like a transfusion. Inserting the blood directly into your system through a vein instead of your mouth. I'd think that would be more efficient anyway, since no matter how evolved your digestion, you're still bound to lose some of the oxygen-carrying traits in the digestive process." Everyone continued to stare at David as if he were speaking in Elvish. "Wait—hasn't anyone ever *tried* that?"

"Nobody ever needed it before. Kristof is the oldest vampire on the planet. We assumed it was the normal end-of-life for his kind."

David jumped out of his chair and glared at Alun, fists on his hips. "This is the kind of thinking that gets people—or vampires—dead. Even if it doesn't work perfectly, it's bound to make him feel better. If there are other nutritional requirements besides the oxygenation, I bet we could find an alternative. Does it need to be liquid?" Who knew? Maybe vampires would go for green juice or Gatorade. "Unless..." David tried to figure out if Alun's perma-scowl was slightly more appreciative than disapproving. With Alun in beast mode, it was hard to tell. "Do the supes have hospital facilities? A blood source? The IV equipment?"

Alun assisted Mr. Czardos to rise. "We can acquire the supplies, but we need to get you to the health center immediately."

"Hans can take him." Mrs. Tomlinson strode across the waiting room to the door. "Joachim will be back momentarily with the other car to pick up Benjamin and me."

She opened the door for Alun and Mr. Czardos, signaling to Hans, who escorted them to the elevator. When Alun returned to the waiting room, he looked at David with a glow in his eyes that for all David knew was normal for the Sidhe, cursed or not. He gestured for the Tomlinsons to re-enter his office, but paused before he followed them.

"I'm so proud of you," he rumbled.

Warmth spread from David's chest to points south. How often had anyone aside from his indulgent aunts been proud of him? He took a step forward, but Alun held up one hand, palm out.

"But it doesn't change anything." He turned and walked into his office, closing the door behind him.

David stomped back to his desk and flopped into his chair. "*Shit.*"

CHAPTER ✦ 24

Goddess, David was remarkable. Perhaps growing up outside the confines of the rigid supe infrastructure was an advantage rather than a drawback. How many other time-worn practices had gotten solidified into tradition or law without regard to whether they were practical or even accurate? Pride and despair warred in Alun's chest. He'd never have a chance to find out because David was out of his reach. Forever.

"Dr. Kendrick." Teresa sat on the edge of the love seat and held out her hand to him across the coffee table. "Alun. May I speak frankly?"

He hesitated. None of his clients had ever touched him. Only Mal—and David—had touched him voluntarily since the day of his curse. He took her deceptively delicate hand—as a dragon shifter, she could probably fling him against the wall without breaking a nail. "Certainly."

"It is obvious that your charming office manager is in love with you."

"No. I'm sure—" He tried to withdraw his hand, but she gripped him tighter, nearly to the point of pain.

"It is equally obvious that you feel the same about him."

Fear coiled in his belly like a restless serpent. *No. I can't. It's impossible.* "I'm sorry, Teresa, but you're mistaken. What I feel for David—"

"Is love." She patted his hand and sat back next to her son. "Do you think that I, a dragon queen, don't recognize the look in someone's eyes when they gaze upon their greatest treasure?"

Leaning forward, he braced his elbows on his knees and propped his head in his hands. "Goddess help me, Teresa, you don't understand. I can't risk touching him."

"Can't or won't?"

"It amounts to the same thing. If he were human, it would have been bad enough, although I'd convinced myself that I could handle the inevitable separation. But he's . . . he's—"

"He's *achubydd*."

"You can tell?"

"I dare say any supe could, if they looked closely enough, and although I know perfectly well what his nature signifies, I'm not certain that you do."

"He has no idea of the consequences of—" Alun glanced at Benjamin, who sat curled in the corner of the love seat with his little plastic toys in his lap "—a relationship with any supe, let alone one like me."

"You mean someone who loves him?"

"Someone broken. Someone with a legacy of pain too great for even the strongest of *achubyddion* to bear without dying." Alun scrubbed his hands over his misshapen forehead. "Even assuming he could bear to look at me as I am now, whatever he feels wouldn't last. He was raised as a human. Humans shy away from the disabled, the deformed."

"I've seen no such aversion. Indeed, he seems a very open-minded and resourceful young man, if a tad impulsive." She smiled fondly down at her son and his toys. "Might I remind you that he's taught members of two of the longest-lived species on the planet that there may be more ways to look at the world, at our problems, than we had believed? Perhaps you give him too little credit."

Alun smiled, and from the astonished looks on the Tomlinsons' faces, the sight must have been as rare as the dragon's breath emerald. "Who is the therapist here, you or me?"

"We can all benefit from advice now and again, regardless of our training or experience."

Could it work? David hadn't been schooled in the ways of his kind, and with no living mentor—let alone any written *achubydd* lore—he might never be. Yet he'd gravitated to the health care field, to nursing. His instincts were there, but they were framed by the context of the mundane world, the only one he'd ever known.

Could that combination of instinct and modern sensibility trump eons of belief about what was possible—not only for David as an *achubydd*, but for all the supe races? Could there be a chance for the two of them to be together, if Alun allowed himself to think outside the confines of his Sidhe biases?

"I don't know, Teresa. He's beautiful, smart, funny. The only flaw I've detected is that he's possibly the worst dancer on either side of the Faerie threshold. He could do so much better than a damaged soul like me."

"What is it you always say to us? 'It's not up to me to make choices for you. You must choose your own path.' Grant him the same courtesy as you would any of your clients. Just as Benjamin made his own choice of treasure, clearly David has chosen as well."

"My history with his race is catastrophic. If it weren't for me, David wouldn't be the last of his kind. You don't know what—"

"You blame yourself for the massacre."

Alun jerked upright. "How did you—" His brows shot together. "Mal. I'll—"

"Your brother is not one to keep secrets, but that's not how I know. In the early days of your curse, you weren't . . . shall we say . . . discreet in your grief." She dipped her chin, her eyes swirling in lazy amusement. "A number of the supe races recorded it. In our case, it was a cadre in Aberystwyth whose hibernation cycle you disturbed."

"I'm sorry—"

"No need to apologize to us for something so long past. But shouldn't you consider forgiving yourself?"

No. Never. How could he so dishonor Owain's memory as to put another of his kind in the same danger?

"I fear I've allowed us to digress. Let's return to the reason for your visit." He nodded at Benjamin, who was crooning a wordless tune to a plastic figure in an improbable black cape. "I think we should discuss transitioning him out of care, don't you?"

"Mama, look." Benjamin held out the caped figure. "This is Batman."

"Is it, my dear?" She stroked his hair and cast a sly smile Alun's way. "Why don't you tell me about him, and your other treasures too, while Dr. Kendrick considers his next move?"

David returned from washing out the coffee urn to find Jackson Hoffenberg toying with a stapler and blocking the path to the desk. Great. Just freaking wonderful. Another unscheduled appointment, this time with the universe's gift to brown suits.

"Mr. Hoffenberg, do you have an appointment?" *I know damn well you don't.*

Hoffenberg set down the stapler and picked up David's coffee mug, rotating it in his hand, running a forefinger around the rim. *That's not creepy in the least.* He continued his cup-porn and stared at David like a shark eyeing especially tasty chum.

"Not with Dr. Kendrick. But I hoped I could prevail on you to have that drink with me."

Danger, Will Robinson. The last time Hoffenberg was in the office, David had felt a definite distaste, but tonight, being less than a car-length away sent warning tingles marching across the back of his neck and down his spine. Was this an achu-whatsis thingy? Because now that he wasn't shielded by Aunt Cassie's talismans, everything felt orders of magnitude *more* than before.

Take Benjy—David didn't just want to keep him occupied, he felt compelled to make him happy. And when Benjy was happy, it made David feel freaking awesome, like a continuous joy feedback loop.

With Alun, he was almost desperate to touch him, to soothe— and face it, to arouse too, but that wasn't his first instinct. When Alun refused to let him near, it wasn't just annoying.

It hurt. A lot.

But with Hoffenberg, something whispered to David's inner nutcase: *There's no help for this guy. Run like freaking hell.*

David glanced around the office, searching for something to do that would let him get as far from Hoffenberg as possible for any reason whatsoever.

Except that's stupid. The man was a lawyer, for goodness sake. What was he likely to do? Litigate David to death?

But that was (a) ridiculous and (b) impossible, so David did the next best thing. He pretended nothing was wrong, detouring to the sideboard to fuss with already perfectly arranged sugar packets and stir sticks, tracking Hoffenberg out of the corner of his eye.

The panic button. Alun had told him to push it if this guy showed up again. But, for one thing, the way Hoffenberg blocked the path to the desk, David couldn't get to it without a dodge and leap worthy of a parkour champ. For another thing, Benjy and his mother were in there. The last thing they needed was Hoffenberg going crazy-pants on a little boy and a woman.

What the heck good was a panic button if you couldn't reach it?

Maybe if he could signal Benjy's bodyguards, they could— *Crap. They're not here.* Unable to justify more fiddling with the coffee paraphernalia, David took a grand tour of the waiting room, shifting magazines from one stack to another, brushing imaginary lint from the chairs, angling his approach to the other end of the desk where he could squeeze between it and the credenza and get at the button.

But every time he changed his trajectory, Hoffenberg countered with seemingly random movements as he examined each of the personal items on David's desk. He picked up a whole handful of Peggy's pastilles, tossed them all into his mouth at once, and chomped away, the sound in the silent room like the crunch of chicken bones.

"Are you sure I can't convince you to have that drink?"

Enough of this freaking dance. David stopped about two yards from Hoffenberg and took his best diva pose. "Look, Mr. Hoffenberg. I don't want to offend you," *oh, yes, I do,* "but even if my position here,*" as Alun's lover, damn it, once the big dope stops being so pigheaded,* "didn't preclude outside associations with clients," *especially bat-guano creepy ones,* "I wouldn't go out with you. I'm afraid you're just not my type."

"I'm sorry you feel that way." He set the empty candy dish back on the desk. "I guess I'll have to convince you otherwise."

Hoffenberg lunged.

Startled, David stumbled as he attempted to dodge, and Hoffenberg grabbed his left arm, twisting it up behind his back. David tried to shout for help, but before he could call out, Hoffenberg clapped a rough hand over his mouth, his erection hard against David's ass.

"You're everyone's type." Hoffenberg's breath was hot and moist against David's neck, and beneath the scent of mint and apple from the pastilles lurked a stench like rotten meat. "I saw that almost right away. Luckily for me, nobody else has caught on. You're coming with me."

No. No-no-no. That was *not* happening. David thrust his right elbow back, connecting with Hoffenberg's ribs. *Ow.* David's eyes watered with the pain, but Hoffenberg barely grunted.

"Go ahead. Struggle. I've heard it's better that way."

As he frog-marched David toward the door, David tried to dig his heels into the carpet, only to get his head wrenched back for his pains. He flailed, and his free hand connected with the sideboard, sweeping the stir sticks and sugar packets onto the carpet with a faint patter. He called Alun's name, but behind Hoffenberg's hand, it made no more noise than the coffee clutter.

"I should have been the next alpha." He jerked David's arm with a vicious twist that sent pain knifing from his wrist to his shoulder. "I *will* be the next alpha. All I have to do is fuck you to death."

CHAPTER ❈ 25

"An' David says Chewbacca shoots a crossbow with *light*."

Alun surreptitiously rubbed his chest as Benjamin related the perfections of his new treasures—and David. The boy had never spoken so much in a session, but Alun wished he wouldn't mention David quite so often, forcing Alun to think about David when he needed most to forget him.

Tomorrow he'd contact Sandra Fischer again and ask her to replace David—however this time he'd provide a glowing recommendation rather than a complaint. *Can I face an office without him in it?* Goddess knew Alun didn't want to, but he had no choice.

All day long, David's presence had taunted him, the glow of his *achubydd* nature tempting Alun like a campfire on a winter's night. Somehow, he'd resisted, and he must have inured himself to the sensation, because as the day had worn on, David no longer burned as brightly in Alun's sight.

Alun shifted in his chair and rubbed his chest again as Benjamin launched a description of how Chewbacca was like Vanessa's husband. *Why can't I focus? It's as if I've got a bone-deep itch that can't be scratched.* If he were still a warrior of the Seelie Court, he'd have identified it as a looming threat, an enemy at the gates. But here—

A muffled cry of distress penetrated Alun's shattered concentration.

David. No!

He surged out of his chair, causing Benjamin to clutch his toys to his chest and Teresa to gather her son and her purse in the circle of her arms.

"Forgive me, I—" He rushed to the door and flung it open.

Alun's heart leaped to his throat. Amid a litter of plastic sticks and paper sugar packets, Jackson was forcing David across the room.

"*Stand down!*" Alun's roar shook the windows. "If your pack finds out that you've threatened a human again—"

Jackson whipped around so that David was between them, his eyes wild above Jackson's restraining hand across his mouth. "He's not human. Anyone with half an eye can see it." He twisted David's arm higher behind his back. At David's muffled cry, Alun's chest burned, his vision narrowing as his battle instincts kicked in. Oak and bloody thorn, if he could get his hands on Jackson, he'd rip his arms off.

"Let. Him. Go."

"Why? This is what his kind is for. Everyone knows it." He giggled, a truly grotesque sound coming from a man of his age and size. "You're pissed because you didn't have the balls to do it first." He pulled David's head back, baring his neck. "On the other hand, a whole clan of *achubyddion* wouldn't be enough to fix your ugly face. I guess you'd know—from what I hear, you already tried that."

"Killing David won't activate your shifter gene."

"It will!" Jackson's eyes glowed red. "It's the only thing that will. I never thought I'd get the chance, but you gave it to me, *Doctor*. I guess therapy isn't as big a crock of shit as I thought. Now, if you'll excuse us, I have an *achubydd* to fuck."

He backed up, step by slow step, David still held in front of him like a shield. Alun kept pace, but couldn't risk a tackle—not with Jackson's arm at David's throat.

A small figure darted out of Alun's office.

"Benjamin!" Teresa called.

Benjamin raised his hand and threw something. It landed on the floor behind Jackson's left heel, and in his next step he trod on it, losing his balance. As he flailed to keep from falling, he released David.

Alun wasted no time. He lunged forward and grabbed David's arm, shoving him behind him.

Jackson fell on his arse with a grunt, and Alan tackled him, flipping him over onto his stomach and pinning him with his hands behind his back.

"Here, Al—I mean, Dr. Kendrick." David's voice shook as he handed Alun a length of blue silk. *His bow tie.* Alun used it to tie Jackson's wrists together, and hauled him to his feet. He shoved the bastard into the nearest chair, standing close enough to block any attempt at escape.

"David, the number for the Clackamas pack is speed dial seven. Would you kindly call and tell them that if they don't come and pick up their garbage, I'll see that it's removed permanently."

"One moment, David." Teresa pulled her cell phone from her bag, her eyes glittering like sunlight on steel. "I'll make that call. In case the Clackamas alpha should imagine that David is without protectors."

While Teresa gave terse instructions to whoever was unfortunate enough to answer the Clackamas pack line, Alun glanced at David, who was standing next to his desk, his collar askew. "Are you all right?"

David nodded, but his face was pale, his lips pressed into a harsh line as if he was trying to hide their trembling. *My fault.* If this incident wasn't evidence that Alun was a threat to David's safety—*Goddess, what was I thinking? I should never have let him return to work.* In fact, he should have insisted David go into hiding the instant his true nature was revealed.

An uneasy silence descended on them all. Jackson had turned sullen, refusing to speak or even look at anyone—just as well. If he'd said one word or made a single move out of line, Alun would have gladly broken his neck.

Several minutes later, Hans and Joachim barged into the room, followed by two enforcers from the Clackamas pack. Alun yanked Jackson to his feet. "Let's go."

Teresa stepped forward. "With all due respect, Dr. Kendrick, this is a shifter matter. You must allow our councils to deal with it."

"But—"

She grasped his forearm. "You may trust me to guard David's interests."

Alun nodded curtly. "Very well. Thank you."

She followed Joachim into the hall, Benjamin's hand gripped in hers. The boy stumbled along next to her, although he was staring over his shoulder at something on the floor. As the door closed behind them, David finally moved, retrieving the thing Benjamin had been staring at.

"What do you know?" He held it up in a trembling hand—it was the black-caped plastic toy. "Batman saves the day."

CHAPTER 26

David managed not to collapse onto the floor, but it was a near thing. He clutched the mangled Batman figure in his fist. *Thank all the stars in the sky for fearless little Benjy.* He glanced at Alun, looming by the door, scowling fiercely at his . . . shoes. *Uh-oh. Not good.*

"Thank you. For rescuing me. Although since Batman struck the first blow, I guess that makes you Robin. Or maybe Commissioner Gordon. Or—"

"Are you truly all right?"

David took a deep breath and attempted a smile. "Well, I—I could use a hug."

"No." Alun pressed his lips together and strode toward his office, cutting a wide berth around David. "It's too dangerous. I can't hug you or kiss you or—Goddess preserve me—make love to you again. If I do, you'll die. Just like Owain."

Anger chased away David's residual shakes. He trailed after Alun, watching him heave papers into his briefcase and slam it shut. *I could slam a few things right now myself—starting with some sense into Alun's head.*

"So what you're saying is I'm not allowed to touch you—or apparently anyone—for the rest of my life? Jeez, no wonder the achu-whatchumacallem are extinct. They probably shriveled up and died from loneliness." David took a step forward, and Alun countered with a step back, running into the corner of his desk. "How exactly did you get your PhD? Because you seriously need a lesson in causality. Owain didn't die because you made love to him. He died because some . . . some psychopathic *fairies* murdered him."

"You don't know the whole story." He walked past David, a good three feet away, to loom by the door.

David glared at him, fists clenched at his sides so he wouldn't give in to the urge to pop Alun one right in the scowl. "That's because nobody will fricking *tell* me the story. How many times do I have to say it? Ignorance does not equal safety. Ignorance equals ignorance, and that can get you just as dead."

"How's this? The first time I met Owain, he nearly died. He . . . he healed a stag that my arrow didn't kill cleanly."

"Maybe *you're* the one who doesn't know the whole story. Maybe animals are different than people. Ever think of that? Maybe he had low blood sugar or had just run a half marathon." *Or had taken one look at you and fallen in love, just as stupidly as I have, although he probably even passed out gracefully.*

"I won't take the chance." Alun switched off the lights, jerking his head toward the door. "We're leaving. Now."

David stomped out of the office, through the waiting room, and into the hallway. "It's not your chance to take, you pigheaded man," he muttered.

"Call me all the names you like, you won't change my mind."

In the elevator, Alun stayed plastered against the far wall, as if David might infect him with a brain-eating fungus. When they reached the parking garage, David headed for his own car, but Alun stepped in front of him, herding him toward the Land Rover as if he were a freaking sheep.

"I can drive myself, Alun."

"No."

"Are you planning to take me to work tomorrow? To the grocery store? To the movies? How am I supposed to retrieve my car? You have a troop of minions waiting in the wings to handle the grunt work?"

"Get in the car, David."

"I hardly think the drivers on I-5 at this time of night care what I am unless I cut them off. Think my achu-gobbledegook can cure road rage? Because then it might be useful except for being another excuse for you to be emotionally unavailable."

"I'm not—"

"Oh, don't even start."

"Fine. Get in my car."

"What*ever*. Jeez." David stormed over to the big-ass SUV, opened his own damned door, and climbed in. Without assistance—*So there, Dr. Knows-Best. I'm not freaking helpless.*

For most of the drive, David stared at his window, arms crossed, watching Alun's reflection in the glass. Alun gripped the steering wheel, hunched forward as if he could urge the car to move faster. *So anxious to get rid of me.* But then David caught his convulsive swallow and his uneven breath. *Could he have been as frightened as I was? Remember, he's still in pain. Confrontation won't help.*

David shifted in his seat until he faced Alun. "Hey." He kept his voice gentle. "Don't you think you might be overreacting just a tad about this achu-doohickey stuff?"

"No."

Breathe, David. No confrontation. "We've both had a pretty full day, so I'll let that pass. For now. But tomorrow at work we need to seriously talk about it."

"You're not coming back to work."

David goggled at him. "What? Why? The supe cat is out of the bag, mine included, so it's not like there's anything to cover up anymore."

"Exactly. You're vulnerable. Jackson knows what you are, and he's not likely to keep his mouth shut. After the disaster at the Revels, the whole Seelie Court knows. How long before the Unseelie hordes find out and come for you as they came for Owain?"

"How will my being unemployed save me from that?"

Alun flexed his fingers around the steering wheel. "You'll have to go into hiding. I'll have Mal talk to the Queen. See if we can—"

"Whoa, whoa, whoa. I am not going into some fairy WITSEC program. This is my life. My home is here. My aunt—"

"Not anymore. Everything's different now."

Not really. Apparently I'm still the guy who causes chaos all around me, then ends up alone.

When they pulled up in front of David's house, Alun slammed the gear shift so hard that David winced. "Stay in the car until I come around."

"I don't think so." David threw open the door and jumped down, leaving Alun to close the dang thing if he was so all-fired anxious to be a chauffeur. He stalked up the sidewalk.

"David. Stop."

He vaulted up the two steps to the porch and whirled, the height of the porch enabling him to look down on Alun for once. "Why? So you can pretend you care?"

"Didn't tonight teach you anything? Jackson was ready to kill you to activate his shifter gene."

David stared into Alun's face. "Would it have worked?"

"Perhaps. I don't know—and that's the point. Nobody knows, not even you, but those who have heard the rumors, the legends—no matter how unlikely—will try them. All of those tales end the same way—with the death of the *achubydd*."

"You want to know what I think?"

Alun's brows lowered further—if that was even possible. "I'm afraid to ask."

"I think the only way to find out if any of that crap is true is to try it." Alun recoiled, ready to spew more of his alarmist manifesto, but David threw up a hand. "Hear me out. There's no way the achu-hoo-hah could have lasted as long as they did if every time they healed somebody, they died."

Alun opened his mouth, then snapped it shut. "You . . . might have a point."

"Of course I do. It's just like Mr. Czardos and his blood aversion, or Mrs. Tomlinson trying to force Benjy to collect stuff he's not interested in. You never *ask*. You never consider that there might be ways other than your moldy oldies."

Alun crossed his arms, his feet planted like the roots of an oak. "Go on."

David hesitated. He knew this next bit would be painful for Alun, but it was time for him to face it. "How long were you and Owain lovers?"

Yup, there it was. The pinched mouth, the tight jaw, as if he were both bracing for a blow and recovering from one. "Nearly a year, by the stars of Faerie."

David raised his eyebrows. "Stars are different there?"

"Time moves slower. It takes longer for a full revolution of the heavens there than in the Outer World."

"So in Outer World terms that would be . . . what?"

"We rarely ventured out of Faerie."

David huffed an exasperated breath. "Estimate, then. Just a ballpark. I don't need freaking decimal precision."

"Time doesn't always move at the same pace—"

"Alun. You're stalling. How. Long?"

"Three hundred years . . . or perhaps a bit more."

Jeez. Three hundred years? Or *more*? David couldn't manage three *days*. "I don't suppose it was a platonic relationship? That you were content to worship him from afar?" Alun shook his head. *Dang it.* "Two years or three hundred, it hardly matters. The point is he was never harmed by any of . . . what you did together."

"Perhaps," he grumbled.

"Don't *perhaps* me, Dr. I'm-Always-Right. You know what I think? I think he got just as much from you as you got from him. Like . . . like biofeedback. A symbiotic relationship."

"How can you know that?"

"Well obviously I don't know for sure, but when I help somebody, when I know I've made a difference, I get a huge rush. I don't feel depleted or used or exploited. I feel fulfilled. If that's my achu-whosis crap creeping out of the woodwork, then imagine how someone who actually knows what to do with it would feel." He descended the steps. "I know you lost your one true love in a horrible way, but people recover from grief. That's one of the reasons you're a shrink, right? To help people recover from grief, from guilt, from trauma."

"Look how well I did with Jackson."

David rolled his eyes. "Not even you can cure bat-shit crazy." He reached out, but Alun dodged before his touch could land. David sighed. "You had the holy mother of trifectas, Alun—grief, guilt, *and* trauma. But after two hundred years of beating the crap out of yourself, aren't you ready to move on? Don't you *want* to move on?"

"Oak and bloody thorn, *yes*."

"That's the first step in recovery, right? Admitting you have a problem and that you want to change?"

Alun's lips finally relaxed into an almost-smile. "Psychologist, shrink thyself?"

Go for the gold, David.

"You said you felt as if you'd been gutted when you found Owain's body—as if that dreadful scar"—*which you no longer have*—"was from a real wound. Alun. Tell me the truth. Who cursed you?"

Alun stared straight ahead, his fists clenched tight at his sides. "I told you. I don't know."

"Well *think* about it, then. Who could it have been? Owain was . . . was gone by the time you woke up, and his murderers were nowhere around."

"The rules of Faerie—"

"Uh-uh. Not buying it. From everything I've learned, Faerie doesn't effect change—it's all about preserving the status quo. Something—or rather, *somebody*—had to trigger the curse."

"Blast it, how many times must I say it? There *wasn't* anybody else. I was the only living person in the circle."

David nodded, waiting for Alun's other size fourteen to drop. *Come on, baby. You can get there. One, two, thr—*

Alun sucked in a breath, eyes widening. "Goddess preserve me. I—*I* did it. I cursed myself."

I knew it—and so did you, deep down. "So now you have to forgive yourself. Owain would want you to. If I were him, I'd want you to."

He shook his head. "No one could be that selfless. He'd want me to suffer."

"Really? If he was that horrible a person, then screw him—he's not worth it." *And I can be exactly that selfish, because I'm not letting you go.* "Two hundred years, Alun. I'd say you've paid your dues."

Alun hung his head, and as if David had suddenly developed some kind of weird x-ray vision, he could see the paths of pain in Alun's body, flowing out from his head and circling his heart like a cage of red thorns. Hot damn, was this what an achu-guy could do? Instant diagnostic ultrasound? *Awesome.*

And just as he could see the pain, he knew—one hundred percent without question—that he could do something about it. He advanced on Alun like a tiger stalking a really surly deer.

"What— Stay away."

"No." He grinned. "How does it feel to have someone tell you no for a change? And you can't even run away, like you've been doing all day. What if some homicidal fairy is lurking in the shrubbery, waiting to have its way with me?"

"David, you don't know what you're doing."

"Maybe not entirely, but I know doing nothing is not an option. Never touching you? Also not an option. So suck it up, Dr. Doom. You're about to become a practical demonstration."

With the bone-deep certainty that Alun would never let him be hurt, David flung himself forward. As he'd planned, Alun caught him around the waist, holding him tight against that broad, scrumptious chest, at the perfect height for a little mouth-to-mouth wrestling.

He grabbed Alun's face and dove in. God, that mouth. It didn't matter whether he was in beast mode or beauty mode, that mouth still drove David wild. Alun moaned, clutching David tighter, the hard ridge of his erection hot against David's belly, and took two giant steps toward the house until David was plastered against the porch railing.

David gasped as Alun ground their cocks together. "Remember that whole 'psychologist shrink thyself' thing? Don't take that too literally."

"Dafydd . . ." Alun's voice shivered down David's spine. "You said I lost my one true love. You're wrong."

"But—"

"He wasn't my one true love. He may have been my first. But he wasn't my last."

This time, Alun took the plunge in a kiss that would have buckled David's knees if he weren't suspended between Alun and the porch. *Yes!* A wave of euphoria crashed over David, swamping his senses. They traded tongues, shared breath, touched *everywhere* that clothing allowed. *No barriers. For the first time, he's not keeping me out.*

David still sensed that lasso of thorns around Alun's heart—tight, but maybe not as tight as it had been? *Because he doesn't belong to Owain anymore. He belongs to me.* With every kiss, David willed Alun to believe it too. *It's time, Alun. Let him go. Set yourself free.*

Then, like the snap of a steel cable—although the sound rang only inside David's head—the bonds burst, and David could *feel* it— the flow of golden energy from Alun to him and back—nothing in the way, no guilt, no pain, no regret. Alun's moan morphed into a possessive growl and his kisses grew positively voracious. *Yes!*

Finally, though, David had to pull away before he passed out from hypoxia, and he leaned his head against the porch, eyes closed. His chest felt twice as broad, his mood so light he was surprised he didn't float off above the rooftops. *Damn, dopamine is some good shit.*

Then he opened his eyes and nearly slid down the post.

Alun was beautiful again.

No more orc-tastic brow ridges or outsized jawbone. No mangled Sir Ian McKellan nose. He was even more gorgeous than after the potion because that persistent worry-wrinkle was gone from between his brows. *And he did it all himself—well, okay, with a little pep talk from me.*

David traced the perfect cheekbones. "Welcome back."

Alun's eyes widened, and he clapped a hand to his forehead, felt the bridge of his nose, the angle of his jaw. "What—" He let go of David and backed away. "I never agreed to this. You had no right to drain yourself for my benefit, to let me feed on you like a thrice-damned parasite."

"Check your assumptions, Dr. Fatalism. All I offered—all I *fed* you—was the truth, something you've been avoiding for the last couple of centuries, give or take."

"No. The energy exchange, when we touched, when we kissed—I should have recognized it." He passed his hand over his face again, fingers visibly trembling. "This is what I was afraid of. You sacrificing yourself for me. If I had drained you—"

Before David's eyes, the bones started to bubble underneath Alun's skin.

"Hey!" David grabbed Alun's shirt front and pulled him back. "None of that. I made exactly zero sacrifice."

"I don't believe you. *Something* happened."

"Of course it did. *You* happened. You finally let go of the past, of your misplaced guilt. Furthermore, I am the complete *opposite* of drained. I'm . . . I don't know, empowered. Like you were finally opening up to me. I mean, do I seem dead to you?" He pressed his still-hard cock against Alun's thigh.

Alun almost smiled—almost. "But Owain . . ."

David clenched his teeth. *Getting really, really tired of hearing about perfect martyred Owain, and if that makes me a terrible person, I'll own it.* "What about him?"

"Doesn't he deserve to be remembered?"

"Oh, sweetheart." David rested his head against Alun's chest for a moment. "Remember him, yes. But don't immolate yourself on his funeral pyre. Honor his life—not his death."

Alun's chest heaved under him. "Goddess, you're right. I almost never think of *him*, only our parting and its aftermath."

"Exactly." He leaned back so he could see Alun's face—his beautiful, uncursed face. "So how does admitting that make you feel?"

"Feel?" Alun blinked, raising his hand until his fingers hovered over David's cheek. "I feel . . . reborn. But you—"

David pressed his fingers over Alun's lips. "Stop right there. I feel better than I have in years. Maybe my whole life, so don't go all guilt-ridden on me again." He tapped Alun's jaw. "It's not a good look on you."

This time Alun managed a full-on smile that turned David's knees to jelly. "I thought you said my looks didn't matter. It was my attitude that was the off-putter."

"That was when I thought you were a victim of circumstance and accident, but, baby—self-pity? Uh-uh. I love you, but I don't hang with whiny guys."

CHAPTER ✥ 27

"**I** *love you.*"

Alun felt as if mead were flowing in his veins instead of blood. Goddess, those words carried more magic than the One Tree itself. Hearing them from Owain had made him feel extraordinary. Powerful. Unstoppable. Hearing them from David, though—a completely different feeling, as if he were just like anybody else—just as deserving, just as worthy of being loved.

If that wasn't magic, nothing was.

Could he finally be free of the curse of his own guilt, his own transgressions? Had he truly found redemption in this incredible man? Could his exile truly be over?

But did he want to return to Faerie, to his old duties and responsibilities? He'd built a life in the Outer World despite his curse. He had purpose here. A lover here. He stroked David's neck, ran a fingertip along the wing of his eyebrow. *A lover who will be in constant danger.* Surely, if Alun had his old resources, his Sidhe powers and connections, he could find a way to protect David. A frisson of alarm crept up his back. Suddenly, the street seemed too open, too indefensible.

He gathered David close and whispered, "Invite me in."

David chuckled. "Good point. If we go any further out here, we're liable to get arrested." He kissed Alun again, then pulled away to dig his keys out of his pocket. When he let them into the house, though, the living room wasn't empty. One member of the druid circle, a plump woman in jeans and a pink sweatshirt, was sitting on the sofa, tying up bags of herbs with red twine. She set them aside and rose, her expression somber.

"Aunt Peggy." David held out his arms to her, obviously expecting a hug. "I didn't know you'd be here this evening." He peered through an arch into the dark kitchen. "Have you and Aunt Cassie been—"

"You're not wearing your earring."

"No."

"Your worry stone? Are you carrying that?"

"No. You don't have to front with me anymore. I know what I am. I'm not trying to mask it anymore."

She raised one hand to her trembling mouth. "That's why."

"Why what?"

"I'm sorry, David. But Cassie is . . ."

David paled and swayed drunkenly on his feet. Alun rushed across the room and wrapped an arm around his shoulders. "Easy, *cariad*."

"Is she—" David gulped and shuddered under Alun's arm. "Is she gone?"

"Oh, my pumpkin." She grabbed his hands. "No. Not yet. But she's in a coma. You see, not all of your protections were held by those talismans. Cassie did a lot of the work herself. That's why she's been failing. As you've grown older, it's gotten harder to keep your power damped down, and the spells have taken more of her energy. She's older now too, so she doesn't have the same reserves."

"You mean she doesn't have cancer?"

Peggy shook her head.

"She never did?" David was still trembling under Alun's touch, but this time it didn't feel like fear. It felt like fury. *Why do I know what he feels?* But as surely as he knew his own name, he knew that David was furious.

David wrenched himself out of Alun's embrace. "You were so fricking worried about other people draining me. Looks like *I'm* the one who's the parasite." He brushed aside his tears. "No more."

He marched past Peggy and down the hall.

She watched him go, wringing her hands. "I told her. I warned her nothing good could come of hiding the truth from him."

"When did she slip away?"

"About half an hour ago. She's been fading all day. Now I know it was because she was trying to compensate for the talismans."

Half an hour ago, he and David had been practically humping each other on the front porch. Had that surge of energy—the burst of glory that had flowed between them, lifting them both, cauterizing Alun's inner wounds—had it been because David was finally free of all the shackles on his nature?

Goddess, if that was a taste of his untutored power, he was a stronger *achubydd* than Owain and his grandfather put together.

"Do you mind if I . . ." Alun gestured down the hall. "I don't want him to be alone."

She nodded and picked up several of the sachets. "We'll both go."

He followed her down the short hallway to a dimly lit bedroom. A trio of squat candles were burning on an oak dresser, their scent heavy in the air. *Vervain. Mint. Meadowsweet.* The three most sacred of druid herbs. Cassie lay in the middle of an enormous sleigh bed, its headboard carved with acorns. She looked as tiny as a doll under a coverlet the color of the sky.

David was sitting on the edge of the mattress, holding her hand, his head bowed. He looked up when Alun and Peggy entered the room, his face streaked with tears. "Did you call the doctor? Why isn't she in the hospital?"

"That's not how we do things, sweetheart," Peggy said gently, giving a stir to a bowl of potpourri next to the candles.

"The way you do things *isn't working*." He slammed a fist into his thigh. "It's time to do something else."

"David." Peggy, despite looking like every child's dream of a cozy granny, commanded the druid power voice too. "The hospital would treat her with drugs and machines, without any notion of what ails her. Will you tell them she's suffering from a lack of life essence? Because that's one way for all of us to be barred from her care."

"But—"

"Dafydd." Alun stood at David's back and put his hands on the trembling shoulders. "Believe her when she tells you this. Druids in many ways are no more human than I am. Than you are."

He shrugged away from Alun's hold. "You know a way for me to help her, to bring her back, don't you?"

Alun moved to stand at the foot of the bed. "Nobody knows for certain. The *achubyddion* have been gone for two centuries."

"Someone must," he said through clenched teeth. "Otherwise why would anybody care about me? Hoffenberg knew. The people who chased us out of Faerie knew."

"They only know tales and legends, so they can do nothing but shoot in the dark. As if you held a guitar in one hand and strings in another, knowing the two could be put together to make music. But without knowledge, you'd be more likely to break the strings, warp the neck of the guitar, than you would be to play the simplest of songs."

"Then tell me the tales. Tell me something. *Please.*" His voice was rough, desperate. "She's *dying*, Alun. Don't you understand?"

"Yes, *cariad*," Alun said softly. "I do."

"Then tell me, damn you. Tell me how to save her!"

"David," Peggy said from her position by the dresser, "do you think she's spent her whole life, the last of her essence to save you, only to have you throw that gift away? That's no way to honor her sacrifice."

"I don't want her sacrifice, don't you get it? I never asked for that. What I want—" His voice broke and he inhaled on a shuddering breath. "I want my aunt back."

"Dafydd, there's nothing I can tell you."

He stared stonily at Alun. "You mean you *won't*. Fine. Go, then. I'll figure it out myself."

Hurt twisted in Alun's belly like a wounded dragon. He reached out to stroke David's hair, but David ducked away. "Everything she did, she did for you."

"So I should shut up and accept the consequences?" He didn't so much as glance at Alun. "How has that worked for you, Dr. Kendrick?"

Alun sucked in a breath as the familiar burn kindled under his sternum. But this time it wasn't the memory of Owain's death that threatened to gut him. It was David's words. "I'll—I'll come by in the morning."

"Don't bother. I'm sure you have other things to do. After all, you don't need to hide in the dark anymore."

So after everything, David was renouncing him? Before the burn could take over and consume him, Alun strode down the hallway to the living room.

"Dr. Kendrick." Peggy's low voice stopped him before he could yank the front door open.

He stood with one hand on the knob, the other pressed to the wall next to the frame. "What?"

"Don't take this too hard. He's had no one but Cassie most of his life. Naturally he's upset at losing her."

"It isn't his losing her that's the problem. It's his refusal to let go." *Just as I refused for two centuries.* "He accuses me of stubbornness, says it makes for hide-bound thinking. Yet he is just as obstinate, with a reckless bent. He won't give up until he kills himself, but if I force him to stop, he'll blame me for her death and I'll lose him just as surely as if he were to die. The best I can do for him is to allow him to take his own path for once in his life, unfettered by any interference."

"Then why are you abandoning him?"

Alun opened the door and stood with his back to her, the low light of the living room lamps casting his shadow across the porch. "I'm not abandoning him. I'm giving him what he wants. The freedom to choose."

"Yet you're leaving."

"I won't stop him. But I can't watch him either."

He strode across the porch and down the sidewalk. The hood of his Land Rover shone in the warring light of the street lights and the gibbous moon. His hand closed around the keys in his pocket.

I can't encase myself in iron and steel, away from the earth and sky. Not tonight.

He turned and walked down the street. When he got to the park at the end of the road, he started to run.

CHAPTER ⚛ 28

*D*amn it, Auntie. How could you do this? How could you imagine that my life was more valuable than yours?

David sat at Aunt Cassie's bedside, willing himself to suddenly figure out what he was supposed to do. All this bull-crap about his magical mystery mojo—complete and utter garbage. What good was it? If he couldn't make people better—or do anything useful at all that he could see—then this alleged ability was as worthless as a rhinestone jackhammer.

But, in that moment on the porch, he'd seen Alun's pain so clearly. *Alun.* David wanted to double over to ease the agony in his middle from Alun's betrayal, his lack of trust. But not now. He wiped the tears off his face with the back of his hand. *Get the job done, David—mourn lost love later.*

He stared at her frail form until his eyes dried out, but he couldn't see the same thing. It was as if she were cocooned in shadow, a shadow he couldn't pierce. *Screw the supernatural shit.* He'd been almost-a-nurse longer than he'd been achu-what-the-hell-ever. So triage—ask the questions, and if you can't treat the problem, treat the symptoms.

"Peggy, do you think she could still be working the—the protection spell?"

"I don't see how. This is an undirected unconsciousness. All the threads of her work are slack or cut."

"So I should have all my potential whatever, right?"

Peggy looked troubled. "Yes. Theoretically."

"So why can't I access it? Why can't I heal her?"

"She has to want to be healed, otherwise nothing you can throw at her, no amount of energy, will ever make a difference."

Just like Alun and his curse; he had to have a reason to move on. So he needed to give his aunt a reason to stay. He scooted closer to her on the mattress and took both her hands. "You listen to me, little missy. You had better let me help you get well. If I can't even keep my own aunt healthy, who will ever hire me as a nurse? You're about to scar me for life. I may never recover."

"You think guilt will work, pumpkin?"

"It damn well works on me. I don't see why I have to be the only one to suffer. She's going to get better whether she likes it or not, because I say so."

David stroked Aunt Cassie's hand, focusing on what he would do if she were one of the patients in the hospice center where he volunteered, although he shied away from considering her death a foregone conclusion. The staff always said a visit from him made the patients' day, that they were calmer, their pain easier to bear, after he'd spent a morning with them—even though the staff was extra-antsy at the end of his shift.

Was that some of his true nature leaking out? What did he do that soothed the patients, yet made the staff lob bagels at each other over the lunchroom table?

Somehow, he'd known what would help Benjy and Mr. Czardos. He'd figured out what Alun needed too. *Me, damn it. He needs me.* Maybe all those other people—the hospice staff, his old boyfriends, the patients who'd rioted in every other medical job he'd held—had needed something too, and had known instinctively that David could provide relief. To need something, to know it was *right there* but be unable to take it—wouldn't that make anyone frustrated and cranky?

"What does she need, Peggy? I know I should be able to figure it out, but I can't."

Peggy moved to the other side of the bed and straightened the coverlet. "Her essence is depleted."

"So what does that mean? Can she get better?"

She shook her head. "None of us has ever gone this far and returned. You must be prepared to face it, Davey. She can't come back."

"All due respect, but I don't buy it. There's always a first time."

And he intended to find it.

Essence. What was essence anyway? He hadn't spent a lifetime listening to new age woo-woo shit without absorbing some of the philosophy. With a jolt, he realized that his aunt and her friends weren't new age at all—they were about as old age as you could get, and he wasn't talking about the number of their birthdays.

Druids. He'd have a hard time believing it except he'd spent the last week having his brain stretched in ways he'd never imagined.

He glanced at the dresser. The candles still burned steadily, their scent mingling with the thread of cedar from the folds of the blanket. He closed his eyes, concentrating on those scents, remembering half-heard conversations between his aunt and her friends about the properties of different herbs for protection and health.

He'd thought they were talking about insect repellent and herbal teas. What if they were speaking literally, about their craft as druids, about the ancient knowledge that had enabled Alun to overcome his curse for one magical night? He'd seen the evidence that their craft worked. Heck, *he* was the evidence.

Maybe it was time to embrace the whole enchilada, or whatever the Celtic equivalent was. Haggis? Rarebit? Colcannon? Who knew? He only knew that he was stalling because if he got this wrong, his aunt would die.

He took a breath to calm his break-dancing nerves. *Center yourself, Davey.* He couldn't count the number of times his aunt had said that to him when he was growing up, awkward and rebellious, uneasy in his own skin. Maybe she'd been trying to teach him something important, something critical to his true nature, and not just attempting to control a hyperactive kid.

He stroked the paper-thin skin on the back of her hand, focusing on the spot under his sternum that she'd claimed was his center. *There.* A glow, bright and blue, like the heart of a candle flame. Was that his essence? *Who cares if it really is—I choose to believe it, so damn it, it's true.*

He visualized the flame elongating, stretching from his chest to hers, feeding his strength into her. He could almost see an answering flicker of wan gold over her heart. *Reach out, Auntie, please. Take what I'm offering. Alun finally did it, and it didn't hurt either one of us. You can do the same.*

The two flames touched, and he gasped, the hairs rising along his arms and at the nape of his neck. Even weakened, Aunt Cassie's essence felt substantial. Powerful. *Ancient.*

"You're too cantankerous to give up, Auntie," he whispered, clutching her hand tighter. "Let me give back what I stole."

Her fingers twitched in his hold, and her chest rose with a deeper breath. *Yes!* He felt his inner flame branching out, joining with hers, twining along pathways that had nothing to do with any physical system. Her hands tightened around his. *It's working! If I can just—*

"Hold," an unfamiliar voice boomed, too large for the room.

From the corner of his eye, David saw Peggy scramble out of her chair. Was it because he wasn't looking at her directly that she seemed taller, glowing with her own inner fire? "Unseelie fae are not welcome here."

Oh shit. Unseelie? David tore his gaze from Aunt Cassie and stared over his shoulder.

The Consort was standing in the doorway, backed by two massive men—fae—whose combined shoulder width kept them looming in the hallway. The smile on his Ken-perfect face was scarier than Alun's worst beast-scowl. "We are not Unseelie. And you have already welcomed Sidhe across your threshold, have you not?" He pointed at David. "You will cease your actions."

David returned his attention to Aunt Cassie. "No." If nothing else, Alun had taught him how to refuse orders from men twice his size.

"Then we shall render them moot." The hiss and clang of metal broke David's concentration again. *Was that a— It was. A sword. The asshole drew a sword in my aunt's bedroom!* And leveled it at the base of Peggy's throat.

David sprang to his feet, his connection to Aunt Cassie broken. "No. Don't hurt her. Don't hurt either of them."

The Consort's sword didn't waver. "Why should we pay any mind to you? You will come with us, yay or nay, and we have heard that druid blood spilled can weave its own power."

Peggy, bless her, didn't flinch. She stared the bastard right in the eye, a zaftig ninja grandmother. "Only when we spill it ourselves, for reasons of our own choosing. Is all of your knowledge this imperfect?"

"Silence!"

David scrambled around the bed to stand next to Peggy. "Please. I'll come with you, do whatever you want. But let me help my aunt first."

"You are right. You will come with us and do our bidding, but you shall not waste your essence on anyone else." He lowered his sword—*thank goodness*—and took a step forward, his nostrils flaring. "We have waited two hundred years for another chance, and Alun Cynwrig delivered it to us, just as he did before."

Anger flared in David's chest, and he wished for a sword of his own, the better to skewer the Consort with. "You. You killed Owain? His grandfather? His clan?"

"They were useless. Their deaths gave us only a fraction of what we needed. But we've learned the way of it now."

"How?" Peggy said defiantly. "From Wikipedia?"

The Consort's alabaster brow wrinkled in confusion. "What?"

"You can't know any more than you ever did, which isn't much, considering how woefully uneducated you are about druids. The *achubyddion* vanished long ago, and left no written lore."

"Ah, but they didn't vanish, did they? Not two weeks past, we found another enclave. Their records were much less ephemeral, although we did not locate the pertinent details until after the blood sacrifice of the two we caught. But now we know the way of it."

David glanced at Peggy. "When he says 'we,' is he referring to the goons at the door, or is he just schizophrenic?"

"Delusions of grandeur. Royal wannabe," she said. "Pathetic, really."

"Silence!" the Consort roared. He took two giant strides across the room and grabbed the front of David's shirt. "You will come with me now." For some reason, his switch to the first person singular sent a chill down David's spine. "I spill my essence into you and all of yours is available to me, and I shall be exalted."

"Where'd you get those instructions?" David forced a bravado he didn't feel. "An Ikea manual? I think something got lost in translation."

The Consort bared his teeth in his male-model smile. "I understand them perfectly." He wrapped one enormous hand around

David's throat. "First I fuck you on the altar stone. Then I slit your throat and bathe in your blood."

CHAPTER ❈ 29

D arkness pooled under the trees in the park, but as Alun pounded down the path, his mood was darker still. His work shoes weren't suited to this kind of punishment, passing the jolt of each step, the bite of every embedded rock, through the thin soles to his feet and legs. He was tempted to take them off and hurl them into the underbrush.

Was he doomed to repeat his own history—rejected once again in favor of family ties by a man he loved? His steps faltered, and he stopped under the gnarled branches of an oak tree. *Goddess. I love him.* No point in denying it: David—fearless, beautiful, honorable David—had danced his awkward way into Alun's heart.

Alun might be free of his curse at last—thanks again to David—but what good was it if the one thing he wanted most was beyond his reach? The pain of renunciation was bad enough, but what if David died trying to save his aunt?

He'd do it, too. As stubborn as he was, as fiercely as he pursued helping others—and as little as he knew about his *achubydd* nature—he could burn himself to a hollow shell without making the slightest impact on Cassie's condition.

Cassie was a druid—an ancient one if Alun was any judge. How much more energy would it take to bring someone with the weight of that much power back from death's doorstep? Owain had collapsed after healing a simple flesh wound in a deer's flank. David would have healed that deer too, regardless of the cost, just as Owain would have probably tried to heal his grandfather, or another of his clan, if they were in the same state as Cassie.

David and Owain were more alike than Alun wanted to admit. Just like Owain, David never let Alun escape the consequences of his own foolish choices. Just like Owain, David had chosen *family* over Alun.

And just like with Owain, Alun had reacted by running away. *Merciful Goddess. What have I done?*

He raced back the way he'd come, bursting out of the tree-cover onto the sidewalk, skidding to a halt in front of David's house. The front door stood open, lamplight spilling down the porch steps to point a pale-golden finger toward where Alun's car stood at the curb.

His pulse hammered in his ears, louder than his footsteps in the still night. He'd closed the door when he'd left, hadn't he? Even if he hadn't, surely Peggy wouldn't have left it open. Not at night, even in a neighborhood as relatively safe as this one.

He vaulted onto the porch and into the house. "David!" No answer, but he heard a murmur of female voices from the bedroom, and the tightness in his chest eased. He took a shaky breath and froze. *What . . .?* He sniffed again and caught the whiff of ozone and steel, the smell of fae on the hunt.

He strode down the hallway, his heart in his throat. *Something's wrong.* He couldn't sense David's presence—that buzz in his blood, a resonance that had been building since their first meeting.

He stopped in Cassie's bedroom doorway, scanning every corner, but David wasn't there. *Gone. Just like Owain.*

Peggy was sitting next to the bed, holding Cassie's hand. And Cassie—she was awake, her bird-bright eyes brimming with tears.

"Where is he?" Alun rasped.

"They took him," Peggy said on a sob. "They threatened us, Cassie and me, and he went with them."

"Who? The Unseelie?"

Peggy shook her head. "No."

"The Consort," Cassie said, no hint of power in her thread of a voice. "It was the Queen's Consort."

Black and white sparks danced in Alun's vision. "The bloody bastard. I'll rip his sword arm off and use it to cut off his own head."

"You can't. The Consort laws are sacrosanct—harm him and suffer the same fate, even unto death."

Bugger the thrice-blasted Consort laws. "I don't care." David's life was worth any sacrifice.

"Something else you should know, Lord Cynwrig." The fury simmering behind Cassie's tears surely matched his own. "This is not the first time the Consort has attacked an *achubydd* with intent to kill. The other times—" She swallowed, her hands clutching the coverlet. "The other times, he was successful."

The blood drained from Alun's head, and he reeled against the doorframe. Peggy rushed over and led him to a chair. "Owain. His clan. *The Consort* was responsible?"

Cassie nodded. "And the more recent murders as well."

Pain seared his chest, as if it were being split open. "My fault. I should have sent David away the first day. Should never have taken him to Faerie." He dropped his head in his hands and felt the bones shift under his fingers. *A beast—you're naught but a beast and you deserve to look as ugly on the outside as you are on the inside.*

"Stop." At the combined power voices of both druids, he jerked his head up.

The hectic color on Cassie's cheeks was startling in her ghost-pale face. "You cannot let your guilt consume you. You must act. Solve the problem. Do not let this monster succeed again."

At her words, Alun pushed back the guilt boiling like sullen lava in his gut. She was right. The only way he could save David was to leave the past behind. Keep the gift David had given him, the gift of redemption.

And use it to take Rodric Luchullain's head.

Alun nodded to the druids and stormed out of the house, dialing Mal as he climbed into his car.

"What?" Mal's voice over the scratchy connection was testy.

Alun put him on speaker. "I need backup."

"Of course you do. You never call unless you need something."

Alun forced his breath to calm, his heart to slow its headlong gallop. "David's in danger."

"He's not the only one. Did you ever consider what the consequences of that little bombshell at the Revels might be to the rest of us?"

Alun jammed his key into the ignition. "The rest of who?"

"The rest of the family. Gareth. Me."

"The Consort attacked you and Gareth?"

"The Consort? What in the hells are you on about? I mean the Queen—her royal pissed-off Majesty herself."

He started the car and roared off down the street. "Why? What did she do?"

"For one thing, she hasn't given Gareth leave to quit Faerie. He's been stuck there since the Revels. His band had to cancel a sold-out concert, so I expect he'll be none too popular with them or their manager when she finally cuts him loose."

"Shite," Alun muttered. "I never thought of that. What about you?"

"I'm on the fucking run, brother. She wants to put a *tynged* on me to bring you in, and she's not particular about whether your head is attached to your body at the time. The only way I can avoid it is if I stay out of Faerie and away from her Royal Bitchiness."

Alun pounded the steering wheel. "Damn them both to all the hells."

"Both?"

"The Consort. He was behind the massacre of Owain's clan."

"You're shitting me."

"He was also the one who murdered those two *achubydd* you found."

Mal's muttered curses shifted to Welsh and increased in rancor. "Do you suppose she's in on it too?"

"I couldn't say. But he's taken David, and if I don't stop him, he'll kill him just like he killed Owain."

"I'd help you if I could—"

"I know." He really did, despite their years of estrangement. "Watch your back."

"Likewise. Luck of the hunt to you, my brother."

Alun ended the call, and reached for his connection to the One Tree, the molten heat of his fae powers infusing his core. He'd need every bit of it tonight—with a price on his head, he'd need to mask his progress or he'd be taken before he could rescue David.

What I wouldn't give for one of my old weapons. But he couldn't spare the time to retrieve his sword or his bow from his apartment.

The Consort had a lead on him already. No telling how quickly he'd— *No.*

Alun couldn't think of David lying lifeless on the altar. He refused to allow it to happen. Not this time, even if the cost was his own life.

CHAPTER ❈ 30

If David had thought racing down the hill between Alun and Mal had been adrenaline-inducing, it was nothing compared to dangling in the air between two massive Sidhe who hadn't had much practice marching in step. His shoulders felt as if they'd been wrenched out of their sockets, and his breath sawed in his lungs as he struggled to keep up.

"The least . . . you could do . . ." he gasped, "is allow me . . . to walk to my doom . . . with a little dignity."

"Quiet." The Consort stopped crashing through the underbrush like a wounded moose and held up one hand. The goons stopped, and David was finally able to catch his breath.

So unfair. He'd just figured out he wasn't a spazzy awkward loser. He'd finally found a man he could love—if the stupid idiot would just take off his stubborn hat. But if he was really going to die tonight, he wasn't about to make it easier for the kidnappers. His nervous response had always been smart-assery, and nothing said nerves like the prospect of being fucked to death by a cross between Ken, Thor, and a giant douche bag.

"You guys need to work on your interpersonal skills, you know? All of you fae are the same. Do this, do that, do what I say—"

The Consort grabbed David's jaw in one massive hand and squeezed until David's mouth puckered like a carp's. "If I were Cynwrig, I'd have cut out your tongue long since."

"No mo' woyal we?" Fish lips made it tough to talk.

"Shut. Your. Mouth." The Consort punctuated each word with an increase in pressure and a vicious shake. David's eyes watered, and the Consort's mouth twisted in a Voldemort smile. He jerked his head at the goons. "The Queen and her coterie are at her pavilion. We detour through the ceilidh glade. The rest of the company will meet us there."

He let go, and David passed a hand under his jaw, certain it had been dislocated. Oddly, he felt a soothing warmth spread from his hand to his bruised cheeks. *Whoa. This stuff worked on himself too? It's my power. Mine. And I get to choose how to spend it.* He might be a mosquito compared to the fae grizzlies beside him, but mosquitoes could be freaking annoying. If that was all he had to work with, he'd own it—and damned if he'd give up without a fight.

The Consort veered off onto a narrower path, forcing them into single file. David glanced back at Goon One, whose shoulders brushed the bushes on either side of the path.

"You guys seriously need a new hobby. Have you tried fantasy football?"

Goon One grunted and glowered. Ha! In a mano-a-mano glower-off, Alun would leave this guy in the dust.

Alun. The tiny glow that his token resistance had afforded faded when he realized he wouldn't see Alun again. That his last words to him had been recriminations. Is this how Alun had felt after his last fight with Owain? This inner maelstrom of regret and want and sorrow? If so, David could understand how he'd want to punish himself for the outcome.

They broke through the tree cover into the ceilidh glade, the place he'd been exposed as other than human. The circle of white stones glimmered in the moss carpet, and at the far end of the clearing, Gareth Kendrick stood on the dais, holding his guitar, a battered leather case open at his feet. He met David's gaze across the empty circle, his eyes widening as he took in the Consort and attendant goons.

A group of about twenty fae, all of them the tall perfect specimens that marked them as Sidhe, strode out of the woods opposite the Consort, who moved forward to meet them in the center of the circle.

David glanced from the stones to Gareth, Alun's words echoing in his head. *"If you venture inside while a true bard plays, you must stay and dance until the music stops."*

Gareth was a true bard.

David glanced at Goon One and Goon Two. Their attention was focused on the confab going on in the middle of the clearing. *Now's my chance.*

So the fae demanded beauty, did they? Well, let them get a load of David's moves. If he could clear any given dance floor of a raft of horny men who wanted to have their twink and eat him too, these jokers stood no chance.

He captured Gareth's gaze, indicating the guitar with a twitch of his chin. Tilting his head toward the group of fae in the dance danger zone, he mouthed, *YMCA.*

A smile, so like Alun's that David nearly faltered, curved Gareth's lips, and he nodded. As he struck the opening notes, David bolted into the circle. Goon Two shouted and followed, but Goon One didn't cross the stone perimeter. *Dang it.*

No help for it. Maybe the hills coming alive with the sound of music would attract enough attention to foil the Consort's little plan.

David's feet broke into a skipping march without conscious orders from his brain, his hands swinging up to clap over his head. Around him, the Sidhe joined in the same moves, although their actions were smooth and as lovely as anyone could be while shaking their booty to vintage Village People as performed by the last living fae bard.

Judging by the expressions on their faces, which ranged from murderous to horrified when their gaze landed on David's best (aka worst ever) moves, they weren't exactly thrilled by the experience.

Too freaking bad.

Gareth's smooth-as-velvet baritone belted out the chorus, and David led the company in a conga line of arm movements. Ha! They followed his lead, as if the horror of his dancing were mesmerizing, just like the people in the trauma group.

This is my true superpower: dance as an offensive weapon.

As Gareth launched into the second verse, David grew breathless. *Shoot.* He had no endgame in mind. Just a nebulous hope that he'd attract enough people to stop the Consort's stealth operation. If that didn't work, what then?

Over the sound of Gareth's guitar and his exhortations for young men to check out the action in the Y, David heard a rustle in the trees from two different directions. *Please let at least one regiment of cavalry be on my team.*

Unfortunately, the Consort apparently noticed the sounds of approaching company too. He glared at Goon One, who dithered on the outside of the circle, as much as a man the size of a WWE champion could dither.

"Kill the bard, you fool."

David stumbled but couldn't stop his feet. He hadn't meant to endanger Gareth. Damn it, he'd acted before he considered the consequences. Again.

Goon One shook his head. "Kill a bard? I cannot. I would be exiled."

"You will be dead at my own hand if you do not stop this madness."

Goon One nodded and pulled a longbow off his shoulder. As Goon One nocked an arrow, David tried to stop dancing, tried to stop flinging his arms in wild abandon, tried to shout anything but "YMCA."

But he couldn't. And Goon One let the arrow fly.

CHAPTER ✲ 31

With a tire iron gripped in his hand, Alun was halfway up the tor to the ceilidh glade when he heard the unmistakable sound of his brother's voice. Surely Gareth wouldn't be so cruel as to play if David were already dead, no matter how much he hated Alun. He couldn't make out the tune, but it didn't sound like a traditional Celtic melody, and was too up-tempo to be a funeral dirge.

He called on the One Tree and put on another burst of speed to scale the last rise and shoulder his way through the trees. When he broke out of the forest, chest heaving, he dropped into a crouch. In the center of the circle, David was capering with the Consort and a full company of Daoine Sidhe warriors.

On the opposite side of the clearing, a cadre of the Queen's guard appeared, armed and battle-ready. Alun had no hope that they were there to rescue David. Far more likely that the Queen had detected Alun's presence and sent them out to capture him. After all, what did the life of one non-fae—last-known *achubydd* or not—matter to her when she had an insult to avenge?

The warriors paused, milling at the edge of the circle, knowing better than to pass the perimeter. If only he could gauge their allegiance. Had they sworn the oath to the Consort that Alun—thank the Goddess—had avoided? Would they follow the Consort, regardless of his horrific plans? Or could Alun turn them sufficiently to save David?

He located David in the shifting throng of dancing warriors—easy to do because even though his lover was at least a foot shorter than the other men, his movements were so disjointed and spasmodic that it was like locating the one frog in a school of angelfish.

But David didn't see Alun—his attention was focused on one warrior who was standing away from the Queen's guard, outside the perimeter. The man raised his longbow, and before Alun could process the scene, the man had loosed the arrow.

It flew across the clearing and struck his brother in the right shoulder. The force of the impact spun Gareth half around; he dropped his guitar with a discordant twang and crumpled to the ground.

Tossing aside the tire iron, Alun lurched toward his brother, but Gareth waved him off before pressing his left hand to his shoulder.

"Never mind me. Stop the Consort."

He whirled to face the chaos in the center of the circle, where the Queen's guard was clashing with the Consort's contingent. *So he's acting alone. The Queen isn't a part of the plot.*

Craning his neck, he tried to sort out the skirmishes amid the crash of swords and differing battle cries. Where in all the bloody hells was the bastard? Where was David? He had been here a bare moment ago—

There. Three-quarters of the way across the clearing, he spied the Consort's silver-blond hair. He was gripping David by the arm, dragging him toward the path that led to the Stone Circle and the altar.

Alun bared his teeth in the fae battle rictus and took off across the clearing, past the fighters. The clang of a nearby sword reminded him that the Consort was armed, even if his guards were otherwise engaged. How could Alun hope to subdue him with nothing but his bare hands and his fury?

"Alun!" Gareth's voice rang out over the cacophony in the clearing. Alun looked up to see his own sword flying toward him, end-over-end. He didn't have time to wonder where his brother had gotten the damn thing, or how he'd managed to throw it with an arrow protruding from his shoulder—he was too relieved to see it. He thrust up his hand, and the hilt settled into his palm with a slap, instantly an extension of his arm again, as if he'd never laid it down.

By the time Alun made it across the circle, the Consort had already disappeared down the path. *Goddess, don't let me be too late.* He knew where they were headed, but he knew an alternate—and quicker—route. He refused to fail. *Not tonight. Not again. Not this man.*

He left the path and circled through a grove of rowan and ash, splashed through a shallow stream, the water turning his shoes into very expensive pulp. *I hate the thrice-damned things anyway.* The soles slid on moss when he scaled the opposite bank, and he cursed his Outer World clothing, so inappropriate for wilderness and battle.

He burst onto the Stone Circle plateau from the north near the king stone just as the Consort dragged David over the lip at the southern edge.

"Rodric Luchullain!" Alun bellowed. "You hold what is mine."

The Consort's face twisted in a sneer worthy of an Unseelie wight. "I see no consort mark on him."

"That doesn't matter. I claim him."

"Hello?" David tossed his hair out of his eyes. "Don't I get a say in this?"

"No!" Alun and the Consort both shouted at once.

"Damn fairies," David muttered, and the Consort wrenched his arm behind his back and placed the point of his sword at David's jugular.

"Mind your tongue." The sword jerked, and Alun saw a trickle of blood trail down David's throat and turn the white collar of his dress shirt dark in the moonlight. "Even a sacrifice must show proper respect."

Alun's grip tightened on his sword hilt, and he willed David to stand down from his brash attitude. A little humility would give Alun time to maneuver into position. If they ignited the Consort's legendary ego-driven temper, though, the fool might forget his intention and kill David out of hand.

Stall. Stall until I can get into position.

David's eyes widened as if he had heard Alun's thoughts. Or maybe David was smarter than the Consort gave him credit for.

"Honestly." David propped his free hand on his hip. "You people seriously need to spend about ten years in kindergarten to learn some common sense. Haven't you ever considered that a willing sacrifice has more power than one taken by force?"

"Blood is the nature of sacrifice." A flicker of confusion crossed the Consort's face. "Who would volunteer to die?"

"Blood. Death. Blah, blah, blah. Sacrifice doesn't have to be that *permanent*. What about an offer to help? Partnership? Cooperation?" The Consort laughed, throwing his head back, his white teeth glinting like a wolf's. Alun took the opportunity to move farther around the circle's circumference until he stood in front of the altar. If the Consort intended to slaughter David there, he'd have to go through Alun first.

"Cynwrig, stand aside. You have no place in this Court anymore."

"You forget my oath of not three days since."

The Consort scowled. "You cannot oppose me lest you be foresworn."

"How?" Alun inched forward. "I swore my allegiance to the Queen and the Realm. Not to you."

"I *am* the Realm!" he roared. There it was—the ego ascendant.

"You are not. You're the Queen's appendage." What did Mal always call him? "Her sidecar, nothing more."

The Consort lunged for Alun, dropping his sword from David's throat.

"Run, David!"

David tore his arm from the Consort's grip and staggered away, stumbling once and falling to his hands and knees. He didn't run, though, damn it—simply scrambled over to slump against the king stone.

Alun advanced on the Consort. They circled one another, each searching for an opening, assessing weaknesses. Alun hadn't wielded his sword for over two hundred years. The Consort had probably used his within the last hour.

Although Alun wasn't his sworn subject, the man was still the Queen's consort, and Faerie consort laws were immutable: harm a consort, and ye shall lose whate'r you seek to take. *Can I kill him, knowing that I'll die too?* His gaze flicked to David, huddled against the towering menhir, blood darkening his throat.

Yes. Without question.

He caught a flash of movement under the trees at the edge of the clearing. White skin, red hair, green gown. *The Queen.*

"I've noticed something different about you, Rodric," Alun said, pitching his voice as he would speak to his most disturbed clients. "You've changed. You're broader."

"I train with the guards. Every day." He bared his teeth in a mirthless grin. "I doubt you can say the same."

"Can training increase your height by four inches?"

"No." He lunged, and Alun parried. Barely. "*Achubydd* blood did that."

"You killed that whole clan—men, women, children—so you could be *taller*?"

The Consort laughed. "No, you fool. I killed them so I could be King. But it didn't work. Not quite." He jerked his chin at David. "That will change tonight. After I kill you, nothing will stand in my way. I'll fuck your little pet, and then I'll kill him. His blood will grant me my rightful place at last."

Alun's vision narrowed to the spot in the Consort's chest where he itched to bury his sword. "Rightful? How is it rightful if you rise by stealing the lives of others?"

"They aren't Daoine Sidhe. They're not even fae. They exist only to serve, so what better way than to grant me this ultimate service?"

A rock sailed over Alun's head and thumped against the ground at the Consort's feet. *Oak and thorn, Dafydd, don't draw attention to yourself.*

But when the Consort's gaze shifted away, Alun took his chance. He lunged, knocking the Consort's sword out of his hand, and aimed his own sword at the man's black heart. "Hold, Rodric. You deserve no one's allegiance, no one's sacrifice. You don't even deserve your miserable, useless life, and I am happy to oblige the gods by extinguishing it."

The Consort smiled, but sweat glistened on his brow. "You would not dare. You forfeit your own life."

"If it sends you to the underworld, it's worth the cost." Alun pulled his arm back for the killing blow, and the Consort cringed, covering his head with his arms.

"Alun, no!" David's voice rang across the circle. "This isn't you. Not anymore. You don't kill. You heal."

As much as Alun wanted to run the Consort through—damn Rodric for a two-faced bastard—he stayed his hand. "He would have killed you, Dafydd. He'll try again. He deserves a worse death than this."

"He may deserve it, but you don't. You've paid for his crimes for two hundred years. Stop." David appeared at Alun's side, and Rodric took the opportunity to scoot farther away. "Don't rob me of a chance to be with you. Don't give him that satisfaction. Besides . . ." He placed his hand on Alun's arm. "If you're dead, you can never have supply closet sex with me again."

A rusty laugh rose out of Alun's chest. With one last contemptuous glance at Rodric cowering in the grass, he gazed down at David and ran his fingers across that perfect cheek. "That's the only thing that could sway me."

He leaned down for a kiss, but David jerked away, eyes wide with terror. "Alun! Duck!"

Out of the corner of his eye, Alun glimpsed the glint of moonlight on steel. But even as he turned, the sword arcing toward his neck disappeared in a sweep of metal, the grate of shattered bone, and a fountain of blood.

"Alun, you idiot!" Mal's voice held nothing but mild irritation. "Never turn your back on a psychopath."

CHAPTER 32

David's knees gave out, and he crumpled to the ground next to Alun while the Consort wailed, clutching his handless arm to his chest. *Blood.* So much blood—splattered on the grass, soaking the Consort's doublet, staining the blade of Mal's sword.

"Mal." Alun reached over David's head and gripped Mal's shoulder. "I didn't expect you."

Mal shrugged. "You said you needed backup."

"I should have known I could count on you. I won't make that mistake again."

"Consider it my way of putting you in my debt." He smiled wryly and let the sword fall to the ground at his feet. "I have a feeling I'll need to collect sooner rather than later."

David could handle the blood—he couldn't be a nurse otherwise—but swords? Not so much. He averted his gaze from the blade. Somewhere above him, Alun and Mal were still talking. Someone else too. The Queen? David wasn't sure, because the Consort's keening was all he could hear now, drowning out all other sounds and setting David's teeth on edge.

I could help him. I could—but why should I? He wanted to kill me. If it weren't for Mal, he'd have killed Alun for sure.

But the notion of ignoring someone in pain cramped David's belly until he could barely stay upright. *Ow ow ow. Maybe achu-majiggers have their own version of the Hippocratic Oath—help or else.*

"Dafydd?" Alun kneeled next to him, wrapping an arm around David's shoulders. David shuddered and leaned in. "Are you all right, *cariad*?"

"I—I don't know."

"Come away. You needn't have anything more to do with Luchullain."

"Don't I?" David stared at the Consort, who was barely whimpering now, although the sound pierced David's brain like a bullhorn. *He's an asshole and a psychopath, but I'm not judge and jury. I'm an* achubydd.

He pulled away from Alun, refusing to lean on him for this. Focusing on his center, as he had in Aunt Cassie's bedroom, as he had when he'd broken Alun's curse, he could make out the Consort's core, throbbing in his solar plexus. *Ewww.* It was dark and mottled, like rotten meat, but the lines of energy were as easy to map as if they'd been drawn with glow-in-the-dark Sharpies. *There*, at the wrist's ragged edge, the lines pulsed and fluttered.

I could do it. I could work with those. I might even—could I make him a new hand?

David reached out tentatively, but Alun gripped his shoulder and held him back. "Oak and thorn, Dafydd, don't. He's not worth it. He'll take everything you've got, just as he planned."

David glanced away from the Consort, and noticed that they'd drawn quite a crowd—the Queen and a whole passel of her guards stood watching, but David couldn't pay attention to them, not now.

"Maybe he's not worth it, but I am. It *hurts*, Alun. Being able to help and refusing? It freaking hurts. Right here." He pressed his hands to his belly. "Did you ever ask why Owain healed that stag? It's because he *had* to. He didn't have a choice. And neither do I."

David turned back to the Consort, but before he could touch him, the stump of his wrist scaled over with new skin, and the energy lines were cauterized.

"Dafydd Evans." The Queen's voice cut off the Consort's whimpers—or maybe the instant first aid had done that. "This burden is no longer yours."

Alun helped David to his feet. "It should never have been his. He should never have been put in such danger. How could you not realize that your own consort was a traitor?"

"Calm down, Alun. It's over now. I'm fine." David turned to Mal and hugged him hard around the waist. "Thank you. Thank you so much for saving him."

Mal chuckled and returned David's embrace. "Why is it that every time I have a hot man in my arms, he only wants to talk about my brothers?"

David stepped back. "I seriously doubt that's always the case, but brothers are—" David's stomach clenched. "*Brothers*. Holy crap, *Gareth*. I have to go."

Alun grabbed David's shoulders. "No. It's not safe. The Consort's men—"

"Shall not touch him." The Queen looked down her nose at—well, everyone. "For the remainder of this night, Dafydd Evans is under my protection."

Alun released David and took a step forward, half-blocking him from the Queen. "With all due respect, Majesty, your guards may be compromised. Did you expect the Consort to betray you?"

She raised one flawless copper eyebrow. "A point. Nonetheless, none shall touch him for the remainder of this night." She cast a disdainful glance at the Consort, huddled on the grass. "We have that much power at least." Her gaze lifted to Mal. "Some would do well to remember it."

David edged sideways, the need to go to Gareth prickling like needles along his skin. "I really have to leave now."

"I'll come too." Alun reached for him, but his hand stopped two inches from David's arm. He grimaced, his muscles straining as if he were pushing a giant weight. "What in all the bloody hells—"

"We said none shall touch him, not here in our realm, not for the remainder of this night. That includes you, Lord Cynwrig. As we said, some would do well to remember who rules in Faerie still."

"Pettiness doesn't become you, Majesty." Alun gestured for David to precede him. "Let's go, *cariad*."

"No." The Queen's tone was hard as stone. "You shall stay here. Dafydd Evans may go."

"I—"

"This is not a negotiation, Lord Cynwrig."

"No, Majesty. It is not."

This time, Alun led the way out of the Stone Circle, and David hurried to catch up.

Finally.

When they got back to the ceilidh glade, Gareth was still on the dais, slumped against a stool. The arrow was still protruding from his shoulder. *Damn it, why didn't I come sooner?*

David rushed across the clearing, leaped up on the dais, and dropped to his knees. "I'm so sorry. If I'd known they would hurt you, I—"

"Never mind," Gareth ground out between clenched teeth. "My choice. My risk."

"Hold on. I'm going to remove the arrow now. It'll probably hurt."

"Can't hurt more than it does now."

Alun joined them and held out his hand. "Hold on to me, brother, if it will help."

Gareth hesitated for a moment, his gaze locked with Alun's, then clasped his hand. "Thank you." He nodded at David. "Do your worst."

David grasped the arrow's shaft, but hesitated as he reached for Gareth's shoulder. "Shoot. That thing the Queen did. I can't touch him, can I?"

"None may touch *you.*" The Queen's voice startled him. *How did she get here? Teleportation?* "The *tynged* does not apply to the reverse."

"Swell." David took a moment to focus on the lines of pain swirling in Gareth's right shoulder. *Crap. He's a left-handed guitarist. If I don't do this right, he won't be able to play again.* "Is this okay with you?" At Gareth's nod, David took a deep breath. *Then I guess I'd better do it right.*

CHAPTER ✤ 33

"Lord Cynwrig. Attend us."

Alun didn't loosen his grip on Gareth's hand. "I'm busy, Majesty."

"Our patience wears thin. Dafydd Evans can manage without you, as can our honored bard."

Gareth squeezed Alun's hand, then released it. "Go on. I'll be fine now. Your lad knows what he's about."

Alun nodded curtly and followed the Queen to the far side of the glade. He frowned, scanning the warriors clustered under the trees.

"Where's Mal?'

The Queen regarded him stonily. "Gone."

"I don't believe it. He wouldn't have left without checking on Gareth."

"He had no choice. Maldwyn Cynwrig violated the sanctity of the consort bond. For that, he is stripped of his rank and privileges, and outlawed from Faerie until he makes whole what he cost us this night."

What in all the hells does that mean? Put Rodric's hand back on his arm? Not likely. "Your Majesty, that hardly seems fair. He prevented a coup. I'd call that a mitigating circumstance."

"Fairness is not the issue. We can allow no convenient bending of the covenants. How do you think our ranks have so diminished over the years? Faerie is built on principles, traditions, and pacts. When you violate any of those, you threaten the fabric of our world."

"In case you hadn't noticed, Rodric shattered most of those when he tried to depose you by destroying an entire race."

She inclined her head. "True. And for that he has been banished and declared no longer our Consort."

"In that case, Mal should be in the clear."

"If he had struck now, that would be true. But his blow landed before our renunciation. His crime still stands."

Anger boiled in Alun's belly. "But—"

"You, Lord Cynwrig, have little room to talk, ready as you were to strike our Consort down. However, you acted in accord with all four of the basic tenets of the Seelie Court, willing as you were to defend your honor to the death. Seeking to protect your true love, who we grant is beautiful, as are you once again. And the balance you sought to restore this night, by discharging the debt to Owain Glenross and his clan, is righteous and proper."

Alun bowed his head, pretending acceptance of the Queen's guarded approval, even though he hadn't given a troll's hairy ass for any of that. He'd only thought of David. Of keeping him safe.

For that matter, he'd seen her outside the Stone Circle during the final confrontation. Why hadn't she intervened? She could easily have renounced Rodric after he'd proclaimed his ambition to take her throne, yet she hadn't.

The anger that had burned in his veins turned ice-cold. "You knew. You knew Rodric was a traitor all along."

Her expression never changed, betraying no guilt, no remorse. "We had our suspicions."

"So the whole charade—starting with that ludicrous oath ceremony—was nothing but a test. A bloody, thrice-blasted, Goddess-bedamned test. You put David in danger, allowed Mal's life to be destroyed, just to find out if your Consort was the monster everyone else has always known him to be."

She pressed her lips together, and her hand tightened on the hilt of her sword. "The test was not only for our former Consort, but for you and your brothers. For Dafydd Evans as well. Any can be corrupted, Lord Cynwrig, with the right incentive—or even with the lack of sufficient reason to remain steadfast."

"And have you remained steadfast yourself, Majesty? You would have let the last known *achubydd* die without lifting a finger. Considering what a gossip mill the Court is, every last one of your subjects will know that you've declared open season on David by morning."

"You overstep. We have no intention of allowing Dafydd Evans to suffer. In our realm from this day forward, no *achubydd* may be touched with intent to harm."

Alun remembered the first days of his own curse, when he'd been mad with grief, shamed by his appearance, and shunned by all who saw him. Rodric was no longer part of the realm, and he'd be desperate—desperate and psychotically vengeful. If he'd been determined to take David's life before to further his political ambitions, how much more determined would he be now that he might see David as his only way back to physical wholeness, his only way back into Faerie?

"That's not good enough."

"We rule in Faerie, not the Outer World. This is what we can offer. We suggest you accept it with better grace."

Alun gazed across the glade, where David was huddled next to Gareth, frowning in concentration. *He won't take steps to safeguard himself. If the Queen won't take responsibility, it's up to me. But how? If the Consort—*

The consort laws. *"Ye shall lose whate'r you seek to take."* If David were Alun's consort, he'd be safe, just as Owain would have been had he accepted Alun's suit that fateful night. This time, Alun wouldn't take no for an answer, because this time he knew the true consequences of a refusal.

"I'll take him for my consort. No one can touch him, then."

The Queen's eyes narrowed. "He has agreed to your claim?"

"He must. He has no choice."

"We wish you good fortune, then. However, because of your actions this night, we have no First Champion. You shall take your brother's place at Court."

"With all due respect, Majesty," Alun drew himself up. "No."

Her face grew as cold and distant as the winter moon. "After so recently regaining your right to enter Faerie, do you wish to become exiled again—and for the same reason?"

Somehow the threat didn't seem as dire—not if Alun had David by his side. "Majesty, if I have learned anything from David, it is that if we expect to prosper in this changing world, we must learn to adapt. How can we do that if we cling too tightly to the old ways?"

"Faerie's very existence is bound by those old ways."

"I think there may be more latitude there than we've always believed. By the old laws, you should never have been able to unify the Celtic fae. And think of your Consort."

"*Former* Consort."

Alun inclined his head. "As you say. Were his actions those we expect from true Seelie fae? Yet he could still pass the Faerie threshold at will." She stilled, clearly struck by his words, and for a moment— *Was that fear in her eyes?* "Do we truly need another pointless tournament or a make-work hunt that accomplishes nothing but to exercise our horses? Shouldn't we consider how fae can make a difference, at least to each other?"

The moonlight gleamed in her hair as she nodded. "Your point is well-taken. However, when we call, you shall answer."

"When you *ask*, I shall consider."

"So be it. But choose your battles wisely, Lord Cynwrig. One day, we shall tire of these negotiations."

"If you will excuse me, Majesty, I have a consort to claim."

Alun strode across the clearing to David, who was sitting on his haunches next to Gareth, a grin creasing his cheeks.

"Check it out, Alun. I didn't screw up. Gareth's all better. And before you go all mother-hen on me, I feel great."

"I'm glad."

Gareth stood, dusting off his pants. "I need to get back to the band. We've already missed one gig. If we miss another, the guys could get rabid." He smiled. "And since they're all shifters, I'm speaking literally."

He reached for David, but couldn't touch him. "I'd hug you but—"

"Leave that to me." David wrapped his arms around Gareth's waist and hugged him hard enough to force a grunt out of him. "Thank you for saving me from a . . . a fuck worse than death."

"Thank you for making it possible for me to play again. Although," Gareth scrunched up his face, "I won't thank you for forcing me to watch the worst dancing I've seen in a hundred raves. I'm surprised I wasn't struck blind." He turned and held out his hand. "Alun. I—I can't promise instant reconciliation, but I think we've made a start."

"Bollocks to that." Alun grabbed Gareth in a fierce hug. "As far as I'm concerned, we're there, but if you need more time, you know where to find me."

Gareth patted Alun awkwardly on the back and nodded. "Thank you." He stepped back and picked up his guitar case. "I'll send you tickets to the next concert. All right?"

David jumped, punching the air. "Yes!"

"Good. Now I'm getting out of this bloody place." He lifted his hand and walked off through the trees.

David sighed. "Your brothers are *awesome*. You know, I wasn't sure about Mal at first, but the way he—"

"Dafydd. We must talk."

"Yeah, sure, but can we go now? I need to get home and see if my aunt is okay. The stupid Consort stopped me before I could be sure, but I think she was getting better."

"She was already recovering when I saw her last."

"Really? Then why are you using your therapist voice? And why do you look grimmer than the day I changed your light bulbs?"

"We must discuss something that I fear you won't like."

"Name something that's happened tonight that I *did* like. My aunt close to death? Nope. Kidnapped by a power-mad fairy? Nope again. Dancing to 'YMCA' with a bunch of guys with really big swords and I *don't* mean the euphemistic fun kind? Nope, nope, nope. I mean, what could be worse?"

"What about going through it all again?"

David blinked, his mouth dropping open. "What? I thought we were done."

"For now. But Rodric could strike again, in the Outer World this time."

"But—" He scanned the glade. "He's not here, right? Isn't he in Faerie jail or something?"

"There is no Faerie jail—there's only death or exile. Rodric still lives, but is barred from the Seelie Court. And, at the moment, the Seelie Court is the only place you're safe."

"No offense, but tonight's little extravaganza doesn't exactly fill me with confidence about that. I was safer in my last medical placement, when I nearly got brained by a flying stapler."

"It is my fault you were put in danger, so I have an obligation to make amends. It's my responsibility to keep you safe; therefore, before we leave Faerie, you'll become my consort."

"Whoa, whoa, whoa. What?"

Alun grabbed David's shoulders, gazing into his eyes. "It's the only way to keep you safe. The consort law states that anyone who harms a consort can't benefit from it, because whatever they take is likewise taken from them. As my consort, you'll no longer be a target because nobody can drain you without draining themselves."

David's eyes turned storm-clouded. How could anyone ever have mistaken him for human? How had Alun? The druids' powers were stronger than any fae imagined, which bore thinking about. But not now. "Is this a proposal, Dr. Kendrick?"

"I— Yes, if you like."

"If I *like*? You say the reason you want to . . . to mate me or consort me or whatever is because of guilt?"

"It won't be as bad now that my curse is lifted. You needn't be shamed or disgusted by my appearance. Now that my connection to the One Tree has returned, I can perform the ritual myself. We don't need anyone else. If we go back to the Stone Circle—"

"No."

Of course. He has traumatic memories of that place. "Very well. It won't be quite as easy elsewhere, but we could pick another spot. Here, for instance, in the center of the faerie circle, or—"

"I meant no, I refuse to be forced into—into *consortdom* because of *obligation*."

Alun scowled. "You have no choice, Dafydd. You'll be prey to anyone outside of Faerie if you do not."

"Well you know what? *Screw* that. Screw that twice. Screw that from here to Orion's Belt and back in a '68 Volkswagen, because I will *not* be anybody's ball and chain."

CHAPTER 34

This time, David was the one who moped on the ride home—and it was freaking hard to maintain his game-face because Alun *talked* to him almost non-stop in The Voice. *Dang it.*

"Dafydd, be reasonable. Although if you were to stay in Faerie permanently, you'd be safe, it has its disadvantages."

No kidding. Like no family, no job, and a boyfriend/husband who wouldn't have committed unless he was forced.

"If you stay in the Outer World, you have to expect aggression from other disgruntled or damaged supes like Jackson Hoffenberg. If you refuse to hide, refuse protective charms from your aunt—"

"Mmmphm."

"All right then, from some other druid circle. You're setting yourself up as a target. Don't you see? Becoming my consort is the only logical solution."

Logic is not what I'm looking for here, Dr. Reasonable.

By the time they pulled up outside David's house, his jaw ached from grinding his molars—Jeez, *not talking* was fricking hard!

A figure was standing on the sidewalk, and for a moment, David thought it might be the Consort—that Alun's alarmist manifesto was actually correct. But then he saw the dark hair and leather jacket. As soon as Alun stopped the car, David hopped out, leaving Alun to follow as he chose.

"Mal!" David rushed over and hugged Mal again, although he only got a one-armed bro backslap in return. "You know, I'd think you could lose the leather in this weather."

He shrugged. "What can I say? Some of us are willing to sacrifice comfort to keep our image intact."

"Come inside. I want you to meet my aunt. If she—"

"Oi. She's a druid, right?"

David frowned. "Well yeah. So?"

"Remember what I said about the fae-druid feud? No offense to your aunt, but druids aren't my favorite people."

"Oh suck it up and deal." He grabbed Mal's elbow and hauled him to the porch, Alun trailing in their wake. He opened the door and rushed inside. "Auntie?"

Instead of lying immobile in her bed as he'd last seen her, or sitting in her rocker with her cane at her side, his aunt was standing in the kitchen, pouring tea fragrant with mint and raspberry into four cups.

David raced across the room and grabbed her in a hug. "Thank goodness. I thought I'd lost you."

"If you don't want me to accidentally pour hot tea down your drawers, *cariad*, you need to release me." Her words were typical of her old tart self, but her voice wobbled.

He let go, took the teapot out of her hand, and placed it on the counter. *Then* he hugged the stuffing out of her, and she hugged him back.

Alun loomed at David's side. "Elder. I'm pleased to see you've recovered."

No thanks to you, as I recall. "Auntie, this is Alun's broth—"

"Maldwyn Cynwrig." *No wobble in her voice now. Sheesh. What did Mal do to piss her off?*

Mal winced. "Elder."

"Be at ease. You are welcome here. As welcome as Lord Cynwrig." *Uh-oh. Guess Alun pissed her off too. Time to redirect.*

"Hey, what's this?" An ornate chest the size of a shoebox sat on the counter. Dragons, complete with scales and tiny jeweled eyes, decorated the top. "Nola usually goes for plant-based themes."

"This isn't one of hers. Three gentlemen, two extremely large and one quite small, delivered this to our doorstep this morning."

David ran a tentative finger over the exquisitely carved dragon. "Did you look inside?"

She took a sip of her tea. "It's not mine to open."

"Maybe the key is in here." David picked up a heavy parchment envelope with his name inscribed in perfect calligraphy. It was sealed with blood-red wax.

"Perhaps. But that arrived by a different method. Pushed under the door sometime last night."

Alun sidled closer and peered at the seal. "That's the crest of the vampire council."

"Um ... should I be worried?"

Mal hitched himself onto a barstool. "If the vampires were pissed at you, they wouldn't send you a greeting card—they'd send an assassin. With fangs. Open it."

David eased the wax away from the envelope and drew out a folded sheet of the same parchment. "I guess if they were sending a letter bomb, they'd have used the cheap paper." The sheet was covered in beautiful calligraphy in a deep-red ink, but ... "What language is this?"

Mal looked over his shoulder. "I think it's Hungarian."

"Seriously? Jeez, for all I know, it could be a death threat."

Alun's hand settled at the small of David's back, chasing a shiver up his spine. *Don't give in. Not on those terms.* "It's a thank-you note."

David peered up at Alun's perfect jawline from under raised eyebrows. "You understand Hungarian?"

Alun shrugged. "Two hundred years of house arrest. I had a lot of time at my disposal." He held out a hand. "May I?"

Not only was he drop-dead gorgeous, a hero, and lord of the freaking Sidhe, but he was a universal translator too? Swell. Didn't mean David wasn't still pissed at him for being a pigheaded control dictator. "Knock yourself out."

"'We, the World Vampire council, recognize the signal service performed by David Evans on behalf of our esteemed leader. In appreciation, we declare David Evans under our protection in perpetuity. Any who seek to harm him shall feel the full wrath of the vampire race.' Signed by Kristof Czardos and the entire council."

Mal whistled, long and low. Even Aunt Cassie looked impressed.

Alun folded the oversized page and handed it back. "By the way, that's not written in ink."

Okay. *Ewww.* David took the note between his thumb and forefinger. "I'm not sure what Miss Manners says about the etiquette of using blood for your official correspondence."

"Davey, you need to put that in a safe place."

"No need for that," Alun said. "It's indestructible. If it's burned, lost, or otherwise destroyed, it will reappear in its original state within twenty-four hours."

"You're kidding me. Even their letters are undead?"

"You shouldn't discount it, Dafydd. The vampire council has essentially promised death to anyone who hurts you."

"Awesome."

"However, you might want to frame it and put it in a prominent location. The protection won't work that well if nobody knows about it."

"Yeah. The whole doomsday thingy. I learned all about that by watching *Dr. Strangelove.*"

Alun blinked at him. "What?"

"We are *so* going to have a movie night. Or twenty."

Alun grinned and moved closer. "We are?"

Oops. "I mean, someday. We might. If I decide to forgive you."

"If you two are done, I want to see what's in the box." Mal tapped the lid. "Shite. You sure there's no key?"

"No keyhole either." Alun spun the box to face him, but failed to open it. "Hmmm. Maybe a little fae magic?"

David rescued the box. "No messing about with magical nukes." He ran his fingers over the dragon's intricately veined wings. "It's too beautiful to mar. Maybe it's not supposed to open."

"It's got hinges."

David gripped the top of the box to turn it around, and the lid gapped. "Oh." He raised it the rest of the way. It was lined with velvet, and full to the brim with a rainbow of faceted jewels.

"Gwydion's bollocks," Mal murmured. "A dragon's hoard?"

"What's that?" Alun pointed to a sliver of matte white amid the sparkling mass.

Fingers trembling, David carefully moved the jewels aside and pulled out a small plastic figure in a white tunic. "Luke Skywalker. Holy cats, these must be from Benjy, but this can't be right. We should return these to his mother right away."

"No, Dafydd." Alun took Luke and set him on top of a thumbnail-sized ruby. "The box opened for you. This is another thank-you note. The dragon shifters are grateful for your aid to their prince. This is how they show their gratitude. If you refuse it, you'll offend them."

"I— But . . . Jeez." David plunked his butt down on a barstool. "What the heck does this mean?"

"First, it means the dragon shifters have got your back too, and where the dragon council goes, the rest of the shifters follow. Second, it means you don't have to temp anymore. You have the means to be a gentleman of leisure."

"Oh, no. You don't get rid of me that easily. I'll go back to school. Get my RN. Maybe even become a nurse practitioner." He poked Alun in the chest. "A psychiatric nurse practitioner. Because the supe community needs me. And so do you."

Alun's glower made a return appearance. "Perhaps, but don't forget my conditions. You need me too, and there's only one way I can guarantee protection."

David tapped his chin. "Hmmm. Let's see. I'm safe from shifters, vampires, and any harm in Faerie."

His scowl faltered. "Yes." He drew out the word, as if searching for the trick.

"Can any fae get crazy with me out here in the human world?"

"Since the Queen has declared you untouchable in Faerie, if any of her subjects break her decree, no matter where they are, they risk her displeasure."

"'Displeasure,' huh?"

"Don't discount it," Mal said. "Her displeasure just dumped a curse—" Mal suddenly found the counter extremely interesting.

"Mal?" *Jeez, I was so focused on Aunt Cassie and Alun, I didn't look closely enough at him. Where the heck is his* glamourie *scruff?* "Are you okay?"

"Never better, boyo." He shot David the same confident, come-on grin as at their first meeting, but if David squinted, he could see the faint tangle of red in Mal's head. *Mental pain—or else I'm a lie-detector now too.*

"Goddess," Alun murmured. "'Ye shall lose whate'r you seek to take.' Mal." Alun shifted into his Dr. Take-No-Prisoners voice—or maybe it was just his big-brother voice. "Show me your sword hand."

Mal sighed and drew his right hand out of his pocket. It looked normal—good color, no wounds, but the fingers curled in toward the palm and they weren't moving.

David reached for it. "May I?" When Mal nodded, David cradled it in both of his. "It's— I can't see the lines. With Gareth, with Alun, I could see the way their pain eddied in their bodies, how to draw it away. But with you—it's like your hand isn't even there. The energy lines end at your wrist, just like the ex-Consort's after the Queen healed him."

"That's because of the way the blasted consort law works," Alun growled. "He took Rodric's hand, so he loses his own."

Mal shrugged. "I'll deal." He was obviously trying to throw down his bad-boy-don't-care attitude, but the worry line between his brows and the pinch of pain at the corners of his eyes gave away the lie.

"Screw that." David stroked his hand from wrist to fingertips. "Can you feel that?"

Mal shook his head. "At least it doesn't hurt. Guess I ought to be thankful for small favors, eh?"

"We'll work on it. I know a PT who can give you some exercises."

"Are you mental? Physical therapy for a Faerie *tynged*?"

David gave Mal his best stink-eye stare, improved by observation of Alun's world-class glower. "Has anyone tried it before?"

Mal scoffed. "Of course not."

"Then how do you know it won't work?"

"Because it doesn't make sense."

David propped his fists on his hips. "In case you haven't noticed, Mr. Skeptic, *you* don't make sense. Faerie doesn't make sense. Druids in twenty-first century Portland don't make sense. Don't be such a big baby. Just because it'll be hard—"

"I'm not afraid of work." He crossed his arms, tucking his unresponsive hand on the inside as if he were afraid David would snatch it and have his wicked *achubydd* way with it. "Or of pain."

"Then what have you got to lose? *Honestly.*"

He rounded on Alun, who stumbled back a few steps. "And you, Dr. You-Don't-Have-a-Choice, what exactly would I gain from being your consort that I don't already have?"

"Nothing, I suppose." From the sorrow in his eyes, he'd already given up. *Jeez, these Sidhe dudes are so fatalistic.* "Only me."

"In that case," David stalked forward and wrapped his arms around Alun's waist, "I accept."

Alun pulled back, a bewildered frown puckering his forehead. "But . . . you . . . I thought—"

"When will you guys learn to *ask*? I love you, but I want the choice. And you deserve choice too. How twisted is it to be forced to marry because some asshole fairy tried to kill me and random supes are too fricking entitled to *ask* instead of *take*?"

Alun smiled, and in his too-handsome-for-his-shirt mode, David's knees turned to water. "You love me?"

David smacked him in the biceps to cover up his extremely unmanly urge to fling himself onto that delectable chest and cling like a bad suit. "I *told* you that, doofus. For a psychologist, you totally suck at listening." He captured Alun's perfect cheekbones between his hands. "Alun Kendrick, Lord of the Sidhe and Shrink to the Supes, will you marry me?"

"Goddess, *yes.* Dafydd—"

David put his hand on Alun's chest to ward off a hug. "I have conditions, though."

"I almost dare not ask."

"You planning on calling me 'the Consort'? Because I gotta tell you, I'm not signing up for that."

Alun's smile widened. "I think we can work around it."

"Good." He stroked Alun's cheek. "Is it weird that I miss your old face?"

"As to that . . ." Suddenly, the brow ridges were back, Alun's skull once more oversized, the nose, the cheekbones—everything but the scar. *Because he's not gutted anymore. He has me.*

"Now *that's* what I'm talking about."

Mal snorted. "*Glamourie* to make yourself ugly? That may be a first."

"Oh shut up, Mal." David caught Alun's hand and drew him out of the kitchen and into the darkened hallway. He nuzzled Alun's jaw and was rewarded with a familiar growl. Alun kissed him, hot and possessive and *his.*

When they broke apart to breathe, Alun leaned his misshapen forehead against David's. "I love you, Dafydd."

Finally. "Excellent. Then let's do the wild thing, Dr. Beast. I'm in a healing mood."

Explore more of the *Fae Out of Water* series:
www.riptidepublishing.com/titles/series/fae-out-water

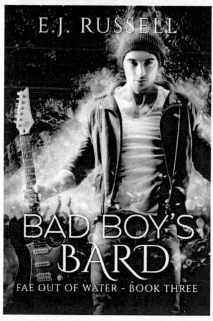

Dear Reader,

Thank you for reading E.J. Russell's *Cutie and the Beast*!

We know your time is precious and you have many, many entertainment options, so it means a lot that you've chosen to spend your time reading. We really hope you enjoyed it.

We'd be honored if you'd consider posting a review—good or bad—on sites like **Amazon, Barnes & Noble, Kobo, Goodreads, Twitter, Facebook, Tumblr,** and your blog or website. We'd also be honored if you told your friends and family about this book. Word of mouth is a book's lifeblood!

For more information on upcoming releases, author interviews, blog tours, contests, giveaways, and more, please sign up for our weekly, spam-free newsletter and visit us around the web:

Newsletter: tinyurl.com/RiptideSignup
Twitter: twitter.com/RiptideBooks
Facebook: facebook.com/RiptidePublishing
Goodreads: tinyurl.com/RiptideOnGoodreads
Tumblr: riptidepublishing.tumblr.com

Thank you so much for Reading the Rainbow!

RiptidePublishing.com

ALSO BY

E.J. RUSSELL

Legend Tripping
Stumptown Spirits
Wolf's Clothing

Geeklandia
Lost in Geeklandia
Clickbait

For a Good Time, Call . . . (a *Bluewater Bay* story,
with Anne Tenino)
Northern Light

Sun, Moon, and Stars (in *Magic and Mayhem: Fiction and Essays
Celebrating LGBTQA Romance*)

ABOUT THE

⚜

AUTHOR

E.J. Russell holds a BA and an MFA in theater, so naturally she's spent the last three decades as a financial manager, database designer, and business intelligence consultant. Several years ago, she realized Darling Sons A and B would be heading off to college soon and she'd no longer need to spend half her waking hours ferrying them to dance class.

What to do with all that free time?

A lucky encounter with Jim Butcher's craft blog posts caused her to revisit her childhood dream of writing fiction, and now she wonders why she ever thought an empty nest meant leisure.

Her daily commute consists of walking from one side of her office to the other, from left-brain day job to right-brain writer's cave, where she's learned to type with a dog attached to her hip and a cat draped across her wrists.

E.J. is married to Curmudgeonly Husband, a man who cares even less about sports than she does. Luckily, C.H. also loves to cook, or all three of their children (Lovely Daughter and Darling Sons A and B) would have survived on nothing but Cheerios, beef jerky, and satsuma mandarins (the extent of E.J.'s culinary skill set).

E.J. lives in rural Oregon, enjoys visits from her wonderful adult children, and indulges in good books, red wine, and the occasional hyperbole.

Find E.J. at www.ejrussell.com, on Facebook at facebook.com/E.J.Russell.author, and on Twitter at twitter.com/ej_russell.

Enjoy more stories like
Cutie and the Beast
at RiptidePublishing.com!

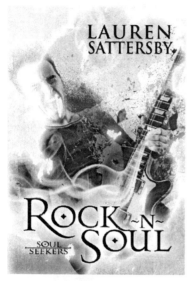

Rock N Soul
ISBN: 978-1-62649-311-7

Half
ISBN: 978-1-62649-520-3

Earn Bonus Bucks!

Earn 1 Bonus Buck for each dollar you spend. Find out how at
RiptidePublishing.com/news/bonus-bucks.

Win Free Ebooks for a Year!

Pre-order coming soon titles directly through our site and you'll
receive one entry into a drawing for a chance to win free books for
a year! Get the details at RiptidePublishing.com/contests.

CPSIA information can be obtained
at www.ICGtesting.com
Printed in the USA
LVOW12s1843050717
540359LV00005B/1037/P